She was just working th[...]
streak when he reached h[...]
hers and covered her hand [...] [...]
diately and shivered a little.

Jack tried hard not to enjoy the feeling of her pressed against him, but he couldn't help it. The sound of her breathing, harsh in the quiet air, made his libido twitch with interest. It made him think of other situations when she might be pressed against him, her breathing ragged. A situation in which they'd be wearing far less clothing and Mira would be feeling far friendlier toward him. It was natural, he told himself, the natural attraction of fire to air.

But give him time and he could seduce her. He knew how to touch her to make her want him . . . beg for him. Even though he shouldn't, he could tempt her into his bed.

The faint scent of her rose perfume teased his nose as he leaned down and placed his mouth close to her ear. "You're incredibly predictable, Mira. Even if you'd gotten out the front door, you never would've been able to call the elevator without my security code."

"What do you mean?"

"I mean my apartment is the only one on this floor. I mean I have the elevator on security mode. You can't access it without my code. No one comes up or goes down without it. No one even stops at this floor without my direct permission. You're a prisoner here." He paused. "A princess in a tower," he breathed silkily into her ear.

She shivered against him . . .

WITCH FIRE

ANYA BAST

BERKLEY SENSATION, NEW YORK

THE BERKLEY PUBLISHING GROUP
Published by the Penguin Group
Penguin Group (USA) Inc.
375 Hudson Street, New York, New York 10014, USA
Penguin Group (Canada), 90 Eglinton Avenue East, Suite 700, Toronto, Ontario M4P 2Y3, Canada
(a division of Pearson Penguin Canada Inc.)
Penguin Books Ltd., 80 Strand, London WC2R 0RL, England
Penguin Group Ireland, 25 St. Stephen's Green, Dublin 2, Ireland (a division of Penguin Books Ltd.)
Penguin Group (Australia), 250 Camberwell Road, Camberwell, Victoria 3124, Australia
(a division of Pearson Australia Group Pty. Ltd.)
Penguin Books India Pvt. Ltd., 11 Community Centre, Panchsheel Park, New Delhi—110 017, India
Penguin Group (NZ), 67 Apollo Drive, Rosedale, North Shore 0745, Auckland, New Zealand
(a division of Pearson New Zealand Ltd.)
Penguin Books (South Africa) (Pty.) Ltd., 24 Sturdee Avenue, Rosebank, Johannesburg 2196, South
Africa

Penguin Books Ltd., Registered Offices: 80 Strand, London WC2R 0RL, England

This is a work of fiction. Names, characters, places, and incidents either are the product of the author's imagination or are used fictitiously, and any resemblance to actual persons, living or dead, business establishments, events, or locales is entirely coincidental. The publisher does not have any control over and does not assume any responsibility for author or third-party websites or their content.

WITCH FIRE

A Berkley Sensation Book / published by arrangement with the author

PRINTING HISTORY
Berkley Prime Crime mass-market edition / June 2007

Copyright © 2007 by Anya Bast.
Cover art by Tony Mauro.
Cover design by Rita Frangie.
Interior text design by Laura K. Corless.

ISBN: 978-0-425-21614-9

BERKLEY SENSATION®
Berkley Sensation Books are published by The Berkley Publishing Group,
a division of Penguin Group (USA) Inc.,
375 Hudson Street, New York, New York 10014.
BERKLEY SENSATION is a registered trademark of Penguin Group (USA) Inc.
The "B" design is a trademark belonging to Penguin Group (USA) Inc.

PRINTED IN THE UNITED STATES OF AMERICA

10 9 8 7 6 5 4 3 2 1

Dedicated to my husband,
who is the inspiration for every hero I write.
The fire has never gone out, baby.
I love you.

Also to all my loop-dwelling friends,
both writers and readers,
you make the Internet worthwhile.
Thanks for the laughter, the information,
and sometimes the commiseration.
You guys rock.

To all the writers who are still trying, write on.
No matter what happens, write on.

Acknowledgments

This book could not have been written without the critiquing attention of Lauren Dane (aka "Scissors"), Megan Hart (aka "Sparkles"), Brent Kellmer, Cathy Pegau, and Jody Wallace, not to mention the wonderful and ever-supportive 3J Crit Group. Thank you all so very much.

An extra thanks to Brenda M. and Lauren Dane for patiently listening to me prattle on while I brainstorm at them. Thank you for your friendship.

Very special thanks to the awesome Laura Bradford of the Bradford Literary Agency for believing in me. Thanks to Cindy Hwang for letting me share this book with the world.

Last but certainly not least, thanks to my family and friends for their steadfast support.

ONE

~❦~

HE LOOKED LIKE SIN AND SEEMED LIKE SALVATION. Salvation for her sluggish libido, anyway.

Seriously preoccupied by the man sitting at table eight, Mira slung plates of liver and onions, the special of the day. She couldn't remember the last time a man had distracted her this way, made her feel like a clumsy fifteen-year-old again. She couldn't remember the last time she'd looked at a man and had an instant, primal reaction. Hell, she'd begun to think she'd completely lost her sex drive.

It was still alive and well.

She tucked her pen behind her ear as she finished taking an order and glanced at the man. He sat at a booth in the corner, sipping black coffee and reading the *Star Tribune*. He'd been there for close to two hours and hadn't wanted any food. Normally that would annoy her, especially since he was taking up prime real estate during the busiest time of the day, but she was prepared to forgive him. Eye candy like him tended to be rare in Mike's Diner. He was so gorgeous she felt like throwing herself at the poor guy, but her boss frowned on scaring the customers. Anyway, recently divorced, grease-stained waitresses probably weren't this man's normal fare.

It wasn't just his physical appearance that made him so attractive. It was his attitude and his mannerisms. It was the way he held himself so confidently. He was one of those men to whom women had a deep, instinctive reaction, a response that harkened back to caveman days when females were most attracted to the biggest, baddest male around.

At least six foot three and powerfully built, the man seemed to walk and breathe sex. Like he'd protect a woman from any threat and take really good care of her body while he did it.

Of course, that was probably just her fevered, undersexed imagination working overtime. That doubtless happened when one unexpectedly rediscovered one's libido.

As a result, she was having sexual fantasies about a stranger during the busiest part of her shift. Instead of worrying if the salt and pepper shakers were filled, she wondered what his hands would feel like on her body, imagined his hard chest rubbing against her bare breasts.

As Mira took care of a table, refilling drinks and making sure the patrons had everything they needed, she glanced at the man again from under her lashes. She felt the need to commit him to memory so he could star in her fantasies later. During the last few months, her vibrator had gathered dust in the bottom drawer of her night table. Now she had a reason to pull it out again.

He was broad-shouldered and leanly muscled. His golden, sun-kissed skin seemed to defy the Minnesota winter and made Mira want to run her lips and hands over it. Silky black hair framed a chiseled, interesting face with black slashes for eyebrows and a sexy dusting of a beard on a sculpted jaw. He was attractive, yet he wasn't a pretty boy. This man had a face that could either freeze someone solid or turn a woman's bones to warm honey, depending on his expression.

The man was sex on legs, but it was his mouth and eyes that really did it for Mira. Long, dark lashes fringed his light blue eyes. They seemed cold at first glance, but when he'd smiled at her, the look in those eyes had made her knees go weak. And he had a positively indecent mouth. The slight curve of his full, sensual lips brought to mind all sorts of tempting images—skin moving on skin, limbs entangled, ragged breathing, mouths and tongues working as two bodies fused amid twisted sheets. . . .

"Hey, watch it!" a customer complained when she nearly plowed him over after clearing off a table.

"Sorry." She pasted on a smile and apologized. She was really off her stride this afternoon. Blowing an errant strand of dark hair out of her face, she carted the tub to the back for the dishwasher. As she passed nearby, she stole her thousandth glance at him.

He wore a pair of close-fitting jeans, a gray turtleneck sweater, a long black coat, and black boots. His dress was casual, but he reeked of money. The whiff she'd gotten of his expensive cologne and the silver Mercedes he'd parked outside were enough to tell her he had lots of that.

Nope. Definitely not her type.

In any case, she'd made a promise to herself to avoid any new relationships for at least a year. She owed it to herself to keep that promise.

Not that he'd want her anyway.

She headed back to the kitchen, hooking a loose hank of hair behind her ear as she went, and placed the order she'd just taken. It was lunchtime, and the diner was crowded with downtowners grabbing a quick bite before they headed back to the office. Nobody wanted to go very far in February; Mike's Downtown Diner was good enough in this kind of Minnesota cold. The sounds of conversation and clattering silverware nearly drowned out the piped-in music, and it felt hot in the small restaurant.

Normally, when she wasn't so distracted, this was the

time of day when she hit her groove. Her whole reality became the synchronization of taking orders, serving food, and refilling drinks. The time went fast and smooth. The rhythm of lunchtime at the diner was like the clackety-clack of well-oiled train wheels speeding down a track.

She was good at her job, able to sense people's needs with a natural intuitiveness that she'd had her whole life. Her regular customers always commented on how she'd show up right as they were thinking about ordering a side of fries or a slice of blueberry pie. Okay, so she wasn't curing cancer, but at least she was being a productive member of society. Plus, the tips weren't bad. Mira was saving up to go back to school and finish her degree in psychology. She had no intention of being a professional waitress for the rest of her life.

"Mira, order up!" Mike called from the kitchen.

She picked up her order and headed out to deliver it, making her way through the crowded diner toward table seven. It was right next to table eight where Mr. Gorgeous still nursed his coffee. She painted on a wide give-me-a-good-tip smile and served the man at table seven his meal. He looked like some middle-management guy struggling his way up the corporate ladder. After working at the diner for the last six months, she'd gotten a good feel for the lunchtime crowd.

"Can I get you anything else right now, sir?" she asked brightly.

The man looked up from his plate and focused on her necklace. "You some kinda Satanist?"

Her smile collapsed and shock rippled through her at the angry tone of the man's voice. Her hand flew to the pentagram around her neck. Damn, she'd forgotten to take it off before her shift.

Scorn followed the shock. This guy never would've said anything if she'd been wearing a crucifix. People instantly equated the pentagram with Satanism, even though it had nothing to do with it. Normally, she'd give him a lesson in religious sensitivity, but this wasn't the time or the place.

"No," she answered coldly. "I'm not a Satanist. Can I get you anything else, sir?"

"So, what? Is it some kinda Goth thing, then?"

"No, it's not a *Goth thing*. Do you want another Coke?"

"Why wear that damned thing around? It offends people."

"Leave the waitress alone."

Her head snapped up. It was Mr. Gorgeous. He hadn't even raised his head from his paper. His deep, resonating voice commanded authority even without his direct attention. "She doesn't want to explain her jewelry preferences. She just wants to know if you want a drink refill."

Middle Management seemed instantly cowed by the note of aggression in Mr. Gorgeous's voice. That's why he probably wouldn't make it very far up the corporate ladder, Mira thought with satisfaction.

"I'm fine," Middle Management answered her, looking down at his plate. "Sorry."

"No problem," she said, turning away.

She glanced at Mr. Gorgeous. He looked up from his paper, and their gazes met for a moment. His mouth curved in a little smile before he turned his attention back to the *Tribune*. She imagined those full lips kissing between her breasts and down her stomach. The image of his dark head working between her thighs as he licked away her deep sexual ache filled her mind.

A baby squalled a couple booths over, breaking her pleasant thoughts. Mira wished she wasn't working and could be home wallowing in her fantasies of this man.

Since she had a little lull, Mira ducked into the break room to remove her necklace and put it in her locker. On her way out, she picked up a pot of coffee and walked back to Mr. Gorgeous's table.

He looked up at her as she approached. "Would you like another cup of coffee?" She held the pot and tipped her head to the side in question.

He shook his head. "The check."

She put the pot down, dug in her apron pocket for his bill, and laid it on the table. "Thanks," she said quietly. "I mean, for saying what you did."

"Are you Wiccan?" he asked while he fished his billfold out and extracted a twenty.

She nodded. "I was raised Wiccan, but I don't practice magick or anything crazy like that. Wicca is my religion. I was raised on it." She snapped her mouth shut so she wouldn't babble on. The man made her feel vulnerable and awkward. Not to mention . . . not many people would instantly take her for Wiccan at the sight of her pentagram.

He threw the twenty on the table and stood. The faint scent of his cologne—spicy, a bit woody—assaulted her senses. He glanced at her necklace-free throat. "Too bad you have to hide it because of the ignorance of others."

Oh. She was in love.

Rendered momentarily speechless, she looked down at his bill. "Uh, let me get your change—"

"No, keep it." He turned and left.

She picked up the twenty and his bill. His coffee with free refills had only been a buck twenty-five.

JACK MCALLISTER CLOSED THE CAR DOOR BEHIND him and focused past the falling snowflakes and the plate glass window of the diner to watch Mira Hoskins consider the tip he'd left her. She glanced out the window, stuffed the twenty and his bill into her apron pocket, and then leaned over the table to take his empty coffee cup and discarded newspaper. Her skirt rode up in the back, revealing the sweet curve of her calf, a little of the creamy skin of her thigh, the tender back of her knee. It was such a sensitive place on most women.

He groaned. The woman had a nice pair of legs, legs he'd imagined wrapped around his waist more than once since he'd been tasked with watching over her. Her hair was long and thick, a rich chocolate brown. Jack had imagined it spilling over the side of his mattress while he sank his cock inside her. He'd imagined fisting it in his hands while he spread her facedown on his bed and took her from behind with long, driving strokes into her wet heat. Jack would make her claw the sheets, make her go slack-jawed and helpless with lust, make her forget everything but the way he possessed her body.

He bet she made the sweetest sounds when she came.

Jack cursed and looked away. He'd known when he accepted the assignment that fire and air had a natural attraction, but he'd underestimated the strength of the magickal affinity. Jack had a huge sexual appetite; however, he'd thought he could resist this woman. She wasn't for him, not on any level. Consciously, he knew that. His cock seemed to have different ideas, however.

He couldn't help thinking about her lush, soft curves and how she'd feel under his hands. Wanting her was powerful, primal—an instinctive response of his magick to hers. Nothing more. All the same, he was lusting hard after the one woman he knew he shouldn't want.

On every other level but the magickal one, she wasn't his type. Mira Hoskins wasn't a woman you fucked and left. This was a woman you kept. One you loved. One you tucked into your life forever.

He watched her gather up the cup and his discarded napkin and head back to the kitchen. She seemed utterly unaware of her beauty. Men noticed her constantly, but she seemed oblivious. She kept her hair natural, long and straight. She never wore much makeup. That unconsciousness about her appearance made her even more attractive.

Jack swore again and started the engine.

Mira was a nice woman, and that meant she wasn't his kind of woman. He usually bedded women who were married and wanting short affairs on the side, or unattached women who were in it for a no-strings-attached good time. Jack stayed away from women like Mira Hoskins.

Especially Mira Hoskins.

He'd taken this job to discharge the debt he owed her. It had to stay professional.

Anyway, she was his boss's cousin. Monahan would have Jack's head off for seducing her, and maybe not the one on his shoulders.

MIRA STEPPED OUT THE BACK DOOR OF THE DINER after closing time. The cold night air snatched her breath away instantly, forcing her to pull the edges of her coat tighter. Mike's was located right in the middle of Minneapolis, making the wind that raced through the corridor of buildings extra frigid. It whipped her skirt around her nylon-clad legs and numbed her calves. All the same, it was invigorating. She'd always loved the wind, even when it snatched the warmth from her lungs.

She picked her way over the icy parking lot toward her beat-up Honda Accord and got in. The cold seat numbed her ass on contact and made Mira gasp. All she wanted was to get home, shower the greasy stink off her skin, and settle down with a TV dinner. She stuck the key in the ignition. She'd break out her vibrator tonight, too. Mr. Gorgeous had inspired her.

The car took several tries to start, but soon the tires were crunching their way over the icy pavement, out onto the street and toward home.

All the way to her apartment, the sense of being watched niggled at her. It was silly. She was in her car alone, after all. Unless the feeling came from being followed. She turned the radio up and tried to ignore her inexplicable paranoia, brushing it off as just her imagination, but that didn't stop her from checking her rearview mirror every five seconds.

She'd been having this feeling on and off for the last couple of weeks. It was ridiculous, of course. Nobody would be stalking her, nobody but Ben, maybe. But Ben probably didn't care enough about her to invest that much time. After all, Ben had moved on to greener pastures and forgotten her. He was far too busy banging his new blonde, buxom girlfriend, Trixie, to bother with her anymore.

Who the hell was named *Trixie*, anyway? It sounded like the name of a stripper, though Trixie was actually a physical therapist who'd moved down from Duluth a couple years ago. When Ben had hurt his knee last year, Trixie had spent a little "overtime" helping him recuperate. The poor baby had required extra TLC, it seemed.

Mira blew out a hard breath that clouded white in the still-cold car. She wished Trixie better luck with Ben than she'd had. Ben wasn't the type to stay faithful for long. She almost felt sorry for the other woman.

But not too sorry.

She murmured the twenty-fifth couplet of the Wiccan Rede to her empty car. "True in love forever be, lest thy lover's false to thee." Mira sighed. Ben had been incredibly false.

She pulled into a spot not far from the entrance of her building on Randolph Avenue in nearby St. Paul. In order to feed her new fear, she made sure no other cars had pulled in behind her before she gathered her purse and made her way in, picking carefully over the barely cleared, snow-covered sidewalk.

She headed through the front door of the old building and down a short flight of stairs. There were only two apartments in the basement and very little luxury. The stairs and walls were all made of unadorned concrete blocks and it smelled a bit musty. A sole light bulb hung from a chain above her head, casting shadows, as she unlocked her apartment door.

Once inside, she took off her coat and kicked the heat

up a notch. Walking into the kitchen, she reached into her apron pocket, scooped out a wad of one-dollar bills, and stuffed them into the pink pig cookie jar on her counter. She was that much closer to night school now. It felt good to have a goal. It gave her life purpose.

Standing in the middle of her kitchen, she smiled. Be it ever so humble. Her apartment consisted of one tiny bedroom, an infinitesimal bathroom, a miniscule kitchen with no dishwasher, and a teeny-weeny living room. The place was dark and decorated with mismatched secondhand furniture.

It was a dump.

But it was *her* dump. Her smile widened. For once in her life she had a place that was all hers. It might not be much, but it was freedom.

The message light on the recorder blinked at her. She walked over and hit play.

"Mira," came Ben's voice. "I want my stereo. I've told you a hundred times, that's my—" She hit Delete. The bastard had cheated on her nonstop during their marriage. When she'd found out, she'd been forced to have a checkup for STDs. STDs! She closed her eyes for a moment, feeling that familiar mixture of betrayal and shame.

She was keeping the damn stereo.

Mira had met Ben in college. He'd been nearly finished with his law degree, and once he'd graduated, they'd married. Ben had somehow convinced her to quit pursuing her degree in psychology to try and get pregnant. He was making enough money to support them both and he'd professed to really want children. He'd landed a job at a local law firm and, while they hadn't been well off, they'd been able to make ends meet in those early years.

Luckily, she'd never managed to conceive. Mira did want kids, but not while Ben had been off trying to make babies with half the female population of Minnesota. Once she'd discovered Ben's numerous affairs and all his lies, she'd confronted him and demanded a divorce that very same day.

She had been heartbroken, but any remaining love she'd had for Ben had evaporated in the ensuing divorce proceedings. Ben had fought her every step of the way. Mira was still paying legal fees, but she'd managed to get some spousal maintenance out of him, at least for the time it took her to finish up her psychology degree.

Anger rose up in her for a moment, so severe it nearly choked her. Ben had lied to her continuously. She'd given him years of her life, her trust, and her love, and he'd treated the feelings she had for him like trash. Treated *her* like trash.

She'd been so stupid to quit school and rely on him financially. At the time, she'd been so in love with him she could never have imagined Ben would be unfaithful. She thought her life would be like the lives of her friends. Even if she didn't have a career, she'd have kids, a great marriage, be happy.

Obviously, such things weren't meant for her.

He'd taken the house in Eden Prairie. She hadn't wanted it. She'd wanted her own place, free of memories and flush with the promise of a fresh start. Besides the temporary spousal support, she'd taken very little from her old residence in a bid to create a new life for herself.

Tears burned her eyes, and she blinked them away. Wallowing in self-pity was the least productive thing she could do. Anyway, she'd been free of Ben and his lies for six months and every day her life got better.

Mira glanced around her apartment a little less certainly than she had a moment before.

Right?

She chased away the flicker of doubt with a shake of her head and hit the button to play the next message. The creepy sound of a man breathing filled the apartment. No words, no voice, just the strangely threatening sound of breathing.

Mira shuddered. After feeling like being watched, she *really* didn't need prank calls like that. She hit Delete and stepped away from the recorder, feeling every hair on her body rise. Normally, she'd laugh it off, but not tonight. Tonight it made dread curl in the pit of her stomach.

Someone knocked on her door—*hard*. Startled, Mira jumped three feet in the air.

"Mira Hoskins?" The man's voice sounded muffled through the door. "We need to talk to you."

We?

She didn't move, didn't breathe. The voice was unfamiliar. There was no conceivable reason anyone should be knocking on her door at eleven at night. Her godmother's voice entered her mind . . . *The Boston Strangler never had to break a lock, you know.*

Bang! Bang! Bang! "Miss Hoskins, we know you're in there. Open up. We just want to talk."

No way was she opening that door.

Silence. She stood rooted in place, hoping they'd go away.

"Miss Hoskins," the voice said softly after a few moments, "let's do this the easy way, shall we?"

Mira's blood ran cold, and her heart rate ratcheted up. That definitely sounded like a threat. She grabbed the phone to call 911—dead. No dial tone. "Oh shit," she breathed. They'd cut her phone line. How the hell had they cut her phone line?

She glanced around at the windows. Tiny basement-level windows, all of them. Almost too small to allow air through, much less a normal-sized woman.

No flight. That meant fight.

Panic making her heart pound and her hands shake, she went to a kitchen drawer, got out a knife, and tiptoed down the short hallway, toward the door, in order to peer out the peephole.

The sound of splintering wood filled her ears, and the door came flying open. It caught her square in the forehead. Blinding pain exploded through her head for a moment, then she felt herself falling backward into darkness.

TWO

MIRA AWOKE TO A THROBBING HEADACHE. SHE blinked, and the hallway ceiling came into view. Wincing at the pain, she reached up to touch her head.

Someone forced her hand down. "Don't touch it," came a gruff male voice. "You got a hell of a knock."

"Wha—"

He leaned over her, coming into her line of sight. Mira gasped in recognition. Forcing herself up, she crab-walked backward until she hit the wall behind her. She instantly regretted the fast movement as nausea threatened to overwhelm her. Eyes wide, she gagged and fought the urge to vomit on the hallway floor.

The man from the diner. The good-looking one. Mr. Gorgeous.

Her mind stuttered over the situation. Mr. Gorgeous in her apartment. The feeling of being watched. The men breaking her door down.

He held out a hand like she was some wild animal to tame. "It's okay, I'm not going to hurt you."

She was supposed to believe that?

Mira glanced past him. The door to her apartment stood wide open, and two huge men she didn't recognize lay unmoving on the concrete floor at the bottom of the stairs. "What the hell is going on? Who are you?" Hysteria edged her voice, making it sound thready to her own ears.

"My name is Jack McAllister. I know you have a lot of questions, but right now I have to get you out of here."

His words barely registered as anything resembling sense. She knew one thing, she wasn't going anywhere with this guy, no matter how gorgeous he was. Lord and Lady, she had bad taste in men!

Her gaze sought and landed on the kitchen knife she'd dropped when the door hit her. It lay between them, closer to her. Mira lunged for it. Her fingers closed around the handle in the same moment Jack tackled her, trapping her wrist. Her breath whooshed out of her at the weight of him. Darkness spotted her vision for a moment, but she curled her fingers around the handle of the knife and doggedly held onto it.

He rolled off her, still keeping his hand tight around her wrist. Mira gasped in relief from having his weight off her and tried to yank her arm away, which only succeeded in hurting her shoulder. She had the knife, but she couldn't use it.

Mira focused on a chip in the wall in front of her, holding onto every shred of willpower she had to stay conscious.

"Don't pass out," said Jack. "You need to stay awake."

No shit, she wanted to say, but she couldn't make the words come. Her life probably depended on staying conscious.

"Look, I'm here to help you. Those men out there in the hallway, they've been following you. We need to get out of here before more muscle shows up. There's a lot to explain and I can't do it now. Just know that I'm here to protect you. Understand?" He sounded like he was talking to a three-year-old.

"Why . . . should I trust . . . you?" she pushed out in a breathy voice, still focusing on the chip in the wall.

"Because you don't have a choice. Now, I'm going to let your wrist go. You can keep the knife if you're so attached to it. I don't think you're in any condition to use it anyway."

He had a point.

Jack released her wrist, and she made a clumsy lunging swipe at him anyway. He jerked back at the last second. The tip nearly grazed his throat.

"Whoa. Maybe I was wrong," he muttered. He grabbed her arm, plucked the knife from her fingers, and threw it across the room.

Mira stared at her out-of-reach weapon with dismay.

Jack grasped her around the waist with unsettlingly large, strong hands and hauled her across his lap. She clutched his shirt. For a moment she struggled against him and then went still. Her head had never hurt as badly as this. She couldn't even draw a breath without pain. Did she have a concussion? Did she need to go to the hospital?

"Why are you doing this?" she gasped.

He stared down at her with stunning blue eyes. It seemed a strange thing to be noticing at the moment, but this was a strange situation. "I told you. I'm protecting you, Mira," he answered in a tender voice that seemed at odds with his brusque demeanor.

Mira blinked and the light-headedness grew more intense. Jack tightened his arms around her, his expression concerned. He felt warm and he smelled sexy. Irrationally, she enjoyed the feel of him against her.

Plus, there were two of him. That made it extra nice.

Her head lolled as unconsciousness threatened.

"Shit," he breathed. "Mira?"

Darkness.

* * *

JACK LOOKED DOWN AT THE WOMAN IN HIS BED. She looked so small and fragile in the king-size four-poster. Her oval face appeared pale, and a huge bruise had bloomed on her forehead. She still wore her pink uniform from the diner and sensible white work shoes.

He had enough healing skill to know she didn't have a concussion. Once he'd carried her to the car and taken her somewhere he could concentrate, he'd ascertained that. Otherwise he'd have taken her to the emergency room, though that would've increased the risk of detection by Crane.

None of this had exactly gone according to plan.

Mira needed to stay hidden now, and his apartment was well warded against magickally prying eyes and ears. She'd have a hell of a headache for a few days, but that was the extent of her injuries. There was nothing for him to do now but wait for her to wake up.

He sat on the edge of his desk and played with a silver Zippo. The flame flared intermittently in the dim light of the room as he reviewed the day's events in his mind. He'd almost been too late. Crane's goons had almost gotten her. Jack knew he'd be hearing all about that little fuck-up from his boss. If he'd been delayed just a few more minutes, he could have lost Mira altogether.

Jack tried to imagine telling Monahan that he'd let Crane take not only Monahan's long-lost cousin, but one of the most powerful elemental air witches they were aware of, all because he'd been pulled over by a cop on I-94 while tailing her home. He'd just been trying to keep up with Mira. Woman drove like a bat out of hell, yet *he'd* been the one pulled over by the ever-vigilant Minnesota highway patrolmen.

He set the Zippo aside, slid off the desk, and walked over to study her.

The light from the hallway spilled in, making her long, tangled hair gleam. Her complexion was dusky, tanned even in the dead of winter, and her skin looked like porcelain, so smooth and perfect. It was the kind of skin that begged to be caressed and kissed. The kind of skin that yearned to be bare, to feel the trace of a man's fingers.

Jack let out a slow, steadying breath and allowed his gaze to follow the line of her slender throat to the edge of her uniform. He cocked his head to the side in contemplation. Her breasts were perhaps a B cup, likely topped with responsive pink nipples. Breasts just large enough to fill his hands and spill out a bit. Nipples perfect to explore with his tongue.

He felt like a lecher admiring her that way right now, but he couldn't help it. It was the natural sexual attraction of fire to air. With Mira it was exceptionally strong.

He reached down and brushed a few strands of her dark hair away from her face. Her long lashes were swept down over her cheeks and her mouth was lovely, full and expressive. She looked like her mother.

Gods and Goddesses. She looked like her mother.

A pang of regret squeezed his chest as the memories came. Jack rubbed a silky tendril of Mira's hair between his thumb and index finger as he let remembrances take him for the millionth time.

He'd just turned ten, and his father had deemed him old enough to observe the casting of his first circle. His father claimed that Jack had too much of his mother in him and it was time to start his training. Jack's mother had died when he'd been five, so he didn't know if it was true, only that his mother's qualities were something his father believed needed to be driven from him. They were a taint, a weakness, a botch on his father's bloodline. His father hadn't been able to force the badness out any other way, so had decided it was high time that Jack begin his education in the art of dark magick.

That day Jack stood near his father's friends and watched as four bound witches were dragged from their holding area to the ritual room in his father's mansion. One witch for each of the elements. Jack could feel their abilities through his magick as they entered. Volatile, unpredictable fire, like himself. Smooth, cool, overwhelming water. Steady, deep, powerful earth. Finally, air. Air was a magick a witch couldn't sense until he or she was smacked with the full force of its strength. Like a tornado on a clear summer day. All of the witches were bloody and beaten, yet all of them still fought their destiny.

All of them except the elemental air witch.

She knelt on her place in the circle, her beautiful dark hair flowing over her shoulders, and focused her eyes directly on Jack. He'd never sensed such a depth of sorrow in a person. She was ready to die. She wanted it.

His father's friends whispered that the woman had watched her husband close a circle the day before and it had broken her will. They doubted her sanity. Of course, they didn't need her sanity for the closing of this circle. They only needed her magick.

Even in his young mind, Jack finally understood that his father sacrificed witches on the altar of dark magick in order to gain power. These were the shoes his father expected him to fill. These were the shoes his father said Jack might not ever be able to fill because he was so weak, so tainted.

If to be strong meant to do this, then Jack knew his father was right—he had too much of his mother in him.

Jack fidgeted and wanted to look away from the elemental air witch's empty eyes, but he felt like he needed to maintain a connection with her. What he really wanted to do was run away. Jack wanted to do something, *anything* to not have to watch the circle being cast. Instead, he held the woman's gaze while his heart thumped hard and his mind raced.

His father and his friends took their places and began

the ritual. The sound of chanting filled the air, making it crackle with their combined power. It raised the hair on Jack's arms and made his ears ring. The power that slid over his skin felt like dark velvet, filling him up, giving him the sensation of light-headedness and euphoria. The magick in his chest reacted by glowing warm and seductively in response, wanting to free itself.

Immersed in it, Jack felt almost invincible. As he looked upon the rapturous expressions of his father and his friends, Jack wondered what they must feel. It had to be much more powerful for the ones working the spell.

The witches making their involuntary sacrifice slipped under the thrall of the powerful, dark forces exerted over them. Their faces contorted into masks of pain as they failed to fight the rape of their magick. That's what jerked Jack from the strange, pleasurable lethargy that had stolen over him. The witches couldn't move, yet their faces showed their agony.

Eventually, they stilled and became submissive. Their bodies slackened as the spell dragged their power into the center of the circle in order to open a doorway for a summoning.

His father had explained this was how to call forth a demon, a supernatural entity capable of great power that would be tied to him and his friends like a servant for a time in exchange for the gift of the four witches, plus a favor or two. It was a beautiful thing, his father had told him, a wondrous sacrifice to bring into being such a magnificent creature.

Jack stood silently, holding the woman's gaze as the magick possessed her and destroyed her. Little by little, Jack watched the light bleed from her eyes until they were dead and glassy, until she'd slumped to the ground like a puppet whose strings had been released slowly. He wanted to do something, fight his father and his friends to save her, but fear held him rooted in place. As each of the witches died in turn, the air in the center of the circle began to shimmer while the demon was birthed.

He never saw the beast in the flesh. Jack ran.

Out of the house, down the long, curling driveway of his father's mansion, past the gate, he'd run as fast as he could. The servants had chased him, but Jack had beaten them to the street and disappeared, hiding among the houses, bushes, and cars until nightfall. Then he'd run straight to Hannah, his mother's sister.

His father had never sought him out after that. He'd let Jack's aunt raise him. Perhaps he'd thought Jack was too much trouble to bother with. Too weak. Too tainted. Jack didn't know.

Ultimately, he'd rejected the name Crane for his mother's maiden name of McAllister. Once he'd turned eighteen, he'd sought the Coven and had been working for them ever since.

His aunt had raised him well and with love, much as his mother probably would've if she'd been strong enough to stick around. He'd chosen this work because of his father and also because of that day.

He could still feel emotion coiled in him like a striking snake. Hatred for his father and at himself for being his father's son, but, most of all, rage at himself for never having done anything to help those witches that day.

The memory lived like a vibrant thing inside him. He didn't know if he'd ever be free of its hold.

Jack looked down to where he fisted Mira's hair and relaxed his fingers, letting the silky strands fall to the pillow. He owed her. He'd watched her mother die and had done nothing to prevent it. He'd stood there in fear, when he could've fought his father and his friends, perhaps could've broken the spell, the circle, something.

Jack walked back to sit on the desk. Thomas Monahan, head of the Coven, had tasked Jack with watching over Mira Hoskins as soon as they'd discovered she existed. If the Coven knew she existed, most likely so did Crane. Jack had been tailing her for about two weeks, sitting in his car in the freezing cold to stake out her work and her apartment. Normally, he didn't do straight bodyguarding jobs like this one, but this was special. Mira was special.

She moved on the bed, waking up slowly. Jack sat on the desk in the dark, flicking the Zippo on and off absentmindedly as he watched her.

Yesterday he'd felt compelled to make actual contact with her, so he'd gone into the diner and watched her work. Her eyes were hazel. Sometimes brown, sometimes green. Her smile was easy and seemed genuine. She actually appeared to like people, which was something he couldn't say about himself.

"Mmmm, huh?" Mira murmured from the bed. She gasped as she caught sight of him in the darkened room and pushed up into a sitting position, her hand instantly going to her head at the abrupt movement.

Jack put the Zippo down. "How are you feeling?"

She took a few moments to answer. "Like I've been hit by a truck, abducted, and am now in fear for my life. How are you?"

"You're here for your own protection."

"That's probably what all serial killers say."

He slid off the desk, walked to the side of the bed, and flipped the light on. She eyed him uneasily and moved toward the center of the mattress, away from him. He watched her glance around the room, taking in the mahogany furniture, the paintings on the wall. She centered her gaze on each exit in turn—the door to the main part of his apartment, the door to the bathroom, and the window.

"Don't try the window," he said. "We're on the fifty-second floor. Are you hungry, thirsty?"

She licked her lips. "I want you to tell me what's going on."

"Your head must hurt. You want an aspirin, maybe?"

Mira hesitated. "An aspirin would be good."

He walked into the bathroom to get the aspirin bottle and a cup of water. By the time he got back, she was gone. Unsurprising. He could hear her fumbling the locks at the front door in desperation.

Jack sighed, set the bottle and cup down, and walked through the living room toward her.

She was just working the top lock and swearing a blue streak when he reached her. He pressed his body against hers and covered her hand with his own. She stilled immediately and shivered a little.

Jack tried hard not to enjoy the feeling of her pressed to him, but he couldn't help it. The sound of her breathing, harsh in the quiet air, made his libido twitch with interest. It made him think of other situations when she might be flush up against him, her breathing ragged. A situation in which they'd be wearing far less clothing and Mira would be feeling far friendlier toward him. It was natural, he reminded himself yet again, the natural attraction of fire to air.

His pelvis cupped her gorgeous ass in this position, his chest bracing her back. He couldn't help but wonder what she'd do if he slid his hands over her breasts, gathered the hem of her skirt and pulled it upward. How would her sex feel bared to his exploring hand? What kind of sounds would she make as he stroked her?

You stupid bastard, he scolded himself. *She'd scream like a siren.*

But give him time and he could seduce her. He knew how to touch her to make her want him . . . *beg* for him. Even though he shouldn't, he could tempt her into his bed.

The faint scent of her rose perfume teased his nose as he leaned down and placed his mouth close to her ear. "You're incredibly predictable. Even if you'd gotten out the front door, you never would've been able to call the elevator without my security code."

"What do you mean?"

"I mean my apartment is the only one on this floor. I mean I have the elevator on security mode. You can't access it without my code. No one comes up or goes down without it. No one even stops at this floor without my permission." Beyond that, the magickal wards in place wouldn't allow her to cross the threshold once she'd opened the door. She wasn't yet ready for that information, however.

"You're a prisoner here. A princess in a tower," he breathed silkily into her ear.

She shivered against him again and her breath shuddered out of her. "I'll be missed, you know. My employers will miss me when I don't come into work. Plus, you made a racket last night. Someone must have seen you, heard you—"

"*I* didn't make a racket, Mira. The men who were trying to kidnap you made the racket." He paused. "Anyway, your neighbors weren't home. That's why the goons chose that time to break into your apartment. You live in the basement of that building, a very isolated place. It's old and well soundproofed. I doubt anyone noticed anything. They planned it that way."

Her breathing hitched. "What do you mean? Who's *they*?"

It was hard to let her go, but he stepped back. She turned. Fear warred with rage on her face, and the latter emotion won. Her eyes were greener than brown now, made bright with anger.

"Your aspirin and your answers are in the bedroom," he answered.

With a baleful glare, she walked back into the bedroom. He followed her. Once inside the room, he pointed at the nightstand and watched as she took the medicine.

Jack picked up the pair of blue silk pajamas he'd draped over a nearby chair. They were probably about her size. "It's late and I'm tired. I found these in one of my drawers. They should fit you." He nodded toward the bathroom. "Go in there and put them on. Feel free to take a shower if you'd like. The door locks from the inside, if it would make you feel better. I swept the room clean, however. Everything that could be a weapon is locked up, so don't waste your time looking."

She just stared at him, her jaw locked and pretty eyes flashing.

"Do it and I'll explain everything when you come back out. I'm not going to hurt you."

She glanced at the pajamas. "Whose are they?"

"Not some woman I just killed, I promise. They were left here by a friend."

"I bet you have lots of *friends*."

Jack shrugged. "I don't do too bad for myself."

Mira snorted. "I'm sure you're the king of one-night stands."

"One-night-stands are not fulfilling for either partner."

She blinked. "I hesitate to ask why you think that. Then here I am, asking why."

He smiled. "One night isn't long enough to learn a woman's body, how she likes to be touched." He paused and dropped his voice a little. "I wonder how many nights with me you could handle, Mira?"

She inhaled sharply. "Damn, you're an arrogant pig."

He shrugged and held out the pajamas again. "Are you going to take them or not? You have to be sick of your work clothes by now, and they won't be comfortable to sleep in."

She hesitated, then took the clothing and went into the bathroom. Obviously, she didn't feel at ease enough to take a shower because she emerged after five minutes dressed in the pajamas. The color made her eyes a little browner, he noticed, and her red-painted toenails peeked from the bottom of the too-long pants.

"Sit down on the bed," he instructed.

She sat, and he sank down next to her. Mira tried to slide away from him, but he held her by the upper arm. "Stay still," he ordered. "I'm not going to hurt you."

He reached up and pushed her hair away in order to

examine her bruise. She flinched. "It's all right. I just want to take a look at it."

She kept her wary gaze on him as he took a closer look at the bruise. He covered the injury with his hand and felt his palm heat up. Concentrating on the area, he did his best to manipulate the cells to regenerate faster. He couldn't do much for her, but he could do a little. Healing, ironically, was in the realm of fire.

"It's hot," she gasped. "What are you doing?"

"I'm almost done."

He took his hand away and noted with approval that the bruise already looked a little better. "How much do you know about your parents?"

"My parents?"

"Yes, you know, the people who created you? They died when you were just a toddler, leaving you to be raised by your godmother."

"I know who they were," she snapped. "I know when and how they died. How do *you* know that?"

He waited a moment before answering. "It's my job to know about the witches who are placed in my care."

She stared at him for a moment, clearly registering the word *witch*. "Oh, you're insane! You think . . . the Wicca . . . in the restaurant. . . . *Hell*." She shot up, yanked free of his grasp, and went for the door.

He grabbed her around the waist before she got very far and held her against his chest. She felt fragile against him and he fought to not underestimate his strength and hurt her. "You need to sit down and listen to what I have to say."

Mira struggled against him, but he only tightened his hold until she stilled. "I don't have to listen to anything you have to say, you crazy son of a bitch!" she shouted at the top of her lungs.

Jack wrestled her back to the bed and sat her down. He wished there was an easier way to do this, to make her understand that he was on her side.

"Screw this." She bolted again, and he caught her around the waist again, swinging her back around to land on the bed.

"Please. Stay. Still."

She glared up at him. Her head had to be pounding by now. She also had to know she had no chance against him. He had a lot more muscle and weight to throw around than she did. She couldn't beat him in a physical fight. The ironic thing was that she *could* best him with her magick; she just didn't know how to wield it.

"I didn't want to have to do this, but you're leaving me no choice. Lay back against the pillows," he ordered. When she didn't comply, he added a menacing, "*Do it now.*"

She leaned back, and he took a length of rope from the drawer in his nightstand. He straddled her waist and drew her hands above her head.

With a deftness that came from lots of practice, he looped the ends around her wrists, tying them tight enough without cutting off her blood flow, and secured the ends to the eyebolt in the wall over the center of the mattress. He left enough slack so she could put her arms down and turn over. She had room to move, but she wouldn't be able to get the rope undone very easily. Jack was proficient at tying knots.

When he finished, he sat down next to her on the bed.

"I see you're a real expert," she growled at him and glanced at the eyebolt. "You use that a lot, do you? Know your way around a length of rope?"

He smiled. "I've had my share of practice with lots of willing women. Key word is *willing*. That's nice rope, by the way. Hemp. It's made to lie against the skin. It won't chafe you."

"I'm not a willing woman."

"You almost slit my throat in your apartment. You're staying tied up." He sat back and admired his handiwork. She looked damn good tied to his bed. *Too damn good.*

Jack forced his mind back to the subject at hand. He sat

down on the edge of the bed. "Tell me what you know about your parents," he demanded again.

She sighed as though tired and fed up. Other women would be crying by now. She was pissed off. Mira might seem meek on the outside, but her spine was made of steel. "My mother was a secretary. My father worked in construction. They died in a car crash when I was three years old. I have hazy memories of them that I can't be sure really ever happened. Maybe I just wished them into existence. I know other things, but it's all secondhand stuff, told to me by my godmother." She paused. "Why?"

"Your parents didn't die in a car crash. They did die, but that's not how they met their end. I'm not going to play around here, okay? I know you're not going to believe me, but both your parents were witches. Their element was air. It's a rare ability that they passed down to you." He drew a breath. "You're a witch, Mira."

THREE

❧

SHE STARED FOR A MOMENT AND THEN LAUGHED harshly. "First of all, you're insane. Second of all, I'm Wiccan, not a witch. There's a difference. Wicca is a religion, and witchcraft is a practice. Wicca is about spirituality, worship of the Lord and Lady, observing the Wheel of the Year. Witchcraft is about casting spells to achieve certain outcomes. I don't practice witchcraft. I don't even believe in that part of it. You can be Wiccan and a witch, *but I am just Wiccan!*" she finished with a shout. Her face had gone beet red.

"Doesn't matter what you believe. Not believing doesn't make it untrue." He shook his head. "Wicca might be your religion, but witchcraft is in your blood. You're a natural witch. You just don't realize it yet. Your element is air, just like your parents. That means your power is centered in commanding air, separating your consciousness from your body, intuitive ability, accessing and directing sound waves. Your abilities lie in manipulating anything in the realm of air, and that, Mira, is nearly everything. It's the most powerful element."

"Insane," she muttered again. "You've been watching too many episodes of *Charmed*."

He ignored her. "You're a real elemental witch, with natural magick running through your veins. I'm not talking about a Goth poser here or a spell caster. There are no bubbling cauldrons, no multicolored candles to burn, no smudge sticks. There's just elemental power and your ability to wield it."

"Sure. Whatever. You probably believe in the Easter bunny, too."

"I bet you've loved the wind since you were a child. I bet you keep your windows open whenever you can, relish a windy day and find excuses to be outside in it, find tornadoes powerful and intriguing. I bet you love the feel of a breeze stirring the hair at the back of your neck—"

"Everyone loves that stuff."

"No, they don't. I bet you've always been predisposed to sound. Sometimes you wake up hearing voices in your room or maybe you hear people calling your name as you fall asleep or perhaps you hear sounds that seem so real it's like they're happening right in your bedroom. Maybe sometimes it seems you hear other people's thoughts or anticipate their desires. People probably call you intuitive, but it goes much further than simple, natural intuitiveness."

She stared at him. Her face had gone a little pale.

"I'm right, aren't I?"

Mira looked away from him with a look of contempt on her face and sniffed. "You're in league with Ben, for all I know. Maybe he put you up to this."

Anger flared within him that she would compare him with an idiot like Ben Williams. He knew all about her ex. He was a selfish, stupid asshole who couldn't recognize gold when it was right in his hands.

"*Don't* associate me with him," he said in a low voice.

She looked back at him, her eyes wide.

Jack ran his hand over his face and forced himself not to give into the irritation he felt. He leaned in close to her. "On some level, you understand what I'm saying. On some level, you've always known you were different." He paused and raised an eyebrow. "Tell me that's not true."

Her mouth snapped shut.

He leaned back. "It takes one to know one. My element is fire." He snapped his fingers and opened his palm. In the center burned a small blue flame. It was a parlor trick, but a spectacular one for the uninitiated.

Mira gasped and backed up as much as she could into the pillows. "How are you doing that?"

"It's magick. My magick. It's the magick of fire."

"It's a trick. Just some stupid trick."

He concentrated on the flame, letting it spread and lick up his wrist and his inner arm, over his sleeve. Mira gasped. "Yes, it's a trick, but not like you're thinking. Took me awhile to learn this one. Fire is a complicated element, dangerous and unpredictable. It takes a lot of time to master. I have my fair share of scars to show for it."

"H-how are you doing that?" she asked again.

"I called fire into being in the center of my hand. I'm holding it in check with my mind so it doesn't burn me. It takes a long time to develop the strength of will and the concentration to command fire."

"That's impossible," she breathed, staring at the flame.

He turned his arm, letting the flame twist around it, gently engulfing it. Fire was like a pet to him, now that he could control the element with confidence. He smiled, watching Mira's face.

"Impossible," she breathed again.

"Your mind has been trained to believe this is impossible, that people can't manipulate their environment and create things from thin air. Reality is so much bigger than you think it is. It's so much more flexible. You can do this too, although with air, not fire."

"I can create . . . air?"

"When there's a lack of it. I meant that with the proper training, you'd be able to create a breeze or a wind."

Her expression changed from awe to skepticism. "So I guess I'll never suffocate then." She shrugged. "Or get caught in the middle of a lake in a sailboat on a windless day. Oh, can I throw away my hair dryer now? And—"

"Mira?" he purred silkily, ignoring her joke. "You know what happens to fire when it's fed by air?" He held her gaze as he blew on the flame circling his wrist. It flared brilliantly. "We complement each other."

MIRA LOST HER TRAIN OF THOUGHT—ACTUALLY, it was more like it had a wreck somewhere in her head. The first impression that popped into her mind after Jack's words cleared everything else out was *fire consumes air*.

Jack's dark, mesmerizing eyes locked with hers and she couldn't look away. "You and I have a natural attraction," he said gently.

Gentle from this man seemed dangerous.

He extinguished the flame with another snap of his fingers and showed her his hand and forearm, so she could see he wasn't wearing anything special on it and that he wasn't injured, though it was true he did have what looked like an old burn scar on his wrist. She sniffed the air, but could smell no chemical.

"You're a good magician, so what?" she said in a shaky voice. "You're an insane serial killer who likes to do tricks for his hostages. You like to pretend there's such a thing as magick."

He ignored her. "Your parents didn't want you exposed to any of this stuff. They hid your birth from the Coven. It was their right to do so. Their last wish was that your godmother let you grow up as a normal kid. But a couple weeks ago your godmother, Annie Weber, got a call that disturbed her. She worried it might be the man who'd hurt your parents, a man who heads a group of witches out for their own gain. Annie was so worried that she defied your parent's last wish and called us."

Mira felt overwhelmed by everything he'd said, but focused on one thing, even if it was a lie. "Who hurt my parents?"

"His name is William Crane. He heads a faction of witches . . . warlocks, really, called the Duskoff Cabal, who betrayed the Coven. Their cover is a multinational, diversified company called Duskoff International. Non-witches need not apply for the executive positions."

"Warlocks?"

"Warlocks are witches who have betrayed their coven, male or female. The Duskoff is an old group. Their history stretches back to the Dark Ages. They don't care who they hurt, and they hurt your parents. Crane sent those men to your apartment, the ones who broke your door down."

She gave him a look of pure skepticism. "So, you're telling me warlocks killed my parents," she said in a dry tone.

He nodded.

Oh, fine. Might as well get the whole fake story. "So what do they want with me?"

"You're a powerful witch who can command the element of air. They need you to close a circle. It's what they used your parents for. A circle is comprised of—"

"Earth, fire, water, and air. I get it."

He nodded. "There aren't many witches like you. You're sought after. I'm here to protect you for my boss, the man who heads the Coven. His name is Thomas Monahan."

Interesting. Monahan had been her mother's maiden name. "So, I'm like . . . what? An endangered species?"

He smiled. "I guess."

She bit her lower lip. "What's Crane's element?"

Jack glanced away as he answered. "Fire, like me."

"What's the circle for?"

"To call a demon. The members of the Duskoff hold high positions of power in the business community and politics. They didn't get where they are without help. Crane forced your parents to close two circles for him. Your father closed one. Your mother closed a second." He paused. "It rapes a witch of his or her magick. A witch can't live without magick. It's akin to a major organ."

Mira laughed. "Okay. Great imagination you have, Jack. How do you explain the fact that I've seen the newspaper clippings of my parent's accident? If you expect me to believe any of this—"

"The car accident was staged. It wasn't your parents they found in the wreckage. The Duskoff doesn't leave loose ends. They don't leave mysteries that non-magickal authorities might trace back to them."

She looked away, a sob gathering in her throat. Mira could barely remember her parents. They were just hazy images in her mind that she saw through deep emotion. Her whole life there'd been an empty place where her parents had been.

All she'd ever wanted was to have them in her life. All she'd ever wanted was her father to cheer her on when she'd played soccer in junior high, for her mother to give her advice when she'd gone on her first date. Annie had done a great job of filling both parental roles, but that hadn't taken away the longing Mira felt for her parents.

"You're a bastard to be playing this way with me," she said in a low voice. "You think I don't still grieve for my parents?" She managed to choke back the sob, but a tear rolled down her cheek. "Damn you."

"I'm sorry, Mira." Jack brushed her tear away with his thumb, and she jerked her head away from his touch and stared at him. He actually did look like he regretted his words. He looked miserable. Wouldn't someone wanting to cause her pain appear triumphant?

This whole situation was so confusing. Why play with her this way? What was the point?

He sighed and took the cordless phone from its cradle on the nightstand. Jack punched in a number and held the phone to her ear. She frowned at him while it rang.

"Hello?" It was her godmother. She sounded groggy, as if the call had woken her up.

"Annie?" Mira said. "Annie, you have to help me! I've been kidnapped by some crazy guy named Jack—"

"Honey? Mira?" her godmother answered, coming more awake. "That means they went after you. I'm so sorry this is happening." Annie's voice broke on a sob. "I'd hoped I was wrong."

Mira went silent for a moment. "What do you mean?"

"I wasn't sure if the person who called was related to Crane, so I asked the Coven to keep watch over you and intervene if anything happened. This man, Jack McAllister, he's protecting you, Mira. Do what he says."

Speechless, she sat for a moment processing her godmother's words. "But what this man is telling me can't be true," she replied slowly. "It simply can't be."

"I'm sorry I never told you any of this before, sweetheart. I was complying with your parents' wishes. Yes, what Jack is telling you is true. I know it seems unbelievable." She let out a soft sob. "I should've prepared you. Please forgive me. I hoped the Duskoff wouldn't come after you and your life could've remained undisturbed."

A tear rolled down Mira's cheek as everything that had happened overwhelmed her. She fell silent, not knowing what else to say. Jack took the phone from her ear and put it to his own. Mira stared straight ahead as Jack and Annie talked. Something close to catatonia stole over her.

Jack glanced at her with a concerned expression on his

face. "I'll take care of her, Ms. Weber, I promise. I won't let any harm come to her. You have my word." He paused, listening to something Annie was saying. "Yes. I'll tell her." He turned the phone off and set it back in the cradle.

It could be another trick, maybe. Maybe somehow he'd been able to fake Annie's voice?

Her head hurt.

Jack looked down at her. "She said to think back to the time when you were a child and you walked into the back-yard and saw a storm cloud over the garden patch. There had been a drought, and she took the chance no one would see her watering her tomatoes with magick. Annie's a witch, too. Her element is—"

"Water," Mira finished. "I thought I dreamed that."

He turned away. "You have enough to think about for one night. I'm going to sleep."

"Jack?"

He turned back to her.

"Did you kill those men outside my apartment?"

His stony silence was answer enough.

She blew out a hard breath and glanced away. "Did you have to kill them?"

"My job is to protect you. If they'd lived, they would have known I'd taken you and led your enemies here. If Crane gets you, he'll use you to close a circle, and you will die. Their deaths were warranted. It was you or them." He paused. "I chose you."

Their deaths were warranted. He said it without any emotion.

"It's taken care of. Their bodies are gone. Quick and ef-ficient. They won't be missed by anyone but Crane, and there won't be any trail to lead non-magickal officials to your front door."

How did you manage that? The question was poised on her tongue, but she swallowed it, deciding she really didn't want to know the answer. She licked her lips and glanced away from him. "So, there are good witches and bad witches, then? Crane is bad. Annie is good."

"No. It's not black and white. There's the mostly good, the mostly bad, and there's some gray."

"What are you?"

He held her gaze and answered steadily. "Gray."

A wisp of uneasiness curled through her stomach. There was a world of weariness in his eyes when he said that word and she wondered why. "I have questions."

He turned away and drew his shirt over his head. Muscles rippled along his back and chest, and scars marked him here and there. The sight of him shirtless made her throat go dry. She looked away.

"And you'll get answers . . . tomorrow," he replied. "I'm tired. I'm going to sleep."

"Aren't you going to untie me?"

"I don't trust you won't sneak into the kitchen, grab a knife, and finish what you started in your apartment." He turned to fix her with his smoldering blue eyes. His voice dropped to something in the sinfully seductive range. "Anyway, I like the way you look tied to my bed. Maybe one day you'll be bound there willingly."

"In your dreams, psycho."

He chuckled, kicked off his shoes, and pulled his socks and pants off. Jack stood there in his blue boxer briefs while he arranged his clothing over a chair. She let her gaze travel over his strong, hairy legs, his extremely fine ass, and the bulge in front that looked really, *really* bulgy.

"Hey!" she objected.

He laughed. "That was a delayed reaction."

"It was not!"

"Be happy," he said as he went toward the other side of the bed. "Normally, I sleep naked."

Oh, sweet Lady.

He got into bed and turned the light off. Immediately, he

turned over on his side, his back to her, leaving her to the darkness and her jumbled thoughts. She hated that she was so attracted to him. She hated it even more that Jack probably knew she was attracted to him.

Mira tried to move away from him a little. Jack seemed to emanate body heat, an interesting trait considering the magickal ability he claimed. He groaned as he relaxed into a comfortable sleeping position, and the sexy sound shot awareness through her.

She tried not to enjoy the warmth of him and the sound of his breathing in the quiet air. She tried hard not to imagine what his hands would feel like cupping her breasts, rubbing her nipples into hard peaks. What would his mouth taste like on hers? How would his cock feel pressed against the entrance of her sex?

Mira shivered and shut her eyes, driving the thoughts from her mind. It was perverse to be considering any of that in her situation. To the dark room, she grumbled, "You could at least untie me."

"And let you take advantage of me?" he answered in a false, demure voice. "No way. Sweet dreams."

"What if I have to go to the bathroom?"

"Then I'll let you. I'm not a monster, Mira."

"That's open for debate."

He chuckled. "Everything will become clear soon enough. I tied you loose, but if you're really uncomfortable or you have to go to the bathroom, wake me up."

She listened as Jack's breathing went from normal to deep and even, signaling he'd fallen asleep. He'd left enough slack in the rope that she could rest her hands on her chest. She spent some time using her teeth to worry at the knot, but he'd tied it so well she couldn't figure out how to free herself. Knowing she couldn't get out of the apartment anyway, she gave up and drummed her fingers on her collarbone as the events of the day assaulted her mind.

Mira would bet anything that one of the abilities of a

witch with skill in the element of water was the ability to read emotion. Annie had always been empathic to the point of having preternatural ability. Mira had never been able to keep anything from her as she'd been growing up.

Then there were those unexplained incidents in Mira's life. Times when Mira had been very emotional, angry or grieving, when it had seemed like a breeze had swirled around her even when she'd been within buildings on windless days. There had been times she'd felt a warm burst of power in the center of her chest when she drew a lungful of air on a spring day. There were other things too, all so mild that she'd been able to find rational explanations for them.

Could it be that these occurrences had been her magick manifesting independently? Maybe because she'd never trained her power, it had whispered out of her on its own at random moments?

She shook her head. *Silly. Stupid.* Jack was really getting to her.

She leaned back against the pillows, searching for a comfortable place to lie. All of it was almost enough to make her believe, but not quite. Her rational mind wasn't ready to give up its stranglehold on the reality she'd always known. In that reality her parents had died in a car crash. There had been no foul play.

And there was no such thing as magick.

FOUR

~

MIRA AWOKE LYING ON HER SIDE WITH ONE FIST curled against her mouth. The scent of breakfast teased her from sleep, and she opened her eyes blearily to an empty bed and morning sunlight streaming in through the window. Jack had untied her at some point during the night. The rope hadn't impeded her sleep, really. Her mind had done that. She rubbed her wrists. The rope hadn't even left marks on her skin. The man had talent.

Groaning, she rolled over and ended up with her nose in Jack's pillow. She groaned again, this time from the scent of him. The light woody and spicy scent made all her nerve endings shoot to attention.

The man was a menace, pure and simple.

She'd never met a man as attractive as Jack. Since she had *such* good taste in men, it figured he'd turn out to be a raving lunatic.

Maybe.

She sat up, her mind replaying her godmother's voice on the phone last night. If Jack had somehow faked that, he was damned good. But why would he go to such great lengths to concoct this strange story and then do everything possible to make her believe it? None of it made sense, but the alternative was too bizarre to contemplate.

What about the fire? How could someone fake something like that? Unless Jack was a crazy magician with a penchant for elaborate pranks. She rubbed the bridge of her nose. *No.* That just didn't fit.

And even if he had faked the call to Annie, how could he know about the garden incident? No one knew about that except her. Mira hadn't even known Annie had realized she'd walked back there and seen that tiny rain burst over the garden patch.

Not to mention the men laying in her entranceway when she'd regained consciousness the night before, the men who had meant her harm. The ones Jack had . . . she swallowed hard . . . *taken care of*. What about them? She'd intuitively felt those men had meant to hurt her. Mira didn't have that feeling about Jack.

Nothing added up; her logical mind denied any of it could be true. The whole thing made her head hurt even more than it already did.

She blew out a hard breath and slid over to the edge of the bed. Jack banged pots and pans in the kitchen, clearly invested in making breakfast. Curious, she opened the drawer of his nightstand and peered within. Inside laid more rope—no surprise there—and a handful of foil-wrapped condoms.

Her eyes widened and she slammed the drawer closed. The noise made pain flare through her head, but Jack seemed not to have heard it. He was still banging around in the kitchen while he cooked something that smelled delicious.

Mira wondered if he made breakfast for the women the rope and condoms were meant for. Probably, she decided. Right after he twisted their worlds on end by declaring magick existed.

She stood up and walked into the bathroom. Catching sight of herself in the mirror that hung over the white marble countertop, she leaned in and examined her bruise. It was a hideous thing, covering the whole right part of her forehead. *Lovely.* She supposed she should be happy her skin hadn't been broken, or that she hadn't received a more serious head injury.

Looking more closely and frowning, she traced it with her index finger. The color seemed wrong. Mira scowled at her reflection. She was no nurse, but she'd had her share of bruises, and this one looked older than it was. Definitely not pretty, but on its way to gone.

How could that be?

She shrugged. She was probably mistaken. It's not like she ever went to med school.

A towel, washcloth, packaged toothbrush, and fresh bar of soap lay on the small porcelain table near the shower, correction, huge, custom shower. A pair of jeans and a silky soft blue sweater rested on the marble counter. More castoffs from his friend, maybe? She was unaccountably annoyed that she was being forced to wear clothing left behind by Jack's fuck buddies.

Mira wondered if he'd tied them to the eyebolt.

She shuddered, imagining herself tied to it for a moment. The images came without coaxing. Jack's big body covering hers, skin sliding against skin, slick with their combined perspiration. Her wrists bound above her head. Jack between her thighs. Herself, at his mercy and completely possessed by him.

Mira groaned, the sound magnified by the large room. How was she supposed to get through this while she was so attracted to her captor?

Could Stockholm syndrome set in this early?

She turned, locked the door, and checked it twice before she stripped off her clothes. She needed a shower. The smell of the diner still clung faintly to her.

The custom shower could probably fit about four people and had jets that shot water from three different directions. After regulating the temperature controls to her liking, she stepped inside and closed the door. The warm water sluiced down her body, drawing a ragged groan of pleasure from her throat.

Carefully keeping her bruise out of the path of the water's spray, she soaped her hands and rubbed them over her arms and chest. Her body felt sensitized, sexually aware. It had been a long time since she'd felt that way. Her nipples went hard as she passed her hands over them, peeking from the white soap bubbles.

Tipping her head back with a sigh, she ran her palms over her abdomen, passed her fingers through the coarse dark hair covering her mound, and then delved between her thighs. She brushed her sensitive clit. It had been a long time since she'd made herself come.

She stood for a moment with her hand between her thighs, feeling the heat of her sex radiate into her palm. She was a healthy woman with needs that had gone unfulfilled. That had to explain her intense attraction to Jack. She was willing to accept that explanation, anyway, since the alternative was so scary. Did she have some dangerous, secret abduction fantasies she should seek counseling for?

Mira finished bathing, then got out and dressed in the cast-off clothing.

The jeans were uncomfortably too small for her and she ended up annoyed again as she stepped out of the bathroom, running a comb she'd found in a drawer through her towel-dried hair. Her annoyance was probably a result of her inexplicable sexual frustration just as much as having to wear the too-small castoffs from one of Jack's lovers.

Jack stood shirtless and shoeless in the middle of the bedroom. The sight of him there in the morning sunlight with his hair mussed from sleep was enough to drop her IQ about fifty points. She stopped and stared for a moment, slack-jawed, before recovering.

He dangled her pentagram from one long finger. "I found this on the carpet in the living room."

"Must have fallen off while you were accosting me," she snapped. She walked over and took it from him.

He grabbed her wrist before she could pull away and drew her close to him. The muscles of his forearm and chest rippled with the movement. Skitters of pleasure and apprehension ran through her body as he brushed her damp hair away from her face and tipped her chin to the side to take a look at the bruise. "It's better today."

Mira frowned. "I'm not sure, but I think it's already healing. That doesn't seem likely. . . . Anyway, that's what it looks like."

"I helped it a little."

She scowled at him. "Not possible."

His gaze held hers steadily. "You have a lot to learn about what's possible." He studied her face for a moment. "You have very pretty eyes. They can't decide if they're brown or green."

She blinked and fought the urge to lower her gaze, suddenly feeling self-conscious. "Thanks."

He held her wrist for another heartbeat, and then released her.

She pulled away from him and put on the necklace. "I suppose I'm meant to stay here for some length of time?"

"I suppose you are."

"I'm going to need things if I'm going to be a prisoner. I have no clothing, other than that what your . . . *friends* may have left, and they, apparently, weren't human judging by their insignificant size. I need proper soap for my face, non-male-smelling shampoo . . . and, goddamn it, I need fresh underwear!" she finished grouchily.

He walked to the desk, got out a pen and pad of paper,

and handed them to her. "Make a list. I'll get whatever you need."

She took the pen and paper, raising her eyebrows at him. "You're not going through my underwear drawer—"

"Just make the list."

She sat on the edge of the bed and made out the list while Jack finished dressing, then handed it to him.

"I swear I won't go through your underwear drawer," he said. "Now, are you hungry? I made breakfast."

She mumbled "yes" and followed her nose to the kitchen. Mira hadn't gotten a good look at the rest of the apartment the day before since she'd been unconscious the first time she'd gone through it and fleeing for her life the second time.

It was decorated much like the bedroom—expensively. The floors were polished wood and area rugs lay in front of the couch and in the foyer. A matching runner lined the hall-way. Most of the heavy furniture was also wood. Modern artwork hung on the walls and sculptures stood on tables.

The apartment had an open floor plan. A spiral staircase in the corner led to a loftlike area, a hallway, and a series of closed doors on the second floor, probably more bed-rooms or maybe an office.

It looked like a rich man's bachelor pad and had prob-ably been decorated professionally. She couldn't really picture Jack picking out the elegant beige couch with the matching red embroidered cushions, or the gorgeous blue glass vase on the classy pedestal that stood against one wall.

Or maybe one of his *friends* had helped him. Maybe af-ter they'd gone shopping, he'd stripped her, pressed her over the back of the loveseat, and taken her from behind un-til she'd yelled out her climax to his swanky soundproofed apartment.

Mira sighed. Clearly, she needed counseling and medica-tion. The sexual thoughts and images that kept leaping into her mind were unusual for her. Not to mention, the thought of Jack with another woman seemed strangely unwelcome. She glowered at Jack as she passed into the kitchen as if it was his fault she'd taken leave of her senses.

Well, hell. It *was* his fault.

The kitchen was large, with a middle island. Above the island hung a big rack with copper pots and crystal wine glasses. Two places were set at a table in the recessed breakfast nook. Jack walked over with a pan and scooped a couple eggs and a few pieces of bacon onto both plates. Her stomach growled.

She sat down at the place set with a bottle of aspirin. He was so considerate, her abductor. Mira poured herself a cup of coffee from the carafe on the table and dug in only to get a mouthful of yuck. "It's cold," she complained.

Jack reached out and touched her plate. "That should be better."

Shooting him a look that clearly said *I think you're crazy*, she took another bite of eggs and nearly had to spit them out they were so hot. Mira set her fork down and eyed him warily.

"How much proof do you need, Mira?" Jack reached out and gathered her pentagram in his hand. He rubbed his knuckles against her collarbone until she shivered and her nipples hardened.

"How can you blame me for doubting such a crazy story?"

He pulled her gently forward until her nose was a few inches from his. His breath stirred the fine hairs framing her face. Those sensual lips were only a short space from her mouth. Mira's heart hammered in her chest. "This pentagram, I don't need to explain the symbol to you," he purred in his chocolate-smooth voice.

She licked her lips and blinked nervously a couple of times. "It depends on your belief system. To me it symbolizes four points for the elements—earth, air, water, and fire. The top point is for Spirit. I'm aware how closely it aligns to your system of . . . m-magick." She had to fight to get the last word out.

He stared into her eyes for a breathless moment. For half a second she thought he might kiss her, and her eyes went a bit wider. Her feelings regarding that possibility were alarmingly befuddled.

Instead, he released her necklace and leaned back in his chair. "Annie tells me you never go a day without wearing it."

She eased away from him, strangely reluctant to do so, and fingered the pendant. The metal was still warm from his palm. Dropping it, she sighed. "Annie is Wiccan. She raised me that way."

"You could have rebelled against her religion. Kids rebel against their guardians for lots of different reasons. You could have chosen the faith of your parents. They were Catholic, right? Annie tells me you took to Wicca right off, held onto it tight all through your life."

Mira began eating her eggs again. They were good, sprinkled with basil and parsley and cooked to perfection. "So what does that prove?" she asked between mouthfuls.

"Wearing that symbol around your throat every day of your life proves that you can take the woman out of witchcraft, but you can't take the witch out of the woman."

Mira ignored him and kept eating her meal. She didn't know how to respond to that, so she changed the subject. "So," she said, motioning at the room with her butter knife, "kidnapping people must be lucrative."

He paused with a bite of egg halfway to his lips. "I don't kidnap people for a living." He sounded a little amused, but mostly annoyed.

"Really? What is it you do then?"

"I work for Thomas Monahan, head of the Coven. I manage his security." He set his fork down and wiped his luscious mouth with a napkin.

"You make yourself sound like a thug for hire."

He shrugged. "Sometimes I am, but most of the time

more skill is involved. If you compare Monahan to the president of the United States, I would be the equivalent of the head of Secret Service or maybe the NSA."

"How did you get that job?"

"Long story." He took a drink of coffee.

That meant he didn't want to discuss it. *Interesting.*

"So shouldn't you be off protecting Monahan, then?" she asked before she took another bite.

He snorted. "Monahan doesn't need protection. He does that fine on his own. He told me to guard you."

"Because I'm an endangered species? Seems strange that such a big shot like you is spending his time protecting someone like me."

"You sell yourself short. Your kind is rare. But aside from that, don't be too certain that's the only reason Thomas Monahan wants you safe."

She set her fork down and regarded him in silence for a moment. "What do you mean?"

Jack shrugged. "That's for him to explain, not me."

Her voice was poisonously sweet when she answered. "I think if you make a cryptic comment like that, I deserve an explanation."

"It's not my place to say. I've said more than I should already." He shook his head. "You have this way of making me overstep my bounds. Just know you're special to Monahan, that's all, and not for any of the sinister reasons flitting through your mind right now."

She glared at him. The man sure did like to play head games.

He rested his forearms on the table and stared at her with his unsettling blue eyes. Warmth became coldness. His light blue eyes seemed to have the strange ability to contain both ice and fire. His expression hardened.

"It's not my place to say," he repeated with finality.

"Fine," she bit off. That would be an argument for another time.

He set his fork down. "You'll be missed at work today if you don't call in. You have to call the diner and tell them you won't be able to come into work for a while."

"How can you be sure I won't scream bloody murder into the phone to let Mike know I'm in trouble?"

"First of all, you're not in any trouble, not here with me, anyway."

That was debatable. It depended on what kind of trouble he meant.

"Second of all, I think you're curious enough to stick around for a while of your own free will."

She let out a short, derisive laugh. "You assume a lot. How am I supposed to survive without going to work? Some of us need our wages to pay the rent."

"Don't worry about money right now, not when your life is in danger. The Coven has already agreed to pay your bills for a time. Think of this as a paid vacation. Only, it's not."

"What?"

"You need to be trained."

Mira stared at him for a moment before replying. "Why?"

"You're a powerful breed of witch who hasn't had a day of instruction in her life. Don't you want to know who you are?"

Mira winced. The comment hit her somewhere tender. She pushed away from the table, stood, and stalked away from him. "I know who I am, and it isn't a witch," she answered with her back to him.

"You think you know who you are, Mira? I see a woman adrift, not one at all sure of her course. I see a woman who has only deluded herself into thinking she knows where she's going."

Mira closed her eyes, feeling the truth of those words spear through her. Ever since her divorce she'd been fighting so hard to guide her life down a more positive road, but she wasn't sure she'd headed herself in the right direction. Mira had wondered more than once if she might be fooling herself.

She didn't even hear him approach. His hand fell on her shoulder and he turned her to face him. The expression he wore seemed conflicted, but she only had a moment to consider it. His arms wrapped around her, his heat and scent and masculinity closed over her, and he dragged her against his chest while his mouth came down on hers.

And the rest of the world simply faded away.

Slanting his mouth across hers, he flicked his tongue against her lips. She opened her mouth to allow him access and grabbed his upper arms, feeling the bunch and play of his biceps. His tongue stroked erotically against hers. Warm. Wet.

Tasting. Testing.

It wiped all the thought from her mind. Jolts of pleasure skittered up her spine and through her body. A growling sound that seemed part ecstasy, part torture curled from his throat and made her knees go weak.

He broke the kiss and rested his forehead against hers for a moment. Both of them breathed fast and shallow. "Mira," he whispered. That one word seemed ripped from him.

She wondered at the intensity of it, but then he kissed her again and she was drowning. This time his lips slid over hers slowly. Her body felt weakened from the easy silken slip of his mouth across hers. Jack nipped at her bottom lip, dragging it gently between his teeth, before angling his mouth over hers and delving his tongue between her lips once again.

Mira heard some low, helpless sound and realized it was coming from her. The hardness of his erection pressed into her stomach. He was aroused. Very, very aroused.

Jack pushed his hand beneath the hem of her sweater at the small of her back and touched skin. All she could do was hold on for dear life as he caressed her there, his strong fingers massaging her muscles with an authority that made her sex throb with need.

He eased his hand up, lingering for a moment over her

bra strap, then moved down to cup her jeans-clad rear. Jack pulled her flush against his big body and made a low, appreciative sound in the back of his throat.

Apart from the knee-melting kiss, something else stirred inside her. It dwelt somewhere in the center of her chest, a whisper of power unfurling. It pulsed, then tickled, then tingled. Finally, it grew warm. It felt like a bud blossoming into a rose and reaching toward the sun.

As Jack's mouth worked over hers, a tendril of power intensified and extended out, searching. Mira gasped into Jack's mouth as it found the curl of warmth emanating from him and twined with it. The power that bloomed from her felt light, but very strong. Jack's felt hot. It was a heat she knew instinctively had the ability to burn her in more ways than one.

It was magick. Her magick. His magick.

Mira knew it deeply and profoundly. Jack had called her magick out of her by using his own. Even though it was foreign, it felt like a long-lost part of herself, like coming home. She wanted to weep with the joy that filled her, sensing that tendril of power untwine like a waking dragon from somewhere near the heart of her.

Tears filled her eyes and she stifled a moan, gripping his shoulders, as their magick danced together, rubbing up against each other, merging and parting. They seemed to feed off each other, complement each other.

While he alternated sexy little tongue kisses with deeper, penetrating possessions of her mouth, their magick mated. The sensation was irresistible, and Mira's body responded hard and fast. Every little movement Jack made caused friction against her nipples through her clothing and arousal warmed her between her thighs.

Damn the clothing anyway. She wanted to feel him skin-on-skin.

FIVE

❦

HIS HARD COCK PRESSED AGAINST HER, AN OVER-powering temptation. Mira reached between their bodies, running her fingers over his shaft through his jeans. All she could think of was touching it, holding it, putting her mouth on it. She wanted it in her body, wanted to let their magick off their leashes to fully merge as their bodies did the same.

Abruptly as he'd initiated it, Jack broke the kiss.

"No, don't," she murmured before she could stop herself.

He stared down at her for a moment, his eyes unfocused. "Do you feel that power inside you?"

She nodded, biting her lower lip and staring at his mouth.

"That's your magick reacting to mine—air to fire. Tell me you're not a witch now." His voice sounded strained.

For a long, pregnant moment, he stared down at her. Her lips felt swollen from his kisses and her body . . . *wanted.* Oh, how she wanted him, but he released her and stalked out of the room, swearing under his breath.

Stunned at the sudden exit from paradise, Mira staggered

backward on legs that felt like cotton. Her back hit the kitchen wall with a thud and she let herself slide down until she sat on the tile floor. Somewhere at the edges of her mind, she heard the condo door slam.

Mira let out a careful, shuddering breath. Every part of her body still tingled. Her clit felt swollen, and her nipples were hard and sensitive. She wanted to cry because he'd left her that way, yet she was also a little relieved. While he kissed her, she'd fallen under some sort of strange spell. She would've slept with him, and that would've been a mistake.

She grimaced at both that realization and also at the sensation of her magick receding, coiling once again in the center of her chest without Jack's fire to coax it from her. Sorrow welled up at the loss of it. Mira pressed her palm between her breasts and slowly inhaled. She'd never even known it was there, and now she missed its presence.

With one kiss, Jack had clouded some things and made others incredibly clear. All of it was true. His magick, her magick. They were real, tangible things, forces of power within their bodies. Now that she'd held her magick in her hands, so to speak, there was no doubt.

Mira closed her eyes. And, oh, fuck . . . she was a witch. A real one. Not just a Wiccan who called herself a witch. *No.* She was an honest-to-Goddess witch with powerful magick to call.

She looked down at her hands. They were shaking.

That meant that everything else was true. Her parents hadn't died in a car crash; they'd been murdered. Worse, the murderer had gotten away with it.

Mira licked her lips, still tasting Jack on them, and swallowed hard. There was the possibility that she might be able to somehow bring her parents' killers to justice—whatever justice might exist in this case. Adrenaline shot through her just thinking about it. She was not exactly a rough-and-tumble kind of girl, ready to rampage across the country in search of revenge, but they had murdered her parents. She wanted . . . *needed* to make them pay for that.

Jack was right. She would stay here of her own free will.

She got up and searched for a phone. Sinking into an armchair, she took the cordless handset she found on an end table in the living room and punched the number of the restaurant with trembling fingers.

The lie stuck on her tongue, but she told Mike that she was having a family emergency and needed some time off to get it straightened out. It was even sort of true. At least she didn't have to fake the quavering emotion in her voice.

It's not like she could tell him the truth. She couldn't tell him that she'd discovered that some of the things that went bump in the night were actually real and she was one of them. And, oh, by the way, she had to avenge her parents' deaths at the hands of a group of warlocks while trying to prevent those same warlocks from using her to raise a demon.

Somehow she just didn't think Mike would believe her.

Like the great guy he was, Mike assured her they could cope without her for a while and wished her well. Told her to hurry back and that her job would be waiting for her when she returned.

Mira hung up with a lump in her throat and tears burning her eyes. Working at the diner had been her anchor for months, and now she felt adrift. Chaos had engulfed her life within the last twenty-four hours and chaos had a name—Jack McAllister.

Resting her elbows on her knees, she covered her face with her hands, careful not to put pressure on her bruise. The too-small jeans dug uncomfortably into her waist and pulled tight across her thighs. Irritated, she undid the top button, then got up and stalked into one of the guest rooms to find some other clothes. A search of the closets and dressers in both the extra bedrooms yielded nothing.

Mira went into Jack's bedroom. She couldn't stand to

stay in these constrictive clothes one more minute. If Jack became upset with her for rooting through his dresser to find something wearable, she didn't care.

After opening a few drawers, she found a pair of gray sweatpants and a sweatshirt that said *University of Minnesota* on it in faded gold and red lettering. She stripped off the loaned clothes and snuggled into the soft, worn fabric with a sigh. They were way too big for her. The sleeves hung past her hands by a good three inches and the pants billowed around her legs.

Worse, the material still held the scent of Jack. She gathered the front of the sweatshirt and pressed it against her nose, inhaling and closing her eyes. Almost unconsciously, she passed her fingers over her lips, remembering Jack's kiss.

Sex with Ben had never been good. She'd only reached orgasm with him a handful of times. Her clit was either too sensitive or not sensitive enough, or Ben had reached his climax before her. Ben had made her feel like it was her fault, and maybe it was. Maybe she was just one of those women who had a hard time with it unless she was doing it herself.

Mira wondered if she'd have a hard time with Jack.

But Jack didn't want her. Not really. He'd practically run away from her after he'd kissed her. Obviously, he'd done it only to ignite her magick and prove to her once and for all that it was real.

She chewed her lower lip. Of course, his hard-on had seemed pretty genuine.

Mira swallowed hard at the memory of it pressing into her, then remembered the wad of condoms in his nightstand drawer. She was being silly. A man like Jack McAllister probably got a hard-on from kissing a tree.

Shaking her head, she walked to the window in the living room. Downtown Minneapolis spread below her, under a cold, clear blue sky. There would be a full moon soon.

She knew the exact date and time of every full moon. There was no available earth on which to make her monthly offering, however. Not way up on the fifty-second floor. She doubted she'd be allowed to go outside to conduct her monthly ritual.

Not since there were men after her, wanting to kill her.

Mira shuddered as that realization finally registered. She backed away from the window and tried not to think about it. Tried not to think about her parents. Tried not to think about Jack's kiss. Tried not to think about her new status as a witch.

Instead she explored Jack's apartment, tracing her fingers over the smooth mahogany tables, the expensive fabric of the sofa and chairs, over the objets d'art. Expensive Frederic Remington sculptures seemed to be a favorite. There wasn't a speck of dust anywhere, which led her to believe he must employ cleaning people.

Eventually, she reached the spiral staircase and climbed it. At the top on her left was a door. She tried it, and a blast of cold air hit her face, making her gasp in surprise. The roof. So Jack had the penthouse.

It was freezing, but she poked her head out long enough to get a glimpse of the Minneapolis skyline and a medium-sized greenhouse. Greenery showed through the panes of glass. That meant Jack kept it heated and grew plants within it.

Well, he was full of surprises.

She shivered and closed the door. Perhaps she'd found a solution to her full moon problem. It wasn't ideal, but she could find some earth in the greenhouse at least.

Behind her was an open area that looked down on the living room. The nook had a couple more bookshelves and a comfy looking overstuffed chair and ottoman in the corner. Two doors led off this little reading room.

The first room proved to be an office, complete with state-of-the-art computer, printers, and various other electronics.

The other door was locked.

Hmmm.

The man had a locked room in his apartment. This was his personal residence, and the voice of politeness whispering in her head demanded she respect that. On the other hand, she was looking for answers.

They could be behind that door.

She tried the knob again and then knelt to examine the lock. It was just a chintzy one, nothing too complicated. She was no master locksmith or accomplished thief, but she'd jimmied a lock like this one on Annie's back door several times in the past when her flighty, distracted godmother had misplaced her house keys. She wouldn't break it. Jack wouldn't even know she'd been in there.

What Jack didn't know wouldn't hurt him, but what she didn't know could kill her. She needed answers, period.

Decided, Mira whirled and headed back into the office. She searched through the desk drawers until she found a paperclip and returned to the door. Her lock-picking skills were based solely on rooting around and manipulating the pins until the door opened.

It took awhile.

Finally, the knob turned and the door opened. She pocketed the paper clip, stood, and flicked on the light.

"Oh, wow," she breathed.

Another surprise. She never would've taken Jack for an artsy kind of guy, even with the expensive Remington cowboy statues displayed in the living room, but it must have been Jack who'd taken the gorgeous photos that hung in this room.

Both glossy black-and-whites and color portraits hung framed on the walls and were pinned haphazardly to easels scattered throughout the room. Mira walked around, studying them. She stopped at several photos of an older woman with salt-and-pepper hair. Perhaps it was his mother?

There were pictures of snow-covered barns, long four-board fences shot at the height of summer, and other nature-related shots. There were pictures of children and older people, bright, shining young faces juxtaposed with knotted, wrinkled hands. They all seemed to make a statement about the beauty of life and its fleeting nature.

Her brow wrinkled. Jack was capable of making deep philosophical statements through artwork?

Shelves stood against another wall, filled with camera equipment and electronics. A desk sat beside it, holding what had to be fifty photo albums.

She walked over and ran her finger over a black-bound album lying on his desk and opened it. A sensual photo of a beautiful blonde in a revealing negligee met her eyes and she quickly shut it.

Really. She should've known better.

This was Jack's private room and if gorgeous, scantily clad women wanted Jack to take their picture, who was she to judge? Hell, women probably fell over themselves wanting attention like that from Jack McAllister. Unwelcome jealousy pricked for a moment before she forced it away.

Abruptly, she grabbed another album, finding it filled with what looked to be surveillance photos of an older, heavyset man and a few of his cronies. *Interesting.* Jack took pictures of some of the witches or warlocks he was tasked with watching. She replaced the album and surveyed the others.

She ran her finger back and forth over a pricey-looking leather-bound album sticking out a little from the rest. It was so pretty. Mira opened it and gasped.

Her own face stared up at her.

SIX

"No, no, no," she chanted, flipping through the pages. All of them were of her, shots taken while she'd been on her way to work or coming home. When she'd been on break or at the grocery store . . .

She put her hand to her mouth. She'd never known Jack had been watching her so closely. He must've practically been her shadow for a good two weeks. He'd told her he'd been watching her, but taking pictures?

That was kind of creepy.

Except . . .

She started from the beginning of the album once more. The first pictures were like a photo record of her day, unconcerned with lighting or her facial expression, just documentation of her daily activities. Midway through the pictures took on a personal quality.

Mira stopped at one showing her about to get into her car. She'd drawn her coat around her against the frigid day, the cold, bright sun shining high above her head. Her car was in the middle of the badly plowed street in front of the diner. There was not one other vehicle on the entire stretch of road, not one other person. She didn't know how she'd never noticed someone watching her. The road itself was shot so that it looked as though it stretched into infinity.

And she was on it alone, wearing a forlorn expression on her face.

Another showed her at a coffee shop down the street where she went sometimes for her lunch to get a change of scenery. He'd been in the crowded restaurant that day with her, sitting in the corner, judging by the angle of the shot. The place had been filled, but she'd been alone in her booth, staring out the window. He'd focused in on her, blurring the people around her. Her reflection in the window appeared bleak.

Did she really wear that expression on her face so often?

Mira closed the album, swallowed hard, and stepped away from it. The first shots were businesslike, but toward the end Jack had used her as a subject for his art. He'd seemed to capture things about her that no one else saw. Feelings and emotions she'd never shared with anyone. He'd captured her intimate moments without ever having spoken to her.

She turned, flipped off the light, and locked the door.

Her mind a jumble of confused thoughts, Mira headed back downstairs.

She understood why he'd originally begun taking the photos. Those were for surveillance purposes. She *should* feel creeped out, since he'd followed her around snapping photos of her like some stalker. That fact pissed her off, but the other, later photos muffled that response. Why had his focus shifted to such an intimate angle toward the end? What had made him view her through a more personal lens?

For now she wouldn't tell Jack that she'd seen the photos. She had enough on her plate dealing with everything else. Not to mention she'd have to admit she broke into a locked room in his residence. Although in light of things, that seemed hardly to compare as far as intrusions went.

Still distracted, she wandered over to the bookshelves, which seemed to house every classic title ever written, along with a few political thrillers and a mishmash of horror novels.

On a lower shelf, she spied a leather-bound copy of Mary Shelley's *Frankenstein*. She grabbed it, knocking a small wooden box off the shelf and onto the floor in the process. A silver ring rolled out onto the floor.

Holding the book in one hand, she knelt and examined the piece of jewelry. It was a man's ring, heavy and well crafted. A *C* marked the flat of it in fancy script and arcane symbols ringed the edges. She frowned. *C* for what? *The Coven*, maybe? Maybe it was some nifty secret decoder ring that she might eventually also receive. She deposited the ring back into the box and replaced it on the shelf.

After fetching a glass of water from the kitchen and tidying up from breakfast, she curled up on the couch with the book. It engaged her for a while, until weariness took over. Nodding off, she set the book aside and lay down for a nap, her head on one of the fancy throw pillows.

The sound of the door opening woke her. She looked up drowsily at Jack as he dropped a bunch of shopping bags on the coffee table in front of her. He wouldn't even meet her eyes.

Maybe the kiss really had repulsed him and he couldn't bear to look at her now.

Her body still felt the press of him against her. The memory of his warmth, the feeling of his body, had clung to her all afternoon. A lazy, honeyed heat seeped between her thighs when she thought about his mouth on hers. It eclipsed everything, even finding the strangely intimate photos he'd taken of her on the sly.

She was so pathetic.

She sat up and peered into one of the bags, seeing fabric

folded in tissue and a tangle of sales tags. "You bought everything new? That must have cost a fortune! I just meant you should go to my apartment and grab some of my stuff!"

"Couldn't do that. Crane is most likely watching your place. He probably doesn't know where you are, and it's better it stays that way."

Oh. "*Probably* doesn't know where I am? That's not very comforting. So what did you get?"

Self-consciously, she ran her fingers through her sleep-tangled hair, remembering she wore his clothes and probably looked ridiculous in them. He wasn't answering her, so she glanced up and found him staring down at her. The memory of their kiss seemed to linger in his eyes. Mira saw a flash of sexual heat there, need laid bare, before he looked away.

Her stomach fluttering, and wondering if she'd imagined it, she stopped fussing with her hair and forced herself to lower her gaze and stare at the bags.

He ran a hand over his chin. "I got everything on your list. Your soap and shampoo, some clothes that will probably fit you better, new underwear. Got you a few other things I thought you might appreciate, too, some perfume. I noticed you wear rose-scented stuff." He cleared his throat. "Got you some gunk for your hair, junk like that. I hope you don't mind."

That was awfully thoughtful. How had it occurred to him to do that? She raised her eyebrows. "Really? Thank you. Do you have a sister or something?"

"No, but I've had my share of—"

"Girlfriends." She gave him a thumbs-up. "Gotcha."

She reached into a bag, pulled out a sexy black thong, and let it dangle from her index finger. Mira looked up at him with a raised brow. Why did Jack buying her lingerie seem more intimate than having him go through her underwear drawer?

He cleared his throat and shifted uncomfortably. "I didn't know what kind you normally wear. I bought a few different styles."

"I'm kind of a bikini-cut girl. I don't enjoy the dental floss look. Nice thought, though." She dropped the lacy bit of nothing into her lap and sighed. "How much was all this? Right now I can't afford a lot."

"Don't worry about it. Like I said, the Coven has agreed to cover your expenses in order to keep you away from Crane."

"Well . . . thank you." She'd still pay them back every penny when she could.

"Not a problem." His mouth twitched a little. "What are you wearing?"

Mira felt herself flush. "Sorry. I went through your drawers." She bit off the end of the sentence and winced at the double meaning.

"They're huge on you. You look like you're drowning." A note of amusement tinged his voice.

"I needed to find something more comfortable. I hope you don't mind."

"No, I don't mind." Jack walked toward his bedroom.

"Jack?"

He turned.

"When you said that our magick had a kind of . . . attraction. What did you mean?"

"Air and fire have a natural affinity, as do water and earth. They always have a magickal attraction. But sometimes there's an intensification of physical attraction too, if both parties are so inclined."

"So inclined?"

"If they would've been sexually attracted to each other without the magick being present, there is an intensification. It's what's happening between you and me."

Mira's mind fumbled for a moment. Her draw to him was because of their magick. Just the magick. Only the magick. That made sense. Everything fell into place.

She stood and walked toward him, with the panties still in her hand. Mira licked her lips and twisted the silk, forcing herself to not look anywhere but at him. "I just wanted you to know that, uh, about what happened in the kitchen." She glanced away. "You proved things to me by doing . . . that."

Jack took a step forward, grasped the undergarment, and used it to pull her toward him a step. She almost stumbled against his chest. Suddenly she found herself enveloped in all that seductive, heady maleness.

"When I did . . . *that*?" he drawled with silky menace. "Don't you mean when I kissed you, Mira? You do remember that part, don't you?"

Her stomach dropped to her toes. His gaze had centered completely on her mouth. Like her lips were food and he was starving. "Yes, of course."

"Do you have any idea how hard it was for me to stop kissing you?"

"Really?" she asked in genuine surprise before she could stop herself.

His voice lowered. "I want you in a powerful way. I want to do things to you that your joke of an ex-husband never dreamed of doing. That's what happens when fire and air meet. Understand? Do you feel it? That intense attraction between us?"

"It's incredibly powerful."

"Yes," he murmured. "Damn near irresistible."

She watched, fascinated, as a muscle in his jaw worked. It seemed like he endeavored to hold himself back from her.

"You're a sensual woman. It's like you have all this dry tinder piled up inside you, waiting for a spark. I could be that spark, but—"

"My husband always said I was frigid," she blurted. She put a hand to her mouth, wishing she could call back that intimate secret.

"What?"

She forced her hand down to her side and drew a steadying breath. *Too late to turn back now.* "You tell me I'm sensual, talk about tinder waiting to be lit. Ben had a hard time giving me an orgasm. He said it was my fault, that I was incapable of it during intercourse."

Jack gritted his teeth. The muscle in his jaw worked again. This time he didn't look like he was holding himself back from her; he just looked pissed. "Frigid, hmm? That's what he told you?"

She opened her mouth to give a better explanation, but then his lips were on it. His fingers threaded through her hair, and his tongue met hers in a possessive sweep that made her whimper.

Yesterday, in the diner when she'd fantasized about kissing Jack, she'd known it would be sexy as hell. However, the tenderness he displayed was a surprise. Jack didn't just kiss. He made slow, easy love to her mouth, making her body respond in kind as sure as if he stroked her. Her nipples grew hard and she became hot and achy between her thighs.

He wrenched the panties from her hands and threw them to the floor. Mira slid her arms around him, kissing him back, spearing her tongue into his mouth with abandon. She wanted to taste him, know him, feel the heat of his body against her. He walked her backward a little, until she felt the nearby wall against her back. He bracketed her there, pinning her with his big body.

Lord and Lady help her, she didn't want to get away.

Her magick unfurled from her chest lazily, looking for Jack's. She let it go, let her power free itself to seek his, to twine and dance and merge. It intensified the pleasure she felt at being in his arms, and Mira gave into it with a little sigh.

Jack found the hem of the sweatshirt and pushed his hand past it to caress the small of her back. His thumb rubbed back and forth, ranging lower, until he'd slipped down past the waistband of the sweatpants and let his hand come to a rest on her hip. She gripped him for support for her suddenly shaky legs.

Mira wanted this, wanted his touch more than anything right now. Was it just the magick making her desire him? At the moment, she didn't care about the reason behind it. All she cared about were his hands on her body.

He stilled abruptly and pulled away from the kiss. Turning his head to the side, he closed his eyes and swore under his breath.

"J-Jack? What's wrong?"

"Fuck it," he murmured, then his mouth closed over hers again and he eased his fingers further down past the waistband of the voluminous sweatpants in the back . . . and found out she wasn't wearing any underwear.

"Hell, Mira," he growled as he cupped her bare behind, delving his fingers between her cheeks and making Mira squirm against him and gasp. "You trying to kill me?" He slid his hand over her hip and threaded his fingers through her pubic hair. Mira gasped into his mouth and jerked in surprise at the intimate contact.

Jack stilled, his hand warm against her mound. "Let me touch you," he murmured. "Just once. Just a little."

The spell he'd woven over her and the way her body responded to his kiss, his touch . . . she was too far gone. This was a bad idea. Jack probably knew it. She *definitely* knew it. But she'd die if he didn't touch her now.

Mira nodded, breathing hard.

"Come on," he groaned. "Open for me. I want more of you."

Her breath caught in her throat and a heady combination of adrenaline and sexual need filled her. It made her wonder if this was all some out of control dream. She spread her thighs a little wider for him.

"That's it." His fingers touched her folds, sliding through her wetness. "Oh, yes, you feel so good."

Mira sighed, and he slanted his mouth over hers, catching the sound of it on his tongue. He stroked her labia and eased the pad of his finger over her clit. It plumped under his attention, growing so sensitive that every brush made pleasure pulse through her body.

His other hand slid to the nape of her neck, then fisted gently in her hair. Jack used it to tilt her head to the side, baring the length of her throat for him. He trailed his sensual lips over her jawline and down her neck as he worked between her thighs. He touched her with patience, rubbing her clit over and over, until he'd skated her to the edge of a powerful climax.

Jack pressed his middle finger against her entrance, breached it, and slid inside. Her breath whooshed out of her as all those nerves flared to life. It had been a long time since a man had touched her there. Jack shuddered against her, pulled out, and thrust back in. She'd creamed readily for him, and his finger slid in and out easily.

"Mira," he breathed against her throat. "You're so hot and tight. Like silk. Silk and honey. Damn. I want my cock here." He added a second finger to the first, making Mira's breath hitch.

"Jack," she whispered raggedly.

He thrust his fingers in and out of her, rocking her against the wall behind her with the movement, and rubbed the heel of his palm against her swollen clit that he'd coaxed to such exquisite attention. Her whole world had become his hand stroking her sex.

Jack ran the tip of his tongue from just below her earlobe to the place where her neck met her shoulder. "Do you like the way I'm touching you?" he drawled in a low voice.

"Y-yes."

"Are you going to come for me?"

"Uh, huh," she breathed.

Jack bit her gently, right where her neck met her shoulder. It was an act of dominance, possession. As though he meant to mark her in some primal way. She shivered and dug her fingers into his upper arms to maintain her balance on trembling legs. At the same time, he increased the thrust of his fingers, rubbing purposefully against her sensitized clit. The first skitters of an orgasm rolled through her, increasing in strength as Jack thrust into her.

The pleasure Mira felt intensified, exploded, shattered through her body. She climaxed against his hand, her soft panting and sighs filling the air between them. The muscles of her sex pulsed and contracted around his pistoning fingers.

He thrust gently into her until she calmed and the waves of her powerful climax had faded, then he released his mouth's hold on her skin and laid a soft kiss. Jack was breathing as heavily as she was as he withdrew his hand from the sweatpants.

"That's how *frigid* you are, Mira," he murmured brokenly. "You only need a man to touch you the right way. With patience and care. Understand?"

She nodded, her body trembling.

"Despite what just happened, I am not the right man. Understand *that*. I'm the last man on Earth who deserves you."

Jack released her, walked into the bedroom, and closed the door.

Mira leaned against the wall and stared at the door with a mixture of deep physical satisfaction and incredible confusion. Her body still tingled with the awareness of him. Her sex throbbed with the memory of his touch. The taste of him still lay on her tongue and the rawness of his words still rang in her ears.

I'm the last man on Earth who deserves you.

SEVEN

❦

MIRA TUCKED HER LEGS BENEATH HER ON THE couch and flipped through Jack's copy of *To Kill a Mockingbird*, only half paying attention to it, though she loved the novel. Mostly, she watched Jack stomp around the living room.

He'd barely had a conversation with her during the last two days, limiting his communication to single-word answers and grunts. The man had brooding down to an art form.

What had passed between them after he'd returned from shopping remained like an elephant in the living room. It was there. It was huge. But they were both ignoring it.

Dinners, while yummy (as evidenced by the pound or two she'd gained), were especially awkward. They ate quickly and made minimal conversation. A television would have been good, would've covered up the lack of human voices in the apartment. They played music instead, and Jack spent a lot of time in his office or the "secret" locked room upstairs.

Clearly, he wanted to get as far from her as possible, but couldn't. Not while a threat remained against her.

It was awkward for her too. She barely knew the man, and she'd not only allowed him access to the old love grotto, he'd brought her to orgasm.

The worst part was that she'd let him do it again in a heartbeat. He'd touched her just right. She shivered at the memory, her body growing warm.

With Ben it had always pretty much just been about him. They'd have sex missionary style; maybe sometimes she'd be on top. Occasionally, he'd fumble a bit at her clit to try and make her come, but he'd give up fast. She'd been too afraid to touch herself during sex, fearing she'd offend him.

They just hadn't been a good fit in the bedroom. They'd lacked trust and good communication from day one. Mira bit the inside of her lip until it hurt, remembering the things Ben had said about his reasons for seeking sex outside their marriage. In hindsight, they hadn't been a good fit in any respect. She wished she'd seen that when she'd first met him.

She tossed the book to the coffee table and watched Jack stand at the wall of windows that overlooked downtown Minneapolis, idly flicking a chunky silver Zippo on and off.

Mira let her gaze trace his broad, tall frame. She had to admit that he made her feel safe, even though what she knew about him should've made her feel less than reassured.

And she wanted him with a bone-deep yearning she'd never had for a man before. Logically, she shouldn't want him. She'd promised herself, *promised*, that she would have nothing to do with men for at least a year, until she had a chance to regain her footing after the divorce. Yet here she was, lusting after a man who seemed conflicted at best and dangerous at worst.

She needed to get a handle on herself. She couldn't let this attraction between air and fire get the better of her.

Jack seemed to be handling it more effectively than she was, in his stoic, stomping way.

The only good thing about the last couple of days was that her bruise had almost completely healed. And even though he still insisted she sleep with him, at least he wasn't tying her to the bed at night anymore.

That was a *good* thing, she reminded herself.

She picked at the couch with her thumb and forefinger. "Jack, I have questions."

He mumbled something at her in response.

She sighed. "Jack, I need you to stop brooding and talk to me."

He turned. "I don't brood."

"Oh, really? Then you're doing a really good impression of a man who does."

He blinked.

She patted the couch beside her. "Come and sit down a little? I promise I won't bite, though I'm not sure you won't."

He gave her a dark look and took the chair near the couch instead.

She flicked her hair out of her eyes and angled her gaze downward. "How did Crane kidnap my parents?"

He shrugged. "We don't know much. We know it was well planned and well executed. It's hard to sneak up on an air witch, and Crane managed to kidnap two at once. We suspect your parents were overwhelmed by warlocks and then drugged somehow." He paused and his voice grew softer. "We do know that your father fought them and was badly injured in the process."

She looked up at him. "How was he injured?"

Jack held her gaze. "Fire. Probably from Crane. He has an ability to kindle white-hot fire that even powerful air and water witches are hard-pressed to extinguish."

"And my mother?"

Jack looked away, out the window. "The story goes that she was forced to watch your father in the first demon circle.

That it sucked away her will to live so she was very pliant when it came for her turn the next day."

Mira shot from the couch and walked to the window, hugging herself against a sudden chill. Her mother had lost her will to live? But Mira had only been a baby then. Hadn't Mira been enough to make her mother want to survive?

Jack's body heat warmed her from behind. "You asked."

"I needed to know." Resolved, she turned toward him. "Tell me more about Crane."

They were close together, too close for Jack's comfort apparently. They stared at each other for a moment before he moved to sit down.

"William Crane," derision was audible in his voice, "was born to a line of powerful fire witches who can trace their heritage back to the 1200s. They were a noble magickal house until Crane joined the Duskoff. He had it all, wealth and the respect and social standing that a good magickal pedigree affords you." He glanced at her. "Like you, Mira. Hoskins is a very well-respected name."

She smiled. "Really?"

"Yes. Both your mother and your father came from strong lines. That's likely one reason they kept your birth a secret. Everyone wanted them to have offspring because the children of two witches of the same element always bear that element. They were both a rare breed and powerful." A brief smile curled his lips. "You would've been famous."

She let that sit a moment in her mind. Had that been why they'd kept all this knowledge from her? Were they trying to spare her the expectations of the magickal community? The danger of being a rare kind of witch? Had they simply been trying to protect her from the Duskoff?

This was information she needed to digest at her leisure, although she'd probably never divine the reasons behind her parents' actions.

"If Crane had everything he needed, why did he join the Duskoff?" she asked.

He said nothing.

"Well?" she pressed.

"Crane was on the straight and narrow, a part of the Coven, until he hit about twenty-three. At the time he turned warlock, he was married to a woman who was a positive influence in his life. Once Crane had a taste of the dark, that influence ended. Crane took the betrayer's path because of greed. He was a very strong witch, seduced into the Duskoff by the promise of the immense wealth and power not offered by his family name alone."

"I guess he moved quickly into the upper echelons."

Jack grimaced. "Crane had a knack for thinking deviously. He arranged many of their demon circles and controlled the creatures once they came through."

Mira shivered. "I still can't believe demons are real."

"Demons are entities who live in, well, I guess you'd call them alternate realities, but that's not really right. They're different planes of existence, with different vibrational frequencies. The magick in a demon circle—all four elements drawn together—creates equilibrium in the differences of the vibrations and makes an opening that calls a demon through."

"Okay, I have a headache now. What does the Duskoff use them for?"

"The demons are under their control for a negotiated period of time, but the creatures require favors in return as payment, along with the gift of the magick that is provided by the sacrifice of the four witches."

"I don't even want to know what they ask for as favors."

"No, and it's better I don't tell you. It's pretty grisly. The Duskoff use the demons to influence elections, kill people, improve a company's profitability. There's not a lot a demon can't do, and they're unencumbered by morals."

"What happened to Crane's wife? Did she ever go warlock?"

Something flitted through his eyes. He glanced away.

He always got those shadows in his eyes when he spoke of Crane or the Duskoff. Had he come up against Crane and been hurt in some way? Had Crane hurt someone he cared for?

Jack pushed a hand through his hair. "Listen, question and answer time is over. I'll tell you later, all right?" He stood. "I have things I need to do now."

Mira frowned up at him. That was rude. "Fine," she snapped.

He walked toward the bedroom, his refuge of choice.

"Jack?"

He turned.

"When will you start training me to use my magick?"

He grimaced. "That requires me to touch you."

Mira's eyes widened and she felt herself flush crimson with embarrassment and anger.

Jack blinked slowly, seeing her expression. "No, Mira. It's not because I find you unattractive. It's the opposite of that. If I touch you a little, I want to touch you a lot. Understand?" He glowered at her for the hundredth time that day, then palmed his Zippo, stalked into his bedroom, and closed the door.

Oh.

Mira sank down on the couch and touched her still burning cheeks. He might make her feel safe, but she hardly felt welcome.

EIGHT

❧

MIRA SLID OUT OF BED IN THE EARLY MORNING hours. The clock on Jack's dresser read 3:05 A.M. Moonlight spilled in through the uncurtained window, pooling on the hardwood floor beneath it.

She stared at it for a moment. That pale silvery light called to her.

Carefully, she eased away from the bed and grabbed a pair of jeans, socks, shoes, and a sweater. The floor creaked on her way out the door and she froze in place, glancing at the bed.

Jack lay on his back with one arm flung over his head in an unconscious pose that defined his biceps. He'd pushed the blankets to the end of the bed, in spite of the chill in the room. He never wore a shirt to sleep and the position revealed his very lickable, muscular chest. Her body tightened at the sight of him.

A light dusting of dark hair marked his chest and tapered into a trail that went down his stomach, past the waistband of his cotton PJ bottoms. The thought of where that trail stopped made a hot, hard flush overcome her body.

Her fingers tightened on the clothes she held. How long would he resist her if she crawled in beside him and set her mind and body to seducing him? Probably not long. Mira had never seduced anyone in her life, but Jack tempted her to explore new horizons.

A gentle snore reached her ears. It broke the spell that had her balancing on the balls of her feet, nearly ready to return to bed. She continued on. In the living room she dressed, found Jack's wool navy peacoat in the closet and a pair of gloves.

She tiptoed into the kitchen to look for an offering. Normally, she used red wine, but Jack's wine rack was empty. Stymied, she turned a circle in the center of the kitchen, too warm in Jack's wool coat, searching for a suitable substitute.

Nothing. Well, there was a two-liter of Coke on the counter, but that wouldn't do.

She went to the refrigerator and found milk, orange juice, and lime Gatorade. When she'd been a kid she'd always used milk. A few times she'd even used grape Kool-Aid. Annie had always told her it was the intention that counted, not the offering itself.

Not seeing much of a choice, she grabbed the milk and filled a glass with it, then headed upstairs to the roof and the greenhouse.

The cold snatched her breath away when she opened the door. She inhaled the clean, fresh air, feeling a subtle warm pulse in her chest in response. Her magick. What stars she could see through the city's light pollution sparkled in the sky, free of insulating cloud cover, which meant it would be frigid in the morning.

Mira opened the smooth glass door of the small greenhouse, flicked on the lights, and stepped into the temperature-regulated building. Jack only had a few plants in here now. Some ferns, hostas, and other things she couldn't identify.

Bare planting beds circled the room. In the center was a grassy area with a fountain and a few stone benches. The sound of running water met her ears.

She closed her eyes, enjoying the small taste of life in the dead of winter. It seemed out of character for Jack to have a place like this, but it seemed out of character for him to be taking artsy photographs, too. Basically, that only proved that she didn't really know him.

She flipped the light back off to let only the moonlight fill the small room. It was enough to see by, if not see well. She slipped off her gloves and coat, laid them on a stone bench, and took her glass of milk to an earth-filled planting bed near the door.

To her right the full moon hung in the sky, silver and swollen, visible through the glass wall of the greenhouse. Normally, she did this outside, no matter the temperature, but she needed earth and that was hard to come by on the roof of a ritzy downtown apartment building.

Mira set the glass down and mounded the earth with her hands, enjoying the feel of it against her palms. Then she closed her eyes and murmured a small prayer.

In her chest, the warmth of her magick purred strongly, responding to the meditation, perhaps, or the prayer. Her breath caught in surprise. It was an alien sensation, and it made her uneasy. As she finished her prayer, her voice trembling, the magick warmed through her body. She wondered how to call it, how to control and use it.

She opened her eyes and picked up the glass.

"From my lips"—she took a deep drink of the milk—"to your bosom," and poured the rest of the glass of milk into the mounded earth.

The door to the greenhouse opened, startling her. She dropped the glass to the planting bed. The lights snapped on.

"Mira?" came Jack's voice.

She let out a slow, careful breath. "You scared me near to death."

"What are you doing out here?"

She gripped the rim of the bed, the metal chilly against her fingers. "Making my monthly offering to the full moon."

"To Artemis? Is that the goddess you follow?"

She shook her head. "Not specifically. It's just a ritual to show respect for powers greater than I am and for the earth."

He took a few steps toward her and she turned to face him. Oh, hello . . . he was barefoot, wearing only his dark blue pajama pants and no shirt.

His lips twitched. "You have a milk mustache."

Horrified, she went to wipe it away, but he caught her hand. His eyes heavy-lidded, Jack reached out and slowly drew the pad of his thumb across her upper lip. The touch made her feel warm in places that had nothing to do with her mouth.

She'd never had any idea milk mustaches could be so sexy.

"How did you know I was here?" she asked.

"You couldn't be anywhere else. I have wards set on all the entrances, but the door to the roof is the only one regulated to allow you passage. I figured you might enjoy the greenhouse. I forgot to show it to you, but I see you found it on your own."

"You could've stayed in bed. I would've been right back."

He reached into his pocket and pulled out a key. "The door locks automatically when it shuts."

"Oh."

"Do you want me to leave you alone for a while?"

She shook her head. "Aren't you cold?"

"Fire witch, remember?"

"Why do you have this place?"

"You ask a lot of questions." He reached out in an easy, unhurried gesture and took her hand. With his index finger he lazily brushed the dirt from her palm. "There's a conservatory at the Coven. It's my favorite place there. I guess I wanted to recreate a little part of it in my home." He looked up at her. Small laugh lines crinkled around his so-blue eyes as he grinned. "All witches have a thing for the earth, don't they?"

She cleared her throat and fought the urge to pull her hand away from his before she did something she'd regret. "I don't know. I've known very few honest-to-Goddess witches, just lots of people who labeled themselves witches but didn't really have any true magick to call."

He dropped her hand. "All the ones I know have a thing for the earth, you included."

It felt so strange to be called a witch. She fidgeted and glanced away. All she wanted was a little normality in her life, a little stability. Was that so much to ask? Instead she got bizarre magickal powers and a hunky witch abductor named Jack.

Her life had really taken an overwhelming and strange turn. As if cheating husbands and messy divorces weren't enough.

"So you do this every month?" he asked.

A distracted smile flitted over her mouth. "Every month since I was a child. I've only ever missed giving an offering twice."

"I'm impressed. Why did you miss those times?"

"I had the chicken pox when I was eight. The other time was . . ." She flushed.

"Was?" he prompted.

"When I was out on my first date with Bryon Richards. It was the night I lost my virginity." She laughed.

He smiled. "Come on, let's go in."

She put his coat on, picked up the gloves, and followed him back into his apartment and down the stairs. He eased the coat off her shoulders when they reached the living room.

She paced to the kitchen and back, feeling out of sorts because her routine had been disrupted.

"Is there something wrong?" Jack asked, hanging up his coat in the closet.

"Sorry. I've been doing the same thing for so long. Normally, I drink rose verbena tea after I make my offering. I don't suppose you have any green tea leaves, dried rose petals, and a dash of lemon verbena?"

He smirked. "Gee, I'm fresh out. I think I have a package of chamomile tea someone left here."

She shrugged. "Sure."

He moved to the kitchen to make the tea, and she sat down on the couch. She curled up in the corner of the couch and rested her head against the cushion and listened to him making noises in the kitchen, feeling safe and comfortable. Despite the edge of awkwardness that remained between them, being in his apartment felt good. She nodded off, but she woke when he came back with two mugs of steaming beverage.

He took a drink and leaned back against the couch. "Your magick, it smells faintly like fresh linen and lemon."

She looked up in surprise. "My magick . . . smells?"

He nodded. "Not all magick has a distinctive scent or taste, but yours does. I just thought you'd want to know that."

"Fresh linen and lemon. Interesting."

"About Crane: you have a right to know everything you can about him. I'm sorry I ditched out on an answer earlier today."

"It's no big deal."

"Crane's wife never went warlock. She committed suicide. His son left to live with his aunt at age ten, and Crane adopted another little boy, one with qualities he could nurture and mold."

"He lost his heir so he obtained another. So Crane's biological—"

"You likely know the adopted son," he interrupted. "His name is Stefan Faucheux."

She gasped. "Stefan Faucheux?" He was always in the society pages, a darling of the media. The man was wealthy, gorgeous, and always seemed to have a movie star on his arm.

Stefan Faucheux's story was famous because it was such a compelling rags-to-riches one. As a child he'd run away from France's protective services, preferring to live on the streets. One day billionaire W. Anderson Crane had come across him and adopted him.

W. Anderson Crane . . . William Crane.

She closed her eyes, realizing she knew exactly who Crane was. She hadn't made the connection before. Her parents' murderer had been staring at her out of the pages of magazines and newspapers her whole life.

Jack nodded. "Crane found him in Paris. He did a good job raising him. Stefan is a powerful witch, loyal to Crane as far as we can tell, but still deadly ambitious. So you see why it's important for you to train your magick. Crane and Faucheux have more than just magickal power, they have real-world power, too."

"If I want to keep my soul attached to my body, I understand I need to control my abilities, Jack. I thought you were supposed to help me learn." Mira gave a melodramatic sigh. "But since I'm all sexy and you can't resist me, I guess I'll have to wait."

He took the cup away from her and set it on the coffee table. Then he nestled his warm palm between her breasts. Mira's breath caught in her throat, her amusement abruptly gone. Her magick instantly responded to his touch, flaring in her chest.

Her body reacted, too, flaring in places further down.

She licked her lips nervously. "Uh, Jack?"

"Can you feel it there inside you?"

She nodded. "I felt it when I made my offering just now, too."

He held her gaze while he spoke. "Your magick is powerful and you are an intelligent witch. You'll learn how to wield this sooner than you think."

Jack removed his hand. Her skin felt cold with the absence of his touch. She rested back against the couch, and her magick withdrew, coiling back into her center. Mira willed the last remnant to stay, and it did. It sat there inside her like a little warm fuzzy, relaxing her.

He picked up his cup and took a drink. Mira noted that his hand was shaking just a little. "Tell me about Annie."

Jack listened to her ramble on about her godmother, her childhood, even about Byron Richards. He seemed interested, and she talked until fatigue overtook her and she fell asleep there on the couch.

The last thing she remembered was Jack gently lifting her and tucking her into his bed.

MIRA SAT IN THE LIVING ROOM, PRESSING A HAND to the place between her breasts.

Jack's kiss, touch, his presence, his fire . . . something about him had awakened her magick. But it had been Mira who'd willed it to stay instead of recede.

Now, it was an ever-present warm glow, reminding her that all she'd ever thought was true about her reality . . . wasn't. It reminded her that she was more than she'd ever thought she was, and not quite human. Despite these uncomfortable truths, she'd grown used to its presence. It was a part of her, a constant companion.

She felt compelled to let it free from its prison inside her. The compulsion had been growing steadily. It was almost as though the power needed to be bled off.

Mira knew there had to be a way for her to access that magick on her own, without Jack's fire to draw it out, she just wasn't sure how to do it.

Jack was in the bedroom. He had shown no interest in helping her learn, so she'd just have to do it on her own.

Mira found a comfortable position and closed her eyes. She'd always been faithful in practicing meditation. Maybe her skill in that area could help her now.

She allowed herself to drift a little, find a comfortable place in her mind where she could rest. Her breathing deepened and the sounds in the penthouse—the gentle click of the grandfather clock in the corner, the soft noises of Jack rustling paper on his desk in the bedroom—faded to the back of her mind.

Once she felt centered, she shifted her awareness to the middle of her chest, feeling for the magick she knew resided there. But it didn't feel any different to her in this slightly altered state of consciousness than it had before. It felt locked in a box, and she didn't have the key. With her mind, she explored the edges of the "box," looking for any way in, some fissure in the walls that penned the power.

Mira quickly grew frustrated. There seemed to be no way to access it at all. Would she always need Jack's fire to draw it? She hated that idea. If this was her power, she should be able to access it on her own.

She clenched her hands in her lap. This magick was *hers* to command, no one else's.

The power in the center of her chest exploded into a flare of brilliance at her declaration. Wind rushed through the penthouse, making her hair swirl around her face and practically toppling her from the couch.

Mira opened her eyes to see something akin to a wind-storm sweeping through the room. The pretty blue vase on the pedestal crashed to the floor, papers on the table in the corner were swept up high into the air and scattered, something in the kitchen smashed.

The center of her chest glowed with warmth and the magick brushed over her skin like a velvet-gloved hand.

She stood and walked a couple of paces to the center of the room, letting the air rush around her, buffet her hair, and pull at her clothes. Euphoria rushed through her and a smile spread across her face.

It wanted out of the confines of the apartment. It begged her with big puppy dog eyes to let it off its leash. As tempting as it was to release the power and allow it to play, Mira clamped down with all her will, forcing it to stay within Jack's walls.

"Mira!" Jack yelled over the sound of the rushing wind. "Tamp it down!"

She turned with wide eyes to stare at him as he stood in the doorway of his bedroom. Chaotic winds buffeted his hair and tugged at his clothing. Paper swirled in a mini cyclone around him.

The gravity of what she'd done struck her, dampening her exhilaration. She tried to direct the power like she had before to keep it within the penthouse, but when she reached with her mind . . . there was nothing to control. Freed, it was uncontainable.

"How?" she yelled back.

He gave her a withering look and raised his hand. Something bright glowed in his palm and suddenly all the air in the room was . . . gone.

Mira gasped in panic, unable to breathe for a few moments as the very oxygen disappeared from her lungs. She collapsed to her knees, wheezing. Air from beyond the apartment rushed to fill the empty space immediately, pouring in from under the door and through the tiniest cracks. Closing her eyes, she breathed it in big gulps.

Jack stood holding his hand and swearing a blue streak. "Gods, I hate doing that."

Silence descended. Mira opened her eyes and surveyed the destruction. Broken glassware, scattered paper, an up-ended office chair, drapes partially ripped from the rod, books fallen from the shelf.

What had she done? She struggled to her feet. When she'd tapped her magick, she'd felt intoxicated. She hadn't realized the damage she'd been doing.

"Don't do that again," Jack said in a low, angry voice, still holding his hand.

"I won't do it again on purpose, but I didn't know I was doing it just now!" She chanced a glance at his grim face. "I'm sorry, Jack. I really am. I'll replace anything I destroyed."

He only stared stormily at her.

She sighed and walked to him. "Let me see."

He let her take his hand. "It looks worse than it is. It'll heal."

She grimaced. A burn marked the center of his palm where he'd drawn the power to suck the air out of the room. "Jack, I really am sorry."

He withdrew his hand. "Don't be." He flicked a hank of hair out of his eye. "It's my fault. I should've been training you to your magick these last couple of days. I should've realized that you'd be feeling pressure to access it."

"I was, but I should've waited."

"Yeah," he answered, "but it's still my fault." He walked around the couch, glancing at the vase that lay in shards on the floor. She followed him.

"Could've been worse," he continued. "We're lucky you didn't release more than you did. An untrained air witch sparked a whole line of tornadoes in Missouri once. Nobody could stop the power she unleashed. Thirty-five people died and a state of emergency was declared."

Mira sat down on the couch abruptly.

Jack sat down beside her. "It's important you learn how much to draw at one time."

Wow. That seemed like such an understatement considering his last remark. "How do I learn to do that without having the National Guard called in?"

"You have to *know*, to *believe*, that this power is yours to command. It's as simple and as complicated as that. It sounds easy, but true belief in your power isn't something that comes right away. If it does, you'll never be a good witch because that means you have too much ego. Assumptions with these kinds of abilities can be devastating and very dangerous."

"Dangerous?"

"The funny thing about magick is the more you use it for violence and chaos, the more it twists you inside. A witch's magick is an integral part of her. Every time a witch uses her magick to harm, it's like adding a pollutant into the body and mind."

"Crane must be a cesspool."

Jack's lips twisted into half smile. "Something like that."

"Well, he's definitely not following the tenet of *harm ye none*," she muttered.

"The time has come for me to train you." He sounded resigned. "I'm going to touch you now," Jack said.

She jerked. "Uh . . . what?"

"It's okay." He reached out and touched between her breasts with his uninjured hand, right in the sensitive hollow of her cleavage. "This is the seat of your magick, but I see you've already figured that out," he said wryly.

He stroked her there, and she tried really hard not to purr. Her magick warmed in response to the pad of his index finger brushing over her flesh. She closed her eyes, enjoying the warm, soft glow filling her chest.

"Feel it?"

It took a moment for his question to register. She felt so relaxed. "Yes."

"Concentrate on drawing a wisp of that power out. Nothing more. Just the tiniest thread of your magick. Visualize it in your mind."

Mira forced herself to switch her attention from Jack's stroking finger to her magick. With care, she imagined a single smoky tendril of power, extracting it from the small bundle of magick tingling in her chest. It was hard to grab. Once she thought she had the edge of a wisp, it was difficult to draw it outward. Finally, she managed it, letting it hang in the air between them.

"Good," he murmured. "I can feel it rising."

"What does it feel like?"

"Soft, beautiful, and tentative, but with an edge of unrealized power. Filled with possibility." He drew a breath. "It feels a lot like you."

That comment left her speechless.

"Smells like fresh linen and lemons, too," he murmured.

It was very hard to concentrate under these conditions. His voice seemed like melted chocolate to her—rich, sinful . . . and very, very bad for her. His hand so near her breasts was even worse. It took all her concentration to pay attention to the task he'd set her.

"Now, what do you want to do with that wisp? It's yours to command."

Mira concentrated on raising a breeze, just a small one. It felt cool and smelled of the woods. She let it blow over herself and Jack, let it play in their hair and caress their cheeks. The tendril dissipated easily as it expended itself.

Smiling, she opened her eyes and found Jack looking at her intently, his hair mussed from the breeze. Slowly, he removed his fingers from between her breasts. "That was excellent."

Her smile widened.

He stood. "Now, do that one hundred and fifty times and we can move on to something bigger." Jack walked back into his bedroom.

Oh. That was a buzz kill.

Mira's smile faded as she watched him close the door. She sighed, glancing around at the carnage her magick had wrought, then stood and started cleaning up.

* * *

JACK STOOD AT THE EDGE OF A DEMON CIRCLE IN the same place his father had stood when Jack had been a child. The sound of chanting filled his ears.

Mira's mother knelt in her place, her gaze fixed on him as she endured the ritual theft of her power. Jack tried to look away, but couldn't. As he stood there watching her die, her face slowly morphed to Mira's.

The scene changed. Now he stood in a cemetery under a night sky in high summer. Grass and weeds choked the bases of the crumbling tombstones around him, the air redolent with the scent of decay and rotting flowers. The stink gathered in his nostrils, in his throat. He gagged on it.

"Jack," called a soft, feminine voice.

He turned toward the sound and saw a woman lying at the foot of an enormous granite angel. Pieces of the sculpture broke off and fell in slow motion around the prone figure at its base.

It was his mother as she'd appeared in the pictures his aunt had shown him, only the beauty she'd possessed in life was half rotted in death. Jack fought the urge to turn away.

"Jack," his mother crooned, reaching out for him with dirt-encrusted, moldy hands. "Let me have Mira. I'll take good care of her, Jack. Jack—"

"Jack!"

Someone gripped his shoulders and shook him. Jack came awake with a jerk. He shuddered, disoriented, his eyes unfocused as reality settled over him.

It had been a dream. All the Gods and Goddesses, only a dream.

Mira rocked back on her heels. The moonlight streaming in through the window painted her in pale silver hues. One of the spaghetti straps of her nightgown had fallen down over the curve of her silky shoulder. Her long, loose dark hair shadowed half her face, but he could tell she wore a concerned expression.

"You were yelling in your sleep," she said. "A nightmare?"

He took a deep breath and pushed a hand through his hair. Gods, the dream had made him sweat. The nightmare still held him in its clutches, and he didn't trust himself to form words yet.

He could still see Mira's mother in the circle, her face morphing into her daughter's. The cloying scent of the cemetery still clung to his nostrils and his own mother's voice echoed in his mind.

"Do you want some water? I'll go get you some." Mira moved to climb off the bed, and he was on her in a moment.

He caught her up and rolled her beneath his body, needing to feel her warm and alive, needing to feel the beat of her heart.

NINE

~

SHE YELPED IN SURPRISE AND FOUGHT HIM FOR A
moment, but when his mouth came down on her throat to
feel the flutter of her pulse under his lips, she let out a little
sigh and relaxed. Her hands brushed uncertainly over his
biceps before her arms closed around him.

He inhaled the scent of her skin and hair, the light rose
perfume mingling with the clean smell of her soap, and
closed his eyes. The impulse to touch her had been sudden
and uncontrollable, and now the situation had become dangerous.

Jack dragged his lips over her throat, up her jawline to
her mouth. He hovered there, not quite kissing her, simply
enjoying the sensation of her hot breath on his lips. He
dropped his head a degree to kiss her and groaned. Beneath
his mouth, her lips felt like warm silk. When he flicked his
tongue, she opened for him and he slipped inside sweet,
hot heaven.

His magick pulsed in his chest, sensing the physical
contact of an air witch. Their magicks rose, brushed each

other, and then settled down. It was a sign that her constant
proximity was dulling the reaction of his magick to hers
and vice versa. They were finding their balance.

Finding that balance didn't dampen his desire for her,
however. That was something to worry about.

Her tongue rubbed against his, causing pure sexual need
to jolt through him, and he forgot all the things he had to
worry about.

Jack reached down, found the hem of her nightgown, and
dragged it upward slowly. His palm rubbed the smooth skin
of her upper thigh, the sweet curve of her hip and waist. He
savored every inch of revealed flesh.

Mira moved beneath him, making soft sounds. He inserted his knee between her legs and settled himself in the
cradle the apex of her thighs made, grinding his cock
against her through his pajama bottoms and the tangled
sheets. She felt hot against his shaft through the thin material that separated them. He wondered if she was slick and
sweet the way she had been that day in the living room.

When she broke the kiss and arched her back, spreading
her thighs for him, Jack nearly had a meltdown. He fisted
the blanket with his wounded hand beside her head, using
the pain shooting through his burn mark to try and maintain his control. With his other hand, he stroked her waist,
loving the sensation of her silky skin.

How easy it would be to slide that hand on her waist
down, to stroke sweeter, more responsive parts of her body.
How easy it would be to pull away the sheets between them,
yank down his pajama bottoms, and bury his aching cock in
all that soft, damp heat, to fuck her long and hard until she
screamed his name.

He closed his eyes, fighting the powerful urge. It would
be a mistake, but it was a mistake they'd both really enjoy.
They'd have one night of heaven before they hit hell full-
on. *Damn it.* How could he want this woman so much? Mira
was the one woman in the entire world he couldn't have.

Gods, maybe that was why. If so, it was the wrong reason.

Jack forced himself to roll away from her with a guttural groan of frustration. He lay on the mattress beside her and pressed his palms into his eyes. This was torture. Either Thomas had to call soon with permission to move to the Coven, or he would give in to the urge to seduce her.

Mira had gone silent. The only sound in the room was their harsh, labored breathing and the gentle tick-tock of the grandfather clock in the living room.

"Jack," Mira said slowly. "What the hell was that?"

"Mira—"

He reached for her, but she moved, abruptly sitting up and scooting to the edge of the bed. "I can't take much more of this," she said in a soft voice with her back turned to him.

"Damn it. You're my charge, my job, but I'm attracted to you." He ground his palm into his eye. "I fucking want you."

"Okay. Ditto, Jack. I want you too." She gave a little laugh. "We're both adults here, so what's the problem?"

Needing to tread carefully, he took a moment to answer. Thomas had instructed him not to tell her about his past yet. Thomas believed Jack to be the best person to protect Mira—and Jack believed that too—but Mira needed to trust him while he did it.

"It would be wrong," he answered. "I'm your bodyguard. I have a job to do and I need to keep my mind on it. I can't guard you if I'm preoccupied with you in my bed. Tell me you don't see that sleeping together would be a mistake." All true.

She picked at the blanket beside her. "I agree that it would be a mistake for me to sleep with you," she finally replied. She turned toward him, her voice angry, "But if I'm just your charge, just your *job*, then explain all those pictures you have of me."

He pushed up on his elbows. "What? What—" Realization bloomed. "You broke into my photography room?"

She stood and turned away from him, folding her arms over her chest. "That's not at issue right now."

He bolted from the bed and stalked to her. "The hell it isn't! You broke into a private room, broke the goddamn lock on a door in my home!"

"I didn't break the lock, I just picked it."

"Semantics!"

She turned to face him. "Considering I'd been abducted by a strange man claiming he wasn't quite human, I think I had a right to fully explore my surroundings."

Jack stared at her for a moment and then turned on his heel. He walked through the living room, pounded up the spiral staircase, and kicked the locked door of the photography room open. The door splintered under the force of his anger. The lock was definitely broken now. He flipped the light on and strode to the center of the room. Mira followed.

He swept his arm out. "You want to explore? Go ahead, explore. I have nothing to hide." *Liar.*

Glaring, she stood for a moment with her arms crossed over her chest, then went straight to the oak desk in the corner and flipped open the book containing the pictures of her. Mira motioned at the album, glaring at him accusingly. "Why, Jack? Why did you take all of these?"

He pushed a hand through his hair and went to stand beside her. She turned the pages, revealing picture after picture of herself. *Gods.* He *had* lost control a little.

"Surveillance," he muttered.

She glanced up at him, her eyebrows raised. "Oh, surveillance was it?"

She flipped to a page of her sitting in a cafe on one of her breaks, sipping a cup of coffee all alone in a corner booth. She turned to another picture, this one of her outside, with her coat on and her scarf around her throat. She was looking up at the sky for some reason. The wind whipped dark tendrils of her hair across her pale face. Her eyes were closed and a slight smile played on her lips. He loved that picture of her. It was one of his favorites.

"Why did you need such intimate shots of me for surveillance, Jack?" she asked softly. "These don't seem like business to me. These seem personal."

He stood at a loss for words. They *were* personal. They were pictures of the daughter of the woman who'd haunted him for the last twenty-five years.

Or that's who Mira had been at first.

As he'd watched her at work, at the grocery store, going to old film festivals by herself, Mira had begun to emerge as a person independent of what she'd originally represented to him. A gorgeous woman, adrift in the world around her, alone and looking for pieces of herself she wasn't even aware were missing.

Jack had found reflections of himself in her.

After that he'd wanted to take pictures of Mira for her own sake, because her soul had been on display and he'd been able to capture the truth of her life so easily in those vulnerable moments when she'd thought no one had been looking.

"I took them because you're beautiful, Mira, and my hobby is photography. That's the only reason."

Mira snorted. "Beautiful? Now I know you're lying."

He blew out a breath of frustration. "Yeah, beautiful. I think you're fucking gorgeous actually. I'm sorry you don't see that when you look in the mirror, but I see it every time I look at you."

She closed the album and stared down at it, quiet. He wished he could guess what she was thinking, but he had no idea.

"It was an invasion," she said almost inaudibly.

"I know. It was wrong. I'm sorry." He seemed to be making mistake after mistake with her. Why did it feel like more were on the way? Why couldn't he just stop, just leave her alone? She was irresistible to him and he'd never dealt well with temptation.

Silence.

"I guess we're even then, as far as invasions go, considering I broke into this room," she said finally.

"Okay."

She turned to face him. Scowling, she blew a tendril of dark hair out of her face and crossed her arms over her chest. "What were you dreaming about, anyway?"

"You," he answered. "And my mother." He glanced away, not wanting to reveal with his eyes that he wasn't telling the whole truth. "I dreamt my mother wanted to take you with her into her grave."

Mira shuddered. "Your mother is dead?"

He nodded.

"I'm sorry." She motioned to the photographs on the wall. "I assumed she was your mother."

He shook his head. "That's my aunt. She raised me. I never knew my mom. She was an earth witch, I'm told."

She pursed her lips together for a moment. "Did Crane kill your mother, Jack?"

His gaze snapped to hers. "Why would you ask that?"

She didn't know how close to home she was hitting. His mother had probably killed herself because of his father. The doctors had diagnosed her with postpartum depression, and that may have played a role in her suicide, but Jack would never know for certain. Regardless of the reasons, she'd killed herself and left him behind to suffer life with his father alone.

"I don't know." She shrugged. "I thought maybe Crane had done something to hurt you on a personal level."

Jack glanced away. "He did, but it wasn't that."

"Okay." She paused. "Is your father still alive?"

He could hardly blame her for peppering him with questions, and she deserved all the answers she could get. Jack only wished he could give her the whole truth. "He's alive." His lips twisted into a rueful smile. "We don't talk much."

"If your mother was an earth witch, what element was your father?"

"Fire. I got my ability from him," he answered.

She bit her lip. He watched that pink bit of flesh caught between her white teeth with interest. "Been meaning to ask you. Where do witches come from? I mean . . . you know, are we aliens, or what?"

He exhaled the breath he hadn't known he'd been holding. She'd navigated away from the personal questions. "We don't know. There are theories. Maybe we're a different race, or humans who have evolved a bit further. We know we date back to Sumer. We know that once we lived among the non-magickicals and were worshipped like gods and goddesses for our control of the elements."

"So witches were out of the closet once?"

He nodded. "There's speculation that we were the reason Goddess worship was labeled evil. There were non-magickal factions who feared us, so they tried to destroy us. We were forced to go underground. Once in awhile one of us would be exposed and it would ignite an inquisition. We try very hard not to be exposed these days." He paused. "That's a point both the Coven and the Duskoff can agree on."

"I always thought the inquisitions were all church politics, mass hysteria, or greedy people persecuting others for their own gain."

"There was lots of that, but our own have been killed too. The Salem witch hunts were sparked by a case of demon possession. A demon the Duskoff birthed possessed the bodies of several young girls in a village. The hysteria that followed had nothing to do with us. No real witches were executed."

"So our origins are mostly unknown."

He nodded. "Cloaked in mystery."

"Hmmm." She stared up at him with her deep, penetrating eyes. "A lot like you," she said softly, holding his gaze.

"Mira . . ."

She didn't respond. She only dropped her gaze, rubbed her finger along the photo album meaningfully, and left the room.

"HE'S GOT HER," SAID WILLIAM CRANE, TENTING his carefully manicured fingers on the top of the shiny boardroom table.

David, a tall, thin water witch he treated as a go-to boy, stood in front of him with his pale narrow hands making a fig leaf in front of his crotch. It was an annoying nervous habit of his that made Crane itch to hit him, if hitting people wasn't so loutish.

Frankly, Crane hadn't expected any problem lifting the air witch from her apartment in Minneapolis, but it was true, what they said about having to do it yourself if you wanted it done right. Now they were out some hired muscle, and he was forced to gear up for a goddamn trip northward where it was even colder than his home in New York City.

His bones ached just thinking about it. Time wore on him more and more these days. It was coming to the point he needed Stefan to step in for him once in awhile. Crane clenched his jaw. He hated to admit that truth.

"I'll bet anything Thomas sent Jack to stand between me and this witch." Crane snorted with derision. "It's just like the bastard."

They'd been playing games for years now, he and Thomas Monahan. Just like Crane had played games with Monahan's father, the previous head of the Coven. He'd eventually killed him, and he'd get around to killing Thomas, too, one of these days. Monahan was an annoying gnat buzzing around his head. Unfortunately, once Monahan was gone there'd just be another Coven gnat standing in line to re-place him.

"With respect, sir, we have no reason to suspect Jack McAllister is handling this air witch at all. We've been watching McAllister's place in downtown Minneapolis. We've found no evidence of her presence, or his, for that matter. I've tried to gain knowledge of her presence through the flow of the water in the building, but haven't found anything. Most likely Thomas didn't use Jack be-cause of his . . . history . . . and they moved her directly to the Coven in Chicago."

Crane raised his gaze to David's. Was he daring to tell him he was wrong? He spoke slowly so David would un-derstand him. "Thomas would use Jack because he's the best, regardless of his . . . *history*. If he or the woman be-came injured, or some other unforeseen event occurred, he would likely take her to his Minneapolis apartment for quick, safe cover."

David took a step back away from him at the tone of his voice. His fig leaf tightened a degree. "We'll keep trying to verify her presence, Mr. Crane."

He cast an irritated glance at him. "My son's no fool. He's got powerful wards in place. You're never going to be able to use magick to discover her presence. You can take your water and pour it down the drain."

"We can place men at each of his apartments across the country, though he may have taken refuge in his rooms in the Coven. Perhaps while we keep investigating the Min-neapolis possibility, we should begin to prepare for an al-ternate plan to pry her from the Coven?"

Crane stared at him, letting his anger bleed into his eyes. "I admire your initiative, even though you're second-guessing me, David. You do realize that, don't you?" His voice sounded like a whip in the boardroom.

Another half step backward. David would be out the damn door soon. "I'm sorry, sir."

"Concentrate on Minneapolis. They didn't move her to Chicago yet. They stashed her somewhere close, and it has *Jack* written all over it. I feel it in my gut. He's got the woman. Bring in the best wardbreakers you can find."

Crane sighed, rubbed the bridge of his nose, and cursed himself yet again for his bad judgment regarding Jack. His decision to allow Jack's aunt to raise his son had been the biggest mistake of his life.

When Jack had been a child, Crane had assumed his son had inherited all of his mother's sensibilities and none of his. He'd never thought Jack's magick was that strong, or his will, for that matter. He'd assumed his son wouldn't be useful to him in any way.

It turned out Jack had much of his father in him after all. Tenacity. Strength. Resolve. The ability to do whatever had to be done in order to achieve a certain end, and the capability to do it with unparalleled ruthlessness.

Of all the Coven's operatives, Jack was the one who gave them the most trouble.

The regret tasted bitter. If Crane had raised Jack and twisted him *just so*, Jack would've grown into a fine man. He would've grown into a man like Stefan and would've been his right hand these days. Crane could've used someone like Jack working to further his agenda. As it turned out, Jack was working to hinder it.

It wasn't all bad. Crane had lost Jack, but had gained Stefan, a rare half-breed fire witch with an amazing amount of both power and rage. Crane had discovered him in Paris and taken him under his wing at the tender age of twelve. He'd groomed all that delightful anger and ambition into a dangerous, sharp point.

Yes, he'd lost his son, but he'd still managed to find an heir. Stefan used his good looks to his advantage and showed up often in the society pages. He was a media star and had been voted one of the top five eligible bachelors in the United States by several magazines. Little did anyone know the savage heart that beat under Stefan's polished public facade.

Damn, but he was a proud father.

"She's there," Crane finished. "Give the wardbreakers all the resources they desire. I need that woman. We might have to do this the crude way and break in." He sighed. "I hate doing it the crude way."

"Yes, sir. I'll get right on it."

"And bring in Stefan from Europe. I need him for this. Christ, if we can't get this woman into the demon circle we'll have to use Marcus. I don't want to waste him. He's perfect where he is, not much power to wield against us and nicely broken in. Anyway, I don't even know if he has enough juice to close a circle."

Their pet air witch had been paper-trained long ago. Marcus had just enough power to give the Duskoff some much needed service in the realm of air magick, but not enough to fight them. Not like the woman. Unless they controlled her before she fully came into her powers, she'd be able to wipe them off the face of the planet.

Crane shuddered in pleasure. Ah, she was delectable. If her parents were any measure, she was a fount of untapped potential. She probably had enough magick to close five demon circles. He might just have to play with her a little—while she was heavily drugged, of course—before he left her the honor of performing this most important task for him.

"Understood, sir."

Crane watched David leave the boardroom, then rose from his leather office chair and crossed the room to the bar. He needed a drink. In the mirror above the polished bar, he studied his reflection. Silver marked his hair at the temples. Age and illness now lined his once handsome face.

His light blue eyes were the only thing that had stayed the same over the years. They were the same eyes that stared from Jack's face. They were eyes that people said were strange to find on a fire witch—so icy and cold.

He took a short, chunky crystal glass and poured himself a bourbon and branch. The cancer was growing within him. He could practically feel it eating him up inside. He could heal himself somewhat, but the disease was quickly breaching the limits of his ability. He suffered bouts of severe nausea and fatigue. His leg bones and knees, where the cancer was mostly located, ached.

Fear flickered through him, and he clenched his free hand. *Fear.* He should know none of that.

He had so much power to command, not only in magick but in the non-magickal world as well. Companies thrived or failed at his whim. Politicians won or lost by his will. People lived, suffered, or died by his desires.

Yet his own body was doing him in.

Crane took a long drink of the bourbon. There was nothing he could do to stop this slow deterioration of his health.

Except find that woman.

TEN

SEXUAL AGONY.

That was the only way to describe it.

Jack took a sip of his bourbon and stared over the rim of his glass at Mira. Letting the liquid sit on his tongue a moment before sliding down his throat, he traced the curve of her exposed calf with his gaze.

He supposed she favored his sweatpants because they were comfortable. Despite all the clothes he'd bought her, she still wore them often. Likely, she didn't realize how sexy she looked in them. Maybe she even thought they made her less attractive and would stop him from wanting to make advances on her.

Oh, if only that were the case.

The sweatpants were his, first of all, and the idea of her bare body in his clothing made his cock hard. Second of all, they were charmingly too large for her and made her seem even more fragile and delicate. Third, she went around the apartment barefoot and kept hiking up the cuffs of the sweatpants so she wouldn't trip over them, thus exposing her very lovely, silky smooth calves.

Calves he wanted to lick and kiss. Calves he wanted to stroke with his palms right before he guided her legs around his waist.

He took another sip of his drink and watched her shift on the couch as she read his battered copy of *The Call of the Wild*. It was one of his favorites, though he hadn't told her that.

It seemed like Mira had been through half his library in the last few days. There wasn't much to do but read and surf the Internet. He didn't own a TV. There wasn't one in any of his apartments.

He had a stereo system, though, and they'd been through his entire CD collection. Everything from Mozart to Led Zeppelin to Nine Inch Nails. She liked both classical music and classic rock the best and had the endearing habit of dancing and singing along—badly—when she thought he wasn't looking.

She turned over onto her stomach, totally engrossed in the story. The soft, well-worn material of the sweatpants clung lovingly to her shapely ass, defining each perfect cheek. His mind called up the memory of how that sweetest part of her anatomy had felt in his hands.

He could think of much more interesting ways to pass the time than by reading or surfing the 'Net. For example, he could walk over there right now and charm her right out of those silly sweatpants. He could ease them down her legs, pull her sweatshirt off, and spread her smooth thighs. He could bury his head between her legs and spend hours there. Gods, he bet she was so sweet and hot down there, a pleasure against his tongue. He wanted to lick her swollen, creamy sex until Mira begged to feel his cock.

Jack would wager any amount of money that she'd never experienced a man going down on her in the right way. Never experienced a man who did it slow and knew where to touch a woman. He ached to show her, ached to make her come that way, against his lips, tongue, and fingers. He wanted to hear the sounds she made, wanted to taste her, wanted to feel her sex pulse around his tongue when she finally climaxed.

"Jack?"

He blinked and focused on her face, coming out of his vivid daydream.

She frowned at him. "Are you all right? You were staring at me."

He relaxed his hold on the glass, realizing he'd been gripping near hard enough to shatter it. "Don't worry about me. I'm fine," he growled.

A hurt look passed over her face, making him feel guilty for his gruff tone. "Sorry," she replied. "Just asking. How's your hand?"

He glanced at his palm. The burn had healed to a neat pink slash across his skin. "Almost gone."

She nodded, closed the book, and slid it onto the table.

"Finished already?"

"Yes." She sighed. "I need to get out of this place, Jack. If the Duskoff don't kill me in their circle, boredom will. Can't we get out a little, just, I don't know, let me go to the grocery with you or something? Anything?"

"It's got to be this way. We stay here until we get word from Thomas that it's safe to get you to the Coven. The plan was to take you there immediately, but when you hit your head I had to bring you here."

She nodded. "How is Thomas Monahan making sure it's safe to move? What's the Coven doing to help that happen?"

"The Coven is watching the Duskoff, monitoring their activities, but the Duskoff are watching us too. We're safe within these walls and we can't move until we get say-so."

"The Duskoff are watching." She shivered and rested her head on a throw pillow, staring at him with her wide dark eyes. "Great."

Gods, she looked so fragile, so breakable. He knew she

was a strong woman mentally, but physically . . . "Have you been practicing with your magick?"

"I've been practicing a lot. I'm getting good. I've got lots more control now."

He nodded. "It's probably time to go a little further. You need to learn some basic defensive magick."

"Oh." She lifted her head from the cushion. "Do you think I'll need that? Because, really, I'm more of a lover than a fighter."

And wouldn't he like to find out if that was true.

He shrugged. "Better safe than sorry. We're not sure why the Duskoff wants the demon circle drawn. Could be they'll come after you with guns blazing. Could be they'll let the Coven have you, thinking you're too much trouble to deal with." He pursed his lips. "But I'm betting on the former. They don't let witches like you go very easily."

"Great. I'm stuck in this apartment for the next year. Fantastic."

"Look, I don't like it any more than you do. But Monahan has the Coven on the situation. They think you're safest here right now and so do I. There's no leaving this warded, protected area. Not until Monahan says it's time."

She sat up and blew out a frustrated breath. "Am I going to have to run and hide forever because of my special brand of magick?" She winced and bit her lip. "I hate to whine, but really . . . I don't want to do this for the rest of my life. I just want things to be normal, stable." She sighed. "That's all I ever wanted—normality."

Jack set his glass down and smiled. "You have no idea of the power you wield, do you? Once you're in control of your abilities no one is ever going to be able to hurt you again." He shook his head. "There will be no more running, no more hiding. In fact, Crane might be running and hiding from you."

She blinked. "Oh. Then how do you explain what happened to my parents?"

"Ah. Well, no one is ever completely invulnerable. By

the way, Thomas thinks you'll be more powerful than either of your parents."

"Okay," she said with a shrug. Clearly, she didn't believe him. "Maybe after all this is over I can go into some kind of magickal witness protection program."

"One day you'll have stability again. It will just be a different kind of stability. It will be a house in the burbs with two-point-five kids and magick on the side type of stability."

She grinned. "An *I Dream of Jeannie* or *Bewitched* kind of stability."

He grinned back. "Something like that. As for being normal, Mira, you've never been that. Not from the day you were conceived."

She shot him a dirty look. "Gee, thanks."

"That was a compliment."

She just sighed.

She truly did have no idea of her power. For now, since she was untrained, that was a good thing. He didn't want any unexplainable tornadoes ripping through downtown Minneapolis in the dead of winter, or any of the other innumerable accidents that could occur with uncontrolled air magic.

On the other hand, she needed to know what she was capable of so she could defend herself. The thought of someone hurting Mira was unbearable to him, even more now that he knew her personally. She was no longer merely a responsibility to him, a way to make amends for standing there passively and watching her mother die. He'd come to know Mira to be a warm, intelligent, and caring person over the past week.

He'd learned she had a deep appreciation for classic literature like himself, had a unnatural love for Braeburn apples and Colby cheese, and, despite her faithfulness to the Wiccan religion, was a skeptical person when it came to all things magickal.

She was uncertain of her abilities and definitely lacking in self-confidence, but Jack felt once she mastered her magick, she would also find her true self. Jack already knew she was incredibly powerful.

Now Mira had to come to that understanding.

He set his glass down, stood, and moved some furniture to the side, well out of the way of his anticipated trajectory, and then walked to Mira. "Stand. This is your first lesson in defensive magick."

He offered her a hand up. She took it and stood, looking doubtful and a little nervous.

"Don't be afraid." He took her by the shoulders and turned her so her back was to him, his own back to the area he'd cleared, and pressed his body to hers. "I'm the one who should be scared," he murmured.

She jerked a little and tried to turn, but he held her in place. The heat of her body warmed him, and the light scent of her rose perfume caught in her hair teased his nostrils.

Damn. This was why he'd avoided training her.

He closed his eyes for a moment at the delicious feel of her against him. A muscle worked in his jaw as he gritted his teeth, fighting to control his cock, which wanted to rise and harden at her near proximity. Baseball, he needed to think about baseball.

"Since I'm a fire witch, of all the elements I'm best equipped to defend myself or to cause physical harm," he said softly near her ear. "But we each have the ability to use our magick in a fight. I'm going to show you one way to use yours."

What he had to do now required intimate physical contact. The magick didn't care if it killed him to touch her and not *really* touch her. It was necessary he have contact with the seat of her magick to be better able to help her control it, should it get out of hand.

He eased his arms around her. She shivered against him and her breathing hitched as they felt the undeniable response of her magick to his. The magick receded after that initial brush, but the attraction remained.

This craving he felt for her should have been easing by now. Their magicks were finding a balance. The accompanying erotic response should've been finding equilibrium also, like amounts of water leveling off. Hell, he'd been counting on his lust for her fading away before it drove them both insane. Yet, against all reason and magickal law, it seemed to be becoming even more intense.

How much of this torture were they supposed to take?

He placed his hands on her hips, and she went very still. Dragging her back against him, he fit her sweetly curved ass against his groin—and stopped to think about baseball again for a moment. Then he eased his hands up her stomach and placed his fingertips between her breasts, careful not to actually touch them.

Mira's breathing grew deep and heavy. He could feel the rise and fall of her chest under his fingertips. Was she excited right now? Did she want him as much he wanted her? Was she hot and damp between her lovely thighs? He wanted to find out.

"Close your eyes," he murmured into her ear. "Concentrate on drawing out a wisp of magick just the way you've been practicing, only take a little more this time. Draw about twice as much as you normally acquire, but no more than that."

"Got it," she said in a breathless voice.

"Already?"

"Been practicing."

"Okay. Good. Imagine that I'm an attacker. Imagine that I'm behind you with an intent to do you harm."

"You mean imagine that I don't want you touching me?" she murmured.

Jack took a moment to respond, trying to figure out what that comment meant. Did it mean it was hard to imagine . . . or easy? "Yes. Then direct it toward me with the desire to blow me backward."

Silence. *Nothing.*

"Mira?"

"Don't rush me. I'm working up to it."

"Okay. Don't worry about hurting—"

A gust of wind ripped him away from Mira. He sailed backward and landed on his back. His breath whooshed out of him and he slid five feet on the polished floor before coming to a stop. Jack lay sprawled, staring up at Mira in surprise.

"Oh my God," she exclaimed. "I'm so sorry. I didn't mean to push you that hard." She ran to him and offered a hand to help him up.

He regarded it warily for half a second, then took it and got to his feet. He winced and touched his aching lower back. "Ouch."

"I'm so, so sorry."

He took her face between his hands and forced her to look up at him. "Stop saying that. You did what I asked you do. You might be more of a fighter than you think."

She gave him a wicked smile. "So do we need to practice that another one hundred and fifty times then?"

He stared into her face, trying not to kiss her. The smile faded from her slightly parted lips as she looked up at him. Her pupils dilated, darkening her eyes. She wanted him, wanted him as much as he wanted her.

They stayed that way for a long, heavy moment. Just long enough for all his resolve to resist her to dissipate like the sun hitting the fog in the morning.

Gone.

Jack turned his face from hers for a moment and drew a breath. "Damn it. This is wrong, Mira, but right now I don't care."

She covered his hands with hers. "Me either."

He lowered his mouth to hers, meaning to kiss her nicely. Instead he pulled her up against his chest and angled his mouth over hers, demanding she open for him.

She made a hungry sound deep in her throat and parted

her lips. He swept into her mouth and found her tongue. She tasted hot and sweet, all wild magick and sexual need.

Jack groaned. He wanted her clothes off, her bare flesh under his hands. He wanted her legs parted and his cock thrusting deep inside her, driving her to the point where she shattered for him in sexual release. Jack wanted to feel her come around his driving shaft, wanted to hear the sexy, soft noises she made and see the look on her face as she climaxed.

At the moment, he could think of nothing else. Thoughts of what Thomas would do to him for seducing his cousin, the secret he kept about his parentage and his past—all of those reasons to resist her had receded so far back into his mind they were but a whisper.

"Mira," he murmured as he broke the kiss. He cupped her cheek in his palm. "I want more of you."

"I want you, too, Jack," she whispered against his lips. "I've wanted you since the moment I saw you that day in the diner." Her eyes had bled to a deep brown ringed with green.

Slow. He had to take this slow.

He felt half animal, wanting to simply strip her out of her clothes and take her up against the couch. He could just bend her over the back, spread her legs, and take her from behind until she screamed out her orgasm. But she needed a slower, more expert touch. Besides that, Mira was a woman to savor, to sip and let sit on his tongue. She was a woman deserving of a man who took his time.

Jack limned her jaw with the edge of his thumb, trailing down to caress her throat. Her pulse fluttered underneath his fingers before he dropped his hand to her shoulder and then further down. He stopped briefly at her waist, and then pressed against the small of her back, forcing her to arch against him. He brushed his lips lightly across hers but didn't linger. Instead, he traced his mouth down over her jawbone to her neck.

He twined his other hand in her hair and slowly tilted

her head back and to the side, exposing the line of her throat. All the while, he nuzzled her. Her pulse accelerated beneath his wandering lips and her breathing grew heavier as she became aroused. His tongue flicked out and tasted the sensitive place just under her earlobe.

Mira whimpered and her fingers twined in his sweater at his shoulders. He cupped her rear and slid down between her cheeks a little to feel the heat emanating from her sex. Her body primed itself for him as she grew more and more aroused. He imagined she was all sticky sweet right now, soft and hot.

He nipped at the skin where her shoulder and throat met, and she shivered. He groaned at how responsive her body was. Hell, he'd never get through this without spontaneously combusting.

"Jack," she whispered.

"What do you want, gorgeous?" he murmured against her skin. "Where do you want to be touched?"

He slid a hand under the hem of her sweatshirt in the back and eased it up her smooth, soft skin to the clasp on her bra. He had it undone with one twist of his fingers and her breasts fell free of the cups.

"Do you want me to touch you here?" he asked. Drawing his hand to her front, he held one of her perfect breasts in his hand and brushed the nipple back and forth until it hardened like a little pebble. At the same time, he kissed her again—slow, in sensual little tastings. Sometimes he rasped his tongue against hers, sometimes he nipped at her lower lip.

"Jack," Mira gasped into his open mouth. She pulled away from him, pushing herself out of his arms and turning away. She stood for a moment and then took a couple steps away from him.

He stood watching her retreat, his cock hard as a steel rod and pressing against the zipper of his jeans. "Mira? What's wrong?"

ELEVEN

~

MIRA TOOK A FEW STEPS TOWARD THE KITCHEN, not sure exactly where she was headed or why. She and Jack had reached the point where sexual hunger overrode reason. Jack was right, this was a mistake. Still, it was a mistake she wanted to make.

She found herself over by the wall by the pedestal, where the blue vase had been before she'd broken it. She grasped the smooth edge of the pedestal and looked up at the piece of artwork on the wall just above her head because then she didn't have to look at Jack. One look at Jack and she'd throw herself at him, and she shouldn't do that.

Lord and Lady, she was sick of *shoulds*.

"Mira?" Jack said behind her. He put his hand on her waist, and she closed her eyes. "Tell me what's wrong."

She leaned her forehead against the wall. This was stupid. It was just sex. It wasn't like she was committing herself to the guy. It wasn't like she was marrying him or having his babies. She was a grown woman. She could have meaningless sex once in a while. After what her ex had put her through, she was due a little impulsiveness and reckless behavior, right? If she wanted to tumble into bed with her extremely attractive bodyguard, she could do it.

At her age, she was far below her meaningless sex quota anyway. It was time she sowed some wild oats.

In any case, this was all just the result of their magick— the innate attraction of fire and air. Maybe, if they succumbed this one time, the powerful draw would subside.

Jack gathered her loose hair to one side, baring her shoulder. "Mira?" His breath whispered over her skin as he said her name.

She exhaled fast and hard. "Touch me, Jack. Take me to a place where I can't think anymore."

"I can do that. I *want* to do that." He lowered his mouth and kissed her earlobe. It sent shivers through her. "I'm going to tell you what else I want to do. I want to take this silly sweatshirt off you and ease these sweatpants down your legs. I want to fuck you up against this wall. I want to take you fast and hard in order to get all this out of both our systems. Then I want to put you in my bed and make love to you, slow and easy, over and over."

Mira shivered. She grew warmer and wetter between her thighs, her clit plumping with need . . . and he hadn't even touched her yet. His words aroused her as if he'd been stroking her body with his hands.

"What do you want?" he purred. "Tell me."

Instead of answering with words, she took his hand from her waist and pushed it underneath the bottom hem of her sweatshirt, up to cover her bare breast. Her nipple tightened against his palm. "I want you to fuck me, Jack."

"Ah," he breathed across the skin of her throat. "That's the answer I was hoping for."

He pushed the waistband of the sweatpants down. They were too big for her, so they went easily, pooling at her feet. She stepped out of them and kicked them away. She wore no underwear and the cool air bathed her flushed skin.

"Mmmm," Jack purred, running a hand down her thigh. "Your skin is so soft." He brushed his palm over her buttocks and slipped between her legs to drag his fingers over her excited sex, making her breath hiss out of her.

"Mira, I've been thinking so much about this," he said in a sexy rough-rasp. He eased his hands upward, taking the hem of her sweatshirt with them, and pulled her unhooked bra and sweatshirt over her head.

She shivered, gooseflesh erupting over her skin as his hands roamed her. Her nipples had hardened into little peaks and her sex felt warm and swollen with the need to be touched. The rough sensation of his clothing rubbing along her nude body drove her insane. She wanted him as naked as she was, wanted to feel the slide of his skin against hers.

Mira tried to turn, but he held her in place with his palm flat against her abdomen and her back flush up against his chest. He fisted her hair in his hand and pulled her head to the side, exposing her throat, and laid kisses from beneath her earlobe to the place where her shoulder met her neck.

"I've been thinking about touching you for a long time," he murmured. "Kissing you, licking you. I want to feel you come, Mira, with my cock buried deep inside you."

She closed her eyes. Her heart beat fast and her breath came quick as he drew his hand up from her stomach to cup her breast. He dragged the pad of his thumb over the sensitized peak until she whimpered deep in her throat.

"I like to be in control in the bedroom. Do you have a problem with that?"

"N-no." She couldn't say she had any problems at all at the moment. Hell, she could barely even form a thought. All she wanted was to touch and be touched, to pleasure and be pleasured. She wanted to feel his body stretched over hers, wanted to feel his cock thrusting deep inside her.

"Good," he murmured in that same sexy-sweet rasp. His fingertips grazed her stomach, and then dipped lower to drag over her mound. Gently, he eased his hand between her thighs and stroked her swollen, aching clit. He knew exactly how to caress her, how to skillfully apply the perfect amount of pressure to make her moan. She fisted one hand against the wall in front of her.

"You feel so sweet, Mira, so silky hot against my hand. Does this feel good?" he asked softly.

"Yes."

"Your body was made to be touched. You're so responsive, so beautiful. I love to see you this way, naked and moaning for me, creaming between your thighs because you want my cock."

She shivered at his words, whispered into her ear. He slid his middle finger into her damp heat, and she bit her bottom lip. He added a second finger and thrust in and out very slowly, over and over, finding a sensitive place deep inside her and brushing over it on every outward stroke.

"Jack," she breathed.

She fought the urge to grind down on his thrusting fingers and desperately grasped the edge of the pedestal, splaying her other hand out on the wall. Hell, she was going to embarrass herself and come from just the touch of his hand again.

He ground the heel of his hand against her clit. Pleasure skittered through her body and Mira whimpered. Her body teetered on the edge of a powerful climax. "Please, Jack."

"Please what?"

"Just *please*." She squeezed her eyes shut and willed her mind to form coherent sentences. "I need to feel you. I need to touch you. I want your cock inside me. Please."

He took a moment to answer, then finally responded in a strained voice. "Turn around."

She turned and looked up at him, stared into his dilated eyes. He'd seemed so coolly in charge of his sexual need while he'd been driving her crazy a moment ago, but now she saw that he was poised on the edge. Mira wanted to push him over, make him relinquish all that tightly leashed control.

Because Jack in control was something indeed, but she could only imagine how incredible he would be without it.

She ran her hands over his chest and shoulders, feeling the powerful bunch of his muscles. Under his gaze, she felt beautiful, sexy, and desirable. She hadn't felt that way in a long time—if ever.

Finding the edge of his cream-colored sweater, she pushed it up slowly. As it went, she licked and nipped over his exposed flesh—up his washboard abs and over his luscious silk-poured-over-iron chest. The man was gorgeous, and she wanted to taste every inch of him.

He groaned and threaded his fingers through her hair, releasing her only long enough for her to pull his sweater over his head and toss it to the floor.

Standing there in only his jeans, he lowered his head and forced a kiss out of her, using his grip on her hair to guide her mouth to his. His mouth slanted over hers, his tongue stroking hers at an erotically slow pace. Her hands roved his body and eventually found the button of his jeans. She undid it and pulled down the zipper. Just the sound made Mira grow even wetter.

She pushed his jeans down and slid her hands over the curve of his finely shaped ass, still clad in his boxer briefs, then slowly eased to the front of him, where she slipped her fingers through the slit in the material and took him in her hand.

He had a beautiful cock. Wide and long, so wide she wasn't even sure her fingertips would meet when she gripped his shaft.

And he was very, very aroused.

Mira petted him, letting her fingers play on the underside of his cock and the pad of her thumb caress the satin-smooth crown. She wanted him in her mouth, wanted to explore every vein with the tip of her tongue. Fascinated, she stroked him, feeling him jerk against her palm in response.

He broke the kiss with a hiss and threw his head back on a groan. "I need to be inside you. Now. Fuck. I need a condom." He tried to pull away and her arms tightened around him.

She inhaled the scent of him—soap and the faint fragrance of his aftershave. "No, don't leave me, Jack."

His arms tightened around her. "Mira—"

Without responding, she pushed the waistband of his boxer briefs down. He stepped out of the clothing piled at his feet, leaving him gloriously naked. He was a sight fit to be included in any male modeling magazine.

She stared at him for a moment, taking in the full effect of him completely nude. He gave her a confident smile that was all male. A smile that told her he enjoyed how much she appreciated his masculine beauty. A smile that clearly said *your ass is mine*.

With one powerful movement, he lifted her. Her legs twined around his waist as though meant to go there. Pressing her back against the wall, he found her slick opening and pushed the side of his shaft against her tender, swollen folds, burrowing between her aroused labia. The hard length rubbed her clit as he thrust gently against her . . . but not inside her.

"Awww, fuck," he breathed out, sounding agonized.

All her breath left her in a rush at the sensation of him so intimately pressed against her. She would have preferred it a little more intimate though. No fair pressing all that lovely hardness against her and not inside her. "J-Jack?" she questioned unsteadily.

"I changed my mind. You're too good to take up against this wall for the first time. I want you in my bed so I can savor you." He braced her back against the wall and buried his face in the curve of her neck. "And I'm not making love to you without a condom, Mira." He thrust his hips forward, rubbing against her clit and making Mira cry out.

"Jack," she gasped. "Let's get to the condoms then. *Now*."

His low chuckle drew gooseflesh from her. "Let's go to bed," he murmured as he nuzzled her throat.

With a strength that bordered on the preternatural—and maybe it was—he backed away from the wall and carried her into the bedroom.

Carefully, he laid her on the mattress in the darkened room. The soft comforter brushed her bare body as she moved. She watched him take a foil-wrapped condom from the drawer and rip the edge with his teeth. Mira sat up and plucked it from his fingers. Looking up into his eyes, she rolled it down his length.

Still holding her gaze, he pushed her back against the mattress and suspended himself above her. He cupped her cheek in his palm. "Damn, you're beautiful. Spread those pretty long legs for me."

She did as he asked, and he kissed his way down her body, stopping to worship each of her breasts as he stroked between her spread thighs with skillful fingers. Mira tossed her head and moaned as he gently, so very gently, nipped one of her hardened nipples, making exquisite pleasure flare through her body.

Jack made a low sound in his throat and moved down between her thighs. He spread her sex with his thumbs and licked from her perineum to her clit. He groaned. "Hot and sweet. Just how I imagined."

Mira sank her teeth into her bottom lip as he worked her swollen clit over and over with the tip of his tongue. He eased two fingers inside her and thrust into her with them as he laved her. Just the sight of his dark head bobbing between her thighs was nearly enough to make her come.

His clever tongue slicked over her labia, flicked her clit, then eased deep inside her. Sometimes he used his fingers to pump her, sometimes his tongue. Jack lost himself to it, nibbling and licking at her until she thought she'd lose her mind.

Her orgasm rose fast and hard, ripping through her body so powerfully it made her scream. She ground her pulsing, climaxing sex against his face. He held her down with two strong hands on her thighs and rode her through her long, long orgasm.

Finally, boneless, she relaxed on the mattress with Jack laving over her sex and making low sounds of satisfaction deep in his throat.

Her body still hummed from her climax when he rose up, looking down at her in the half light. "I'm going to fuck you until you can't think anymore," he murmured. "Is that what you want, baby?"

She smiled, wrapped her legs around him, and used them to pull him down closer to her. It was an unsubtle answer, and it made him grin.

He dragged his hand from her cheek to her collarbone, over her breast, to her hip and then eased the head of his cock inside her, all the while still gazing into her eyes.

She moaned and dug her fingers into his shoulders at the way he stretched her. Ben hadn't been small, but he hadn't approached Jack's size either. Slowly, inch by inch, he pushed the rest of it between her swollen labia, into her aroused sex, until she was completely filled and panting. She whimpered at the size of him.

"Damn, you're tight. How does that feel?"

"Good. So good. That's what I wanted." Her hair was mussed and her eyes were glassy with lust, she just knew it. She was lost to him, possessed by him, and she wouldn't have it any other way.

Still holding her gaze, he pulled out and thrust back in slowly. Mira's spine curved as she arched into him, her fingernails digging into his upper arms. She could feel every inch of his cock tunneling deep inside her. Jack eased out and thrust back in again, making Mira's breath hiss out of her.

Jack caught her wrists and pressed them to the bed on either side of her body. She thought of the rope and shivered. He liked his women bound, she knew that. He held her that way for a moment, gazing into her face, then dropped his head and kissed her.

His tongue slid past her lips and he took her mouth possessively while he shifted his hips and shafted her slow and then even slower. Slow enough to drive her insane while he pushed her closer to climax.

Jack shifted his hips again and the head of his cock rubbed that bundle of nerves buried within her on every inward thrust. Her eyes widened at the deep pleasure rippling through her body as he skillfully manipulated that sensitive area. Caught in a thick haze of pleasure, she wondered if this was the fabled G-spot. If so, it was a place Ben had never been able to find. Then the thought—all her thoughts—were gone, washed away in the crest of her rising climax.

He kept her wrists pinned to the bed and his tongue in her mouth as he changed his pace, taking her hard and deep and steady. He increased the pace of his thrusts and forced her blooming orgasm to catch, hold, and explode. The muscles of her sex pulsed around his pistoning cock. Jack caught all her cries and moans against his tongue.

He moved an arm between their bodies and rubbed her sensitive clit as her climax began to fade. "There it is, baby," he murmured. "Come for me again." His stroking fingers made her climax falter, stutter, then flare to brilliant life once more.

"Ah, Jack," she cried as she felt herself pulled under by another intense wave of pleasure.

He found her breast and closed his lips around it, flicking the nipple. Jack's cock jerked deep inside her, letting

Mira know he was ready to come. She watched as he threw his head back, groaning her name. It was the most erotic thing she'd ever seen or heard.

Jack collapsed on top of her, still buried within her. She threaded her fingers through his silky dark hair, enjoying the feel of him skin-on-skin and the rapid rise and fall of his chest. His heart thudded against her breast, and his breath felt hot on her neck.

Her body still tingled with the intimate awareness of him, pulsing with the remnants of the multiple orgasms he'd given her. She'd never thought she'd be capable of coming twice in a row. Mira smiled, flush with a burst of happiness. She wouldn't mind trying for triples.

With a groan, he rolled to the side, leaving her staring at the ceiling, heavy lidded and still a little stunned. Delicious languor stole over her body. Never had she felt so sated after sex.

She turned her head and looked at him. He had his eyes closed and his arms thrown over his head. Smooth muscle rippled over the expanse of his chest. A light dusting of dark hair tapered into a trail that led down his hard stomach and surrounded his unbelievable cock, now lying half flaccid against his thigh.

Mira had the urge to take him into her mouth. She'd never wanted to do that with Ben, not voluntarily, at least. The few times she'd done it, she'd done it out of a sense of duty, and it had been more a chore than anything else.

But with Jack . . . she wanted to give Jack as much intense pleasure as he'd just given her. She wanted to render him helpless against her tongue and lips the way she'd been just moments ago in his arms. She wanted to feel his body bow beneath hers as she slid her tongue up and down his length.

There were many things she wanted in this moment that she'd never even thought much about before.

Suddenly, Mira realized that her magick hadn't reacted

to his, not once for the entire time they'd been together. She opened her mouth to ask about that, but Jack spoke first.

"Mira," Jack said raggedly. "I'm sorry." He pushed to his feet and went into the bathroom without another word.

Confused, Mira pushed up onto her hands. Sorry? Sorry for what? Making her scream in coital delight? "Jack?" she called, but he was already closing the door. A moment later she heard the sound of the shower.

She scowled at the door for a few moments, wondering if she should go after him or not. Finally, she rolled off the bed and stood. She walked across the room, tried the bathroom door, and found it open. Steam rolled out.

"Jack?" she called as she entered the room. He didn't answer, so she approached the shower door and opened it.

Jack stood facing her in the center of the shower with all the jets trained on him. His arms were up, fingers threaded through his hair, eyes closed. Her mouth went dry. He looked like a god standing there all wet and naked. She wanted him again already.

But she was pissed.

"Jack? You're a really moody son of a bitch, you know that?"

His eyes opened and she saw something in them for a moment—something dark and painful. It was gone as quickly as she'd glimpsed it. Like storm clouds rolling through on a summer day. In its wake, he didn't look so much like a luscious, drenched god as he did a lonely man.

She hesitated, then stepped into the shower and walked toward him. The comforting warmth of the water hit her, wetting her hair and skin.

Jack pulled her to him as soon as she was within arm's reach and held her against his body. He plunged his hands into her hair and buried his face in the curve of her neck.

Mira let out a deep sigh of pleasure, feeling him pressed against her and his arms around her. She let her hands roam his warm, wet muscled back and shoulders. "What did you mean?" she asked near his ear. "What did you mean . . . you're sorry?"

He only forced her mouth to his and nipped her bottom lip, demanding she let him in. She opened her mouth and his tongue swept in to brush against hers. That same fire she'd felt in the living room rushed through her body. It was like Jack had opened some floodgate inside her. She practically had to stop herself from climbing his body and impaling herself on his cock.

Jack tangled his fingers through her wet hair and took her in a rough, near-bruising kiss, as commanding and overwhelming as the man himself. It left her breathless and her mind fumbling for coherent thought.

"Mira," he groaned ragged against her ear. "I want you again."

"So, take me. I'm yours."

"No condom."

"Jack, if it's STDs you're worried about—"

"No." He shook his head. "It's near impossible for our kind to catch those. I'm worried about pregnancy."

"Oh, that. Don't I wish. Jack, you know, Ben and I tried for years and never conceived. I don't really think that's an issue."

He held her gaze for a moment before speaking. "Ben wasn't like you, Mira. Ben wasn't a witch like me. A witch and non-witch are damn near infertile. A witch and another witch on the other hand . . ." he trailed off.

Realization dawned. "Oh."

He nodded. "Very fertile."

Well. That explained a lot. "But it's nowhere near my time of ovulation. I don't think there's any way I could possibly get pregnant this time of the month. I think we're safe." She curled her hands around his cock and pumped him until he groaned. "Jack," she whispered in entreaty. "Touch me."

"Mira—"

"I'm all wet," she murmured coyly with a raised eye-brow. She slid a finger over one hard, pink nipple, gathering moisture, to prove the point, and then eased her hand down to catch his and place it between her thighs. "Everywhere for you," she finished.

Hunger flared dark in his eyes. He twined a hand to the nape of her neck, the other to the small of her back, and pulled her flush against his chest as he kissed her. His tongue burrowed past her lips, possessing her mouth.

His hand at the small of her back dropped to cup her ass, then slid between her cheeks where he delved his fingers deep inside her and stroked. Pleasure shot through her sex and she rolled her hips forward, seeking more of his touch. Every breath or slight movement rubbed her stiff nipples against his chest.

She ran her hands up his biceps, over his shoulders. They ate at each other's mouths, licking, sucking, and nipping—like they couldn't get enough of the taste of each other.

They weren't directly in the hot stream of the showerheads, but the spray of it had thoroughly wet them. Their bodies slid against each other—warm and slippery. He broke the kiss and worked his way down her throat to her nipples. He sucked on one while he plumped and caressed the other breast with his free hand. His lips massaged her hardened nipple and his teeth scraped gently across it. Jack worked it thoroughly, until Mira felt a surge of moisture between her thighs.

He licked his way down over her stomach and through the hair of her mound. Then he went to his knees, pressed his palms to her ass, and pulled her to his face. She felt his tongue flick out to lap up her juices and tease her clit in long, persistent licks.

Her knees went weak. She gasped and grabbed his shoulders to prevent herself from toppling over. He supported her by cupping her bottom, holding her with her thighs spread so he could feast on her sex. His tongue played leisurely with her labia, driving her crazy. Finally, he found her entrance and pushed inside. With agonizing slowness, he thrust into her with his tongue.

"Jack," she moaned.

He stood, cupping her ass, and lifted her, bore her back a few paces to press her against the tile wall of the shower. It was the living room redux, though now she thought Jack had every intention of fucking her.

Jack settled her over the head of his hard cock and rotated his hips, pressing against her opening. He rolled his hips forward and impaled her to the base of him. Her breath hissed out of her and she wrapped her arms around his neck.

"Are you sure you want this, Mira?" he asked in a rough voice near her ear.

The muscles of her sex rippled and pulsed around his shaft, adjusting once again to the length and width of him. Mira nodded. "I want everything you have to give me, Jack." She kissed him.

They stayed that way for a moment, connected at the pelvis, their mouths working against each other's and the water coursing down their bodies. Then Jack cupped her rear and began to thrust.

Oh, yes, yes, yes! Now he would take her up against the wall.

She whimpered as his thick shaft slid in and out her. Her legs fastened around his lean waist and she gripped his shoulders to keep her steady. Water from the shower ran into their mouths as they kissed.

Jack pinned her to the wall, bracing her there as he took her harder and faster, his cock slamming up into her and totally possessing her, making her breath come in little pants.

Her orgasm came in a powerful wave that made her cry out. She threw her head back, closed her eyes, and screamed his name as she climaxed around his pistoning cock. Jack followed only a few seconds later with a shout that echoed through the shower.

Panting, Jack placed his forehead to hers. "Damn it, I *like* being inside you."

She grinned. "The feeling's reciprocal, I assure you."

He kissed her first on the forehead, then on the cheek, and finally on her lips. Then he released her thighs and let her stand. His cock slipped from her body and she felt the loss. "I can't resist you. Fuck, once I have you, I want you again. You're addictive," he growled.

His words should have pleased her, but they held an undercurrent of guilt . . . of remorse. The look in his dark eyes was the same. Like she was some sinful treat he knew he couldn't have, yet took all the same.

Jack McAllister was keeping secrets from her.

"Bring her in, Jack," said Thomas Monahan.

Jack stood with the phone to his ear, rubbing a towel through his damp hair. "Right away? It is urgent?"

"Not tonight. Tomorrow morning. There are plane tickets waiting for you both at Minneapolis-St. Paul International, first class, straight through to Chicago. We're sending men to watch your back, but they're going to hang out of sight unless they're needed. Anything else would just draw Crane's attention. He's been watching your place with a little more interest than we like. We think he suspects Mira is with you, and that means it's time to move." He paused. "How is she?"

Jack glanced toward his bedroom, seeing her walk past the doorway as she got ready to sleep. She plucked her nightgown from the foot of the bed and pulled it over her head. He watched the silk sheathe her body. How was she? Beautiful. Wonderful. Luscious. Delectable. Irresistible. *Oh, by the way, I just made love to her twice.*

"She's, uh, okay," he said in a voice too low to carry to Mira.

"Has she tapped her magick?"

"Yeah. I think once she has some more training your cousin is going to be able to kick some serious ass, Thomas. We tried some defensive magick today and she slid me halfway across the living room floor on the first try."

Thomas laughed with pride. "That's that Monahan blood. Hoskins blood is pretty powerful too. Did she come to it easily? How'd she tap it?"

His questions were eager. Jack knew how much Thomas was dying to meet Mira. Family meant a lot to him, and Mira had pretty much been out of the fold since birth. "You didn't mention the strength of the affiliation between fire and air. My magick drew hers. She was unbelieving at first, as you'd expect, but once she felt it rise, it was all over. She came to it pretty quickly after that."

Monahan went silent for several moments. "You just keep your hands off her, okay? I know you've got a weakness for beautiful women, but this one is special. I don't want you messing with her head, got it?"

Too late.

"Yeah."

"Okay. Be at the airport at 7 A.M. Go to the Northwest ticket counter to pick up your tickets. Your flight leaves at 9:09 A.M. Got it?"

"Got it."

"Watch your back. I don't have to tell you twice. It would be best if you got her out unseen, but if you can't, the Coven witches I sent will be there to back you up. I don't want anything to happen to Mira."

"Harm comes to Mira over my dead body," Jack replied vehemently.

"I know, Jack," Thomas said in just about the gentlest tone the man could manage, which wasn't very. "I know what this job means to you."

Mira appeared in the doorway with a comb in her hand. Her hair fell over her shoulders in dark, damp skeins, and her beautiful eyes questioned him.

Jack held her gaze for a long moment. It meant more to him than Thomas realized, more than Jack had ever intended.

"Yeah," he answered, still holding Mira's gaze.

TWELVE

—❦—

CRANE REGARDED THE AIR WITCH WHO SAT IN A
slight stupor before him. Rage swelled from the mere pathetic sight of him.

They kept Marcus drugged with a low dose of Ketamine, which had the effect of a tranquilizer when intro-
duced to a witch's metabolism, with only mild dissociative
side effects. It was important to keep him mollified and a
little confused since any air witch was dangerous, even
weak ones like Marcus.

Marcus's hands were bound in his lap. He wrung them
over and over, a clear sign of his agitation. As if the wide,
wild eyes and gaping mouth weren't enough evidence of
his mental state. He was kept a prisoner all of the time.
They trotted him out when they needed the information
only an air witch could provide.

Information like they needed now.

Crane had hauled Marcus to the frozen wastelands of
Minnesota in deep February, all in order to see if he could
somehow glean any intelligence about whether the woman

resided in Jack's apartment or not. Mostly, Crane had received a big, fat nothing for his trouble, and he'd been worried he might have to admit David had been right about the witch not being at Jack's Minneapolis residence after all.

Then, finally, Marcus had heard something. The video and audio monitors in the room where they kept Marcus had shown him jarred from his sleep by some occurrence. The video footage showed him sliding out of the bed and trying to hide under it, obviously not happy that he'd gleaned information that Crane wanted and too addle-brained from the Ketamine dose to hide it well.

Crane reached out, grabbed Marcus's pudgy cheeks, and shook his head back and forth until his unruly black curls flew. "David says you heard something on the wind tonight, Marcus," he said. "You're going to tell us." He paused for effect. "Now."

Marcus whimpered and rocked back and forth. "No, no, no, no!" he chanted. "I won't tell you. I won't!"

Enforced magickal servitude had driven Marcus a bit crazy, but it still hadn't broken him of these little ill-advised fits of rebellion.

Crane laughed. "Maaaar-cus," he sang softly. "Our ward-breakers have been unsuccessful, and that means I don't have time to play games. He stroked his fingers through his jet black curls, then clenched them hard and fast and yanked his head to the side. Marcus cried out, and spittle, an unfortunate side effect of the drugs, trailed out of the corner of his mouth. "Now tell us, like a good little pet air witch, and maybe I'll let you go back to your room and have a cookie."

Marcus sniveled for a moment, and then clearly enunciated, "No."

Crane sighed heavily. "Marcus, you know why we need to call the circle, correct?"

Marcus nodded.

"So you know I'll do anything in my power to gain an air witch to close it, yes?"

He nodded again.

"Then what do you think is stopping us from using *you* to close the circle?"

Uncertainty flashed through his brown eyes, chased by a dash of fear. *Good.*

"I'll tell you, Marcus. You're not very powerful, that's definitely one reason. Why, our little Marcus can barely call a light breeze, can he?" Crane laughed softly. "Damn those pesky genetics anyway. But the other reason, the far more important reason, is the cooperation that our Marcus gives us." Crane smiled. "Understand?"

Marcus nodded.

"When we need to know things that only an air witch can discover, our Marcus helps us out."

He nodded again.

Now they were getting somewhere. "If you want to keep your sizable ass out of that circle, Marcus, if you value your pathetic life in any way, you'll tell me what you heard right now. Otherwise, I'll substitute you for her and hope you have enough juice to close the circle. After your magick is bled out, I'll just find myself another weak air witch to mold to my pleasing."

He whimpered and a tear slid out of his eye, but Crane kept his tight grip on Marcus's hair. "Okay."

Crane released him.

He sniveled again and snot trailed out of his left nostril. Marcus wiped it away with his bound hands. "I heard a telephone conversation. It woke me up. I think there was a chink in the warding and some of it slipped out. I was so tuned on the apartment that I caught it on the air when it passed. The air witch is in Jack McAllister's apartment, but they're planning to move her to the Coven tomorrow morning."

Crane smiled coldly at Marcus, and then turned to David, who stood near the door. "I don't care how you do it, you get those wardbreakers to find us a way in before dawn." He paused. "Tell them their lives depend on breaking that warding. If they fail, they'll die slowly and painfully. Got it?"

David nodded.

With the proper motivation anything could be accomplished. They had to get in now, because once she was at the Coven, she'd be nearly impossible to take. They could try to snatch her en route to the airport, but that was a last resort because it meant a public magickal showdown.

And that would just be crass.

SOMETIME DURING THE NIGHT, MIRA FOUND HER way into his arms.

Jack buried his nose in her hair and inhaled, letting the faint fragrance of her perfume infuse his senses. Her breathing sounded deep and heavy and her body felt warm against him. Jack closed his eyes and wallowed in it.

But this couldn't happen. Whatever this was that he felt for Mira, it had to end. Once she found out who he was, it would be all over. She'd hate him. How could she do anything else?

The last thing he wanted to see in her pretty eyes was fear or revulsion when she looked at him.

While he didn't regret sleeping with Mira, it had been a huge mistake. He'd started out meaning to resist her and had failed. That lapse in his willpower would hurt both of them in the end, but especially Mira. As much as it pained him, all this had to be nipped in the bud. It would make things easier later on.

His arms tightened around her and she murmured his name in her sleep. *Damn.* He didn't want to let her go, but that's exactly what he had to do.

Jack eased his arms carefully from her warm body so he wouldn't wake her and turned over. It took about an hour of staring into the dark before he finally drifted off to sleep, dreaming of cold places.

Sometime in the predawn hours, Jack awoke from his chilly dreamscape to heat. Skillful fingers curled around his erection, caressing the length of him. His breath hissed from between his teeth at the sensation of her hand stroking him. She'd managed to get him hard while he'd been sleeping. Need rode high in his balls and his cock felt like a steel rod.

"Gods, woman," he groaned. "What do you think you're doing?"

He'd turned over onto his back while he'd been sleeping, and she'd eased the covers down past his hips. Her dark head hovered by his side. The moonlight slanted through the window and caught in her hair. It still wasn't morning.

"Couldn't resist. Hope you don't mind," she answered in a playful tone.

Hell. He did mind. At least, his brain minded even if his dick didn't. His thoughts raced, finding tactful ways to get out of this without making her feel rejected. "Mira, we should—ah!"

She'd slid her lips over the head of his cock and was now tonguing her way down his shaft.

"Mira!" he cried out gutturally at the feel of her hot mouth engulfing him. It was so wet and soft. More than he could defend against. Point to Mira. Every shred of willpower he'd had a moment ago went *poof*.

She slanted her head up at him, revealing a sexy, mischievous expression on her beautiful face. It was an expression he was hard-pressed to resist. Then she dropped her gaze and licked up the length of his shaft . . . like it was a Popsicle. He made a strangling noise.

"I want to do this really badly, Jack," she murmured before she licked him again. "Let me."

"How am I supposed to say no?"

Her hair brushed his upper thighs as she engulfed his cock in her mouth again and worked her tongue against him.

His fingers found those silky moonlit strands and fisted. Just how much could one man take? Mira had pushed him past his limit as soon as her tongue had touched him.

The mere sight of his cock, wet from her saliva, thrusting between her full lips, was nearly enough to make him lose it. She seemed to love having him in her mouth. She'd thrust him in until the crown touched her tonsils, then would spend time licking his shaft up and down and swirling her tongue around the head.

All that playing drove him insane.

The charm of her mouth, and the enthusiasm she showed in having him there, rendered him helpless. Did it have any effect on her? He wanted to know if this made her wet. Was she aroused from this?

"Hell, you're going to make me come," he murmured. He fought the urge to thrust into her mouth, wanting to let her do as she wished with him.

She stopped for a moment and smiled up at him. "That's kind of the idea, isn't it?"

He moved fast, toppling her to the bed and dragging her beneath his body. She yelped in surprise and then laughed. Eager to touch her, he yanked up the hem of her pajamas and stroked her soft pink flesh until she moaned. Oh, yes, having him in her mouth had turned her on.

Jack stared down into her face while he caressed her between her thighs. He tunneled his fingers inside her to feel all that delicious wet heat. "I want to come when I'm deep inside you," he growled. "And I want to feel your climax ripple around my cock before I go."

Her breathing came faster and heavier at his words. She might seem innocent, but it excited her when he talked a little dirty. "I have no particular objections," she murmured.

"But first, I need to taste you." He lowered his mouth to hers and kissed her deeply, his tongue skating against hers in the recesses of her mouth. After kissing her breathless, he worked his way down, yanking her nightgown farther up to expose the sweetly curved hollows and planes of her body, her luscious breasts with their responsive nipples.

He worshipped it all with his lips and tongue, occasionally with his teeth. Mira liked it when he nipped her here and there—the curve of her waist, the sensitive place where her throat met her shoulder. It made her shiver and moan.

Every wrinkle and pucker of each nipple got his full attention. Mira moved restlessly beneath him on the bed, her fingers kneading his upper arms and shoulders, her hips lifting and thrusting in an unconscious, needful way.

Jack enjoyed teasing her, enjoyed having control over her body. He'd love to bind her sometime, make her truly helpless to him. He wanted to tease her body to the edge of climax over and over so that when she finally went, she did it yelling his name and seeing stars.

He left her nipples even though he could spend hours there and ran the tip of his tongue slowly down her abdomen, into the dip of her belly button and over her mons. He kneed her legs apart and planed her leg with his hand before kissing and gently biting the place where her sweet inner thigh met her sex.

Mira's back arched and her hands closed around the blankets on either side of her.

"Do you like the way I touch you, Mira?" he asked.

"Jack, yes." She raised her head and looked down the length of her body at him. "If you just blow on me right now, I'll probably come."

Jack grinned and blew gently over her sex. Mira shuddered and moaned, letting her head fall back against the mattress. He inhaled the scent of her, musky and aroused. His balls ached and his cock had gone harder than steel. This erotic torture was torture for him too.

He lowered his mouth to her sex and licked her swollen, aroused clit. "Spread your pretty thighs for me a little more," he ordered her gently.

Mira parted her legs and he slid a finger into her heat, then another, making her sigh his name as he began to thrust. Her wetness coated his fingers and her muscles clamped down, rippling and releasing.

Her body responded to the touch of his tongue and fingers. Jack used those clues to judge how close she was to coming and managed it, possessed it. When her body tensed and shuddered on the cusp of climax, he eased her from the threshold and built her back up. He did it over and over until the sweet sound of begging spilled from Mira's lips.

Jack sealed his mouth around her clit and worked his fingers around to rub over the sweet spot deep inside her. At the same time, he laved her aroused clit until Mira writhed beneath him on the bed.

"Jack," she gasped. "Please, don't stop."

This time, he had no intention.

Mira bucked beneath his mouth and the muscles of her sex contracted and released. She cried out, her back arching. Her beautiful breasts stabbed up into the air as she rode out the waves of her climax. He never relented, keeping up his attention in order to milk every bit of pleasure from her body that he could.

Gods, she was so sexy when she came. He wanted to make her do it over and over again.

Feral and half-drugged with sexual need, he climbed up her body. She wore a languorous look on her face as she watched him advance on her. The look of a woman well satisfied. It became her. It made Jack want to keep her that way forever.

Jack settled himself between her thighs and hooked the back of her knees around his elbows, spreading her legs for him, and placed the head of his cock to her slick entrance. "I can't get enough of you," he said in a low voice. "You make me crazy. You're not too sore for this?"

Mira bit her bottom lip and shook her head.

He gripped his erection and guided the head of his cock inside her slowly and carefully, so as not to hurt her. Her heat enveloped him. Just having half his shaft in her was enough to make him spill prematurely, but he resisted the urge. He had more control than that, though with Mira it was hard won. Inch by inch he slid within until he was seated balls-deep inside her.

Mira sighed and murmured his name as her body adjusted to hold him, her satin muscles rippling around his shaft.

By the wan light of the moon he could see his cock glistening with her juices as he withdrew and the way it tunneled past her labia when he pushed back in. Jack thrust a couple times, deep and slow, before he let go of her legs and settled down over her, seated within her to the base of his cock. He could feel her velvet-soft rear against his balls and the pulse and ripple of her glorious, perfect sex around his shaft.

Jack eased in and out of her as he covered her mouth with his. Every little moan and sigh, every little needful restive movement against his body drove him right to the edge of a climax.

Yeah, he wasn't going to last long.

"Hard," she murmured. Mira laced her fingers through his hair and ran them over the stubble he needed to shave off his jaw. At the same time she circled her long, slim legs around his waist and gathered him close to her. "I want to feel you hard and fast."

Nope. Not long at all.

"Are you sure? Aren't you sore?"

She raised her head to look at him. Her eyes were dark with lust. "Hard, Jack."

He grinned wickedly, slid a hand over her breast, to her hip, then cupped one of the perfect mounds of her ass . . . and took her hard, deep, and fast.

"Yes," Mira hissed.

Every thrust of his cock penetrated and possessed. He stared down at her, her heavy-lidded eyes, lips swollen from his kisses and parted slightly. He slid a hand between their bodies and stroked her clit. She tossed her head from side to side and then arched her back. Her body went tense as she lost herself to another orgasm.

His own climax rippled up out of his balls. He buried his cock deep inside her and groaned out her name as he came. Breathing heavily, he rolled to the side and dragged her up against him.

The aftermath of the pleasure still rode him, but behind it laid the sharp tang of regret. He closed his eyes. *Damn it.*

"Mira." He swallowed hard and tried to catch his breath. "We have got to stop doing this."

And just how could he do that? He racked his brain. How the hell could he resist this woman? In the names of all the Gods and Goddesses. How?

She snorted, dropped a kiss on his mouth, and murmured, "Why?"

MIRA AWOKE TO SEE THE COLD PALE LIGHT OF THE edge of morning slanting in through the bedroom window. Jack lay sprawled on his back beside her, beautifully nude.

She stretched, feeling a delicious ache all through her body, most especially between her thighs. Mira had never had sex that many times in a twenty-four-hour period, had never wanted it that many times in a row before, but with a man as skilled as Jack . . . Like some incubus, he had the power to make her never want to leave his bed.

It was like he'd opened up the floodgates of her repressed sexuality. As if with his kiss in the kitchen he'd awoken not only her magick, but a door leading from the sexual wasteland where she'd been existing.

Mira thought of how many times Jack had brought her to orgasm. *Frigid? Not quite.*

She touched her lips, remembering how the need to feel his cock in her mouth had ridden her so hard, made her aggressive. Mira had wanted to feel him come against her tongue, wanted to experience Jack losing himself utterly to the touch of her lips on his cock. She'd had that for a little while, until he'd wrested control back from her. Jack was a man who liked to be in command, there was no doubt about that.

Turned out she was a woman who liked him to have it.

Mira curled up on her side and watched the pale light creep over Jack's body, illuminating one of his flat nipples. Her eyelids drooped in fatigue and she wondered for a moment what had woken her in the first place.

Something rattled . . . like a doorknob. Mira sat bolt upright. Voices murmured softly, sounding far away. Still, it was enough to throw her into panic mode.

She shook Jack awake. "Jack!" she said soft and urgently. "Wake up, Jack!"

"What?" he murmured sleepily. "What's wrong?"

"I heard something."

Jack sat up. The sheets rustled with his movement and then they both fell silent. The sound of the doorknob rattling came again.

"Did you hear that?" she whispered.

"Hear what? What are you hearing?"

"The sound of someone trying to open a door and people murmuring." She drew a breath as it came again, louder this time. Her adrenaline spiked. "It's coming from both the front door of the apartment and the door leading from the roof."

"It might be your magick magnifying sounds as a warning." He paused. "Fuck. Mira, get dressed."

She moved quickly, finding clothes and pulling them on while Jack did the same. Jack found his cell phone and called someone, probably the Coven witches Thomas had sent, and quickly told them what was happening.

The sounds that only she could hear got louder. She

stood in the center of the room, listening as the intruders broke the locks on both the doors at almost the same time. She and Jack were trapped in the middle. The wards on the penthouse broke with a snap of vibrating energy that made her flinch.

Jack winced in response, able to feel the wards break, too. It was a subtle, yet alien, sensation. If they'd been asleep they might have slept through it.

She looked wide-eyed at Jack, who stood watching her with his shirt in one hand. "They're in," she whispered unnecessarily. Her chest felt nearly empty of anything but her heart beating and the warm pulse of her power. Mira's breathing came fast and shallow. At least her magick had given her a little warning, and they weren't being caught with their pants down . . . literally.

He shrugged his shirt over his head, grabbed her by the upper arm, and pulled her behind his body as he inched toward the bedroom doorway. Mira glanced around desperately for something to use as a weapon and then remembered her magick. It glowed there in the center of her chest in a reassuring way. Hopefully, she could access and direct it.

The sounds she heard now were less in her mind and more in her immediate physical reality. Feet shuffled on the floor. It sounded like someone not quite managing to be quiet.

Jack pushed her into the corner of the bedroom and put his finger to his lips—as if she needed to be told to be quiet—and waited by the side of the bedroom door. Mira heard someone inch nearer. Before she could draw another breath, Jack sprang through the doorway.

A ball of fire appeared, manifested by Jack, she assumed, lighting the living room so brightly that Mira had to shield her eyes. Jack sent the ball hissing through the air. One of the intruders screamed in pain and a gush of liquid hit the hardwood floor.

Fire, meet water. Of course they'd sent water witches to trump Jack's fire.

Voices rose in anger. Furniture overturned. She inched closer to the doorway, unable to remain idle while Jack risked his life on her behalf.

"We just want the woman, Jack," one of the men said gruffly. "You're outnumbered and out-magicked. Just hand her over and we won't have to kill you to get to her."

"Fuck you," Jack growled. A fist connected with someone's face.

Leave it to Jack to be direct.

An old-fashioned, magick-free knockdown, drag-out fight ensued. Men grunted, cursed, and snarled at each other, feet scuffled, lamps broke, fists met flesh.

How many men was Jack attempting to fight off? The thought left a cold ball in the pit of her stomach.

Feeling for her magick in the center of her chest, she tiptoed closer toward the doorway. She caught the edge of her unpredictable power and prepared to pull it, mold it, and use it if she had to. It was her only defense, and maybe it would be Jack's only defense, too.

"There you are," said a man who'd popped like a jack-in-the-box out of the darkness on her right.

A strong hand twined through her hair and yanked, making Mira yelp in pain and lose her hold on her magick. He dragged her through the doorway and into the living room by her hair. She pitched a fit, struggling against the man and kicking and swearing. He grabbed her around the waist and pulled her up fast and hard against his body. Her breath crushed out of her lungs. Mira gasped and went still as nausea threatened. Everyone in the room went silent.

Jack stood with his hand curled into the shirt of one of the intruders, obviously in midpunch. There were six of them that Mira could see, all dressed head-to-toe in black. Jack had made quick work of two of them. They lay sprawled on the floor.

She stood in the center of the room, taking in the scene. All eyes were on her as she winced and fidgeted against the hold the man had on her hair and body.

"Awww, what a pity. I hate when they're pretty," said the man Jack had ahold of. "It's such a waste."

Jack punched him.

The man holding her started to drag her around the couch, away from Jack and toward the door. Mira struggled against him and only succeeded in making the grip on her hair even more painful. She yelped, feeling like her scalp would rip off in his hand at any moment, but she still managed to kick the man's shin with her heel when he released her waist. He grunted and cursed at her, but didn't let her go.

Jack stalked across the room toward them. "Take your hands off her," he growled low. His rage seemed like a palpable thing there in the room with them. Something you could touch. It heated the very air and prickled over Mira's skin like licks of flame. He spread his hand and a ball of fire ignited. "Or I'll burn every inch of skin off you."

Mira believed him.

The two men behind Jack moved on him. "Behind you!" she yelled. Jack turned at the last moment and threw his fireball, but one of them—a water witch, obviously—extinguished it immediately.

Both men attacked Jack at the same time. One of the men's fists connected with Jack's jaw. The other kicked him in the stomach and then punched him in the head.

Mira screamed as she watched Jack fall to the floor in a heap and instinctively *ripped* a hank of her magick from her chest. Saying it hurt was an understatement. It felt like Jack's fire ball had hit her right between her breasts. She gasped, but ignored the pain. After imagining what she wanted it to do, she tossed the magick up in the air, molded it with her intentions, and exploded it.

And hoped for the best.

Immediately, a blast of air threw the man who had ahold

of her backward. He took some of her hair with him. Mira cried out in pain, her hands instantly covering her aching head.

The room descended into chaos.

Wind swirled around her but did not touch her and, if she'd done it right, not Jack either. Anxiously, she hoped so. She couldn't see him because debris formed a tornado around her. It obscured everything in her view but did not enter the four-foot bubble encasing her. Wind shrieked and furniture smashed.

Mira clamped her hands over her ears and squeezed her eyes shut. She fell to her knees, screaming at the top of her lungs, though she couldn't hear her own voice over the pandemonium she'd unleashed.

Everything fell silent.

"Mira," Jack breathed in a rasping voice.

Mira opened her eyes to find Jack standing in the center of the room, glancing around wide-eyed. His clothes were ripped and blood smeared his face.

Shaking violently and clutching the place in her chest where she'd torn her magick, Mira struggled to her feet and looked around her. The whole room had been swept clean. All the furniture, rugs, artwork, books—everything that had been in the room previously was now smashed and splintered along the edges of the walls. Only she and Jack stood unharmed in the center of the room.

Everything else was . . . destroyed. Every*one* was . . .

Her breath came in short, fast gasps. *No, no, no.* "Tell me I didn't kill them," she said in a rush, glancing around at the debris.

Pain throbbed in her chest where she'd ripped out the hank of her magick. Metaphysically—if one could feel metaphysically—her chest felt bloodied and wounded. The pain reached all the way up through her throat to her head. She tottered to the side a little and caught herself before she fell.

"Mira." He paused, breathing heavy and wincing from his own wounds. "It was self-defense. They would've killed me in a heartbeat. Eventually, they would've killed you, too." He shook his head. "Don't doubt it."

The door to the penthouse slammed open, and more men in black poured through. They all stopped short, expressions of amazement on their faces as they surveyed the scene before them.

Jack shot them a disgusted look. "You're late," he snarled. His sudden anger lashed her with fire, making her flinch.

The pain she'd felt when she'd ripped the magick from her chest fully registered.

Mira met the floor.

THIRTEEN

❦

MIRA AWOKE TO THE LOW SOUND OF VOICES AND
the motion of a vehicle. Her body thrummed with pain, especially where her hair had been ripped from her head. Her
chest hurt too. Every time she drew a breath, it burned.

Merely opening her eyes ached, so she closed them
again after glimpsing the interior of what appeared to be a
limo. There were others in the car, but she could sense Jack
next to her and decided she was safe. Physical discomfort
precluded any further musing on the subject of her personal
security.

Strong hands eased her up and cradled her against a
chest. She winced at the movement. "Jack?" she murmured. She knew the feel of those hands, that chest.

"It's me. It's okay," he whispered. He brushed the hair
away from her forehead. "You keep passing out on me. We
have to figure out how to keep you from doing that."

"Tell her to stop rupturing her magick. That'll help,"
said a woman from somewhere in the interior of the auto-
mobile.

Jack placed his palm over Mira's forehead. The skin he touched grew warmer. The pain slowly leaked away. "Ingrid," he sighed, "if your men had been there a little sooner, she would not have been forced to do what she did. You know Thomas isn't going to be very happy about this mess." He placed a hand between her breasts, and the pain eased there as well.

"Not even Thomas foresaw the Duskoff being able to crack those wards. It must have been their kidnapped air witch who tipped them off to the move. They pulled out all the stops to break in before you left for the airport. Crane wants her badly."

"I'm not talking about the break-in. I'm talking about your men's inability to reach us in time." Jack's voice trembled with threat, and his body grew noticeably warmer with his carefully restrained anger. "If Mira hadn't pulled that magick, I could be dead and she might be gone."

Ingrid, whoever she was, fell silent, clearly chastened.

The pain in Mira's head and body receded enough for her to be able to function, thanks to Jack. She opened her eyes groggily and struggled to sit up. Jack was bruised and battered. A bit of dried blood marked his forehead and he held his right hand as though it hurt.

The woman, Ingrid, was slim and dressed in a charcoal gray suit and sensible heels. Her ankles were crossed primly and a pair of stylish black glasses teetered on her heart-shaped face. Mira couldn't tell how long her blonde hair was since it was pulled up severely in a French twist. She would've been pretty were it not for her scowl.

Two men sat on either side of Ingrid, both hunky and wearing black. What was the deal with these guys in black? Mira recognized them as two of the men who'd burst into the apartment right after—

She put a hand to her temple, remembering. "I killed them, didn't I?"

Jack put his arm around her shoulders. "Mira—"

"Wait a minute." She pulled away from him and held up a hand. "I don't want to talk about that right now. I don't even want to *think* about that right now." She needed time to digest what had happened.

"The cleanup of that incident is under my authority," Ingrid said. "I have Coven witches sifting through the mess. We don't know what became of the warlocks who attacked you yet."

She glared at Ingrid. Had she not just said she didn't want to talk about it? *Incident. Cleanup. Mess.* She'd killed people, and this woman talked about it like she'd dropped the milk carton on the kitchen floor.

Jack sighed. "We're on our way to the airport now. Once we're at the Coven, the Duskoff won't be able to touch you."

Mira put her hand back to her temple. "Does it hurt so much because I pulled a lot of power?" Her body still ached despite Jack's healing, and she felt nauseous.

"Yes. Think about your magick as a garden, Mira," answered Jack. "You tend it carefully and it nourishes you. Abuse it, yank big handfuls out of it, and there are consequences. When you take as much power as you did in the way you took it, it can make you sick. Your magick needs time to replenish itself."

"Where does it come from? The magick, I mean?"

"That's a question for the philosophers at the Coven, Mira," answered Ingrid. She rolled her eyes. "They'll discuss it with you endlessly if you inquire."

Jack sighed in irritation. "Mira, meet Ingrid Harris. She's Thomas's right hand."

Mira massaged her temples and glanced at him. "Does that make you his left hand?"

His mouth twitched. "Something like that."

"You're a very powerful witch, Mira," said Ingrid. "You'll get the training you need in Chicago, and once you've got your magick on a leash"—Ingrid smiled—"Crane will be the one running from you."

Mira moved her hand from her temple to look at the woman. "I would really like to see that," she replied with vehemence she felt to the tips of her toes.

Ingrid's smile widened.

The limo came to a stop in front of Minneapolis-St. Paul International Airport, and the driver opened the door. Light poured into the dark interior of the car. Mira squinted while her pupils adjusted and shivered as cold wind rushed in to fill the warm space.

"Have a good flight," said Ingrid. "I'll be traveling to Chicago in about a week. See you then."

Jack only shot Ingrid a dirty look. There was definitely some tension there. She wondered for a moment what kind. Was it sexual or professional? Both? Then she pushed the thought from her mind. It was none of her business.

After saying goodbye to Ingrid, she gathered her winter coat, which someone had laid on the seat beside her, and climbed out of the vehicle. Jack followed.

Mira quickly shrugged her coat on against the frigid temperature while the driver set their luggage on the curb beside them. Yay for only destroying Jack's living room. The bedrooms, and their clothing, had been fine, apparently.

Jack spoke to the driver, then turned to her. His face was truly a mess, now that she could see him clearly in the light. "Oh, Jack," she said in a rush of breath that clouded white in the cold air.

He'd changed his clothes before they'd left the apartment and had wiped some of the blood away, but his lip was split and his left eye and side of his face was one big bruise.

"Warlock had a wicked right hook," he grumbled as he picked up their bags and headed into the airport.

After they'd checked their bags in—they were booked first class, to Mira's surprise—and navigated through security and the shops on the other side, Mira yanked him into the women's bathroom.

"Ah . . . Mira?"

"You're bleeding again, Jack," she answered, pulling him toward the bank of sinks along one wall and garnering both amused and annoyed looks from the women in the bathroom as they went. "You can't go sit down in first class looking like you went toe-to-toe with a badass flight attendant to get in."

"I fly first class looking like this a lot," he growled at her. Boy, he was grumpy.

She ignored him and wet a piece of paper towel under the faucet. "Just humor me, okay?"

He winced as she wiped away some of the blood on his lower lip. "They have first aid in Chicago? Some kind of doctor there?"

"Of course. There's a full staff of doctors and nurses, ones who don't ask questions."

She moved to a cut near his hairline. "I shouldn't have asked. They probably know you well, don't they, Jack?"

He grabbed her hand, stilling her movement. "I won't see you much when we get to Chicago." He paused, searching her eyes. "My part of this will be done once we cross the Coven's threshold. You'll be safe, and I'll go on to another job."

She masked the sudden stab of melancholy she felt by tossing the paper towel in the trash. *What a stupid reaction to have!* She cussed herself out in her head. The last thing she wanted right now was to get into a relationship. So they'd slept together a few times. *Big deal.* It had been great, but they were both adults. Mira was old enough to understand it had been purely physical. *Fine.* He'd told her he wasn't the man for her right in the beginning. She'd known something like this was coming.

Still, it pinched.

"Okay," she replied with a tight, little smile. "And here I thought for sure you were going to ask me to marry you."

"Mira—"

She rolled her eyes. "Joking." Mira inspected her make-upless face in the mirror, ensured she didn't have a bald spot on the back of her head, and grimaced at her reflection. Finished, she turned on her heel and walked out of the bathroom. "I wouldn't marry you anyway," she called over her shoulder.

"Why not?" he asked as he caught up to her.

"Well, you're great in bed, I'll give you that much. The rest of you is kind of a mess, though."

"Thanks."

"Don't take it personally. I wouldn't marry anyone again, ever." She glanced at him. "I think I learned my lesson the first time. Marriage and I don't get along."

"Don't blame the institution of marriage. Blame your imbecile ex-husband."

Mira shrugged. "He wasn't an imbecile. He was a philanderer." She snorted. "Oh, sorry, I mean he was a *sex addict*. That's the clinical term for his affliction. He just couldn't help himself. Poor man."

"No. He was an imbecile," Jack ground out.

Mira stopped in the middle of the concourse. She turned to face him. A swarm of people flowed around them. "Why do you keep saying that?"

Jack's answer came swift. "Because only an idiot would let you go."

She stared at him for a heartbeat and then said, "Then what does that make you?" Mira bit her tongue, wincing at the words that had rushed out of her mouth without her permission, then pushed past him toward the gate. Her face felt hot and a lump had formed in her throat. Why had she said that? *Stupid, stupid!*

Jack stood alone for a moment before following her.

They found seats at the gate and fell into a silence. Mira kicked herself over and over for speaking before thinking.

Her words clearly displayed the fact that, despite trying to feel otherwise, she was not okay sleeping with Jack without some kind of emotional commitment.

She wished she could say that she was a sexually liberated, cosmopolitan woman who was able to have casual affairs and then go on with her life, but apparently she just wasn't made that way.

Or maybe she cared about Jack.

She glanced at him sitting next to her. He had his hands clasped in his lap and looked like he was a million miles away, lost in some strange place in his head where she couldn't follow. Jack was a man with secrets, ones he obviously had no desire to confide. He'd been right. He wasn't the man for her. Of course, since when did common sense have anything at all to do with emotion?

Mira worried her bottom lip between her teeth and concentrated on the empty seat opposite her. Yes, she cared about him. She'd just have to get over it.

The flight attendant called for first class to board. She and Jack handed over their tickets and settled themselves into two comfortable seats—Mira by the window—and watched everyone else get on while juggling their carry-ons and looking generally harassed.

Mira snuggled into the seat, leaned her head against the window, and closed her eyes. She'd only ever been on a plane once before, when she and Annie had gone to Florida for vacation when she'd been twelve. She'd definitely never flown first class before, but she thought she could get used to it pretty quick.

A horrible thought occurred to her, and she opened her eyes. "Uh, Jack? Could an air witch take down a plane?"

He flipped through one of the in-flight magazines. "Yeah, sure, a powerful one could." Jack glanced at her. "You could."

Mira swallowed hard.

Jack tucked the magazine in the pocket in front of him. "But don't worry about Crane trying it. He needs you alive."

"Ingrid mentioned Crane had a kidnapped air witch?"

He grunted. "A man named Marcus. He's a hostage. He's not powerful enough to defend himself, which makes him pretty much anyone's meat. Crane caught him, drugged him, maybe broke him. We're not sure. The Coven has tried to extricate him on several occasions without success. Marcus has enough power to hear things on the air, but doesn't have enough ability to raise much more than a strong breeze. Marcus couldn't take down a plane."

"Marcus was the reason the men broke in this morning?"

"We're betting there was a crack in the warding of the phone call Thomas gave me to let me know to bring you in. Marcus heard some of the conversation through it, told Crane, and Crane put the thumbscrews to his wardbreakers."

"Can the wardbreakers break into the Coven?"

Jack shrugged. "The Coven is not impenetrable, but it's pretty damn close. Even if they could get in, it wouldn't be in their best interests." He shot her a lopsided grin. "All the air witches of any talent, the few of them there are, work for us."

"But they can still get in," she confirmed.

"Theoretically, yes, but it would be nearly impossible for it to go undetected."

Mira bit her bottom lip and turned her attention to the tarmac outside her window. Images of Jack's apartment after she'd exploded her magick flashed through her mind, and she pushed them away. She still wasn't ready to deal with the fact that she'd killed six men. *Evil men. Duskoff men.* She had to remind herself of that. Jack was right; it had been self-defense.

And she hadn't meant to do it. Not consciously, anyway. But somewhere in her mind had lain the desire to see them dead in order to protect herself and Jack . . . and to give payback for her parents' murders, perhaps.

She leaned her head against the window and stared outside, sorrow choking her throat.

THE CHICAGO AIRPORT WAS LOUD, CROWDED, AND huge. Jack and Mira were met in baggage claim by a brunette Coven witch named Belinda, who was tall, lovely, and far too friendly with Jack, in Mira's opinion.

Another limo picked them up and ferried them away from the airport. They battled their way through construction and headed out to the northern suburbs. Mira had never been to Chicago, and it seemed she wouldn't get to see the downtown area now. Frankly, the landscape outside the limo's window looked a lot like Minnesota.

They'd been near silent for the entire trip. When Jack's cell phone rang, it startled her.

After a series of hostile "yeahs" and "uh huhs," Jack snapped his phone closed. "That was Ingrid. Good news, you didn't kill any of the intruders this morning. You just injured them pretty damn good. Ingrid's team picked them out of the debris, and they're being treated by a local doctor."

Relief swept through her. She closed her eyes for a moment, feeling a little giddy, and took a cleansing breath. "So, they're being treated by a local . . . witch doctor?"

"Cute. Yes, the doctor is a witch."

"What are they going to do with them?"

"I imagine they'll drug them up enough so they can't use their magick defensively and eventually bring them to the Coven. They're captives now." Jack rubbed a hand across his jaw, which was dark with five o'clock shadow. "Be nice to know why Crane wants to raise that demon. Maybe these guys know."

Mira took a moment to respond. "So, you'll torture the information out of them, in other words."

Jack shot her a stormy look. "Look, I know you've got some high morals, but we're fighting a war here, Mira, and you're the spoils."

She pursed her lips together. "And you don't have very many morals, do you, Jack?"

He glanced away, stared out the window at the industrial area they were passing through. "I do what needs to be done. That's my job." He turned his gaze back to her. "And I'll do anything to protect you, Mira." His voice shook slightly. "Anything. Understand?"

"Why? Why do you care? You barely know me. What aren't you telling me, Jack?"

Mira could practically feel the stone wall go up between them. He didn't answer her. He only turned his head and stared out the window.

Fine. He could keep his secrets. For now.

The limo turned down a small road marked Private Property. They drove through a set of towering metal gates and past the little sentry building that stood there. The long, twisting road they traveled after that must have been a couple of miles long. Tall trees shaded the way and beautiful, parklike grounds stretched off on both sides.

They finally breached the canopy of trees and pulled through yet another set of gates, into a circular driveway in front of a monstrously huge mansion.

"Welcome to the Coven, Mira," said Jack before he got out of the limo.

The driver came around the side and helped her from the car. She refused to look at Jack as she climbed out.

She tried to take her bags from the limo's trunk, but the driver wouldn't let her, saying he'd bring them to her rooms. Feeling like minor royalty all of a sudden, she followed Jack up the stone stairs and into the house.

Mira couldn't quite suppress her gasp of surprise as they entered the gleaming marble foyer. Apparently, the Coven had done fairly well for itself. This place was like something out of *Architectural Digest*, all vaulted ceilings, marble, and glass.

A tall man in his midforties with premature salt-and-pepper hair emerged through the doorway on her right and walked toward them. "Jack," he greeted warmly. The man's smile faded the closer he got. "What happened to you?"

"I got the bad end of a fight this morning." Jack shook his hand and turned to Mira. "Mira, this is Douglas. He manages the house. Douglas, this is the witch causing all the activity lately."

"Nice to meet you, Mira. I've heard much about you. We all have."

Oh, good. She managed to smile and shake his hand. It seemed she tasted salt for a moment when their hands touched. Warm salty water, like the sea. Was Douglas a water witch, perhaps? *Interesting.* She'd always had a little ESP, was it growing stronger now that she'd tapped her magick?

"Thomas said to meet him in the library," said Douglas. "Then he'll let you get some rest. I hear you've both had a busy morning."

"What kind of a mood is he in?" asked Jack.

Douglas smiled. "Impatient. Grouchy. Opinionated."

"What's new?" Jack glanced toward the door.

Douglas gave a short laugh. "Well, I'll leave you two to it then." He gave Mira a little salute and a wink and then strolled out the other door.

What was with this guy, Thomas? Was he some kind of ogre or what? It seemed like everyone, even big bad Jack, was wary of this guy. Although Mira supposed a man didn't get to head the Coven without being somewhat the alpha dog on the block.

Jack walked toward the door he'd glanced at a moment ago. Mira followed him.

New books, old books, books of every conceivable shape and size were stacked to the tops of shelves that stretched as high as the vaulted ceiling. The far wall was a mass of floor-to-ceiling windows that looked out over the landscaped grounds. Several desks stood in the room with computer equipment.

The rest of the room was decorated in leather and expensive wood furniture. A wet bar stood along the wall to her left, in between the bookshelves. A library with a bar. Well, perhaps one needed a drink now and again while perusing the stacks.

The room was empty save for one man. He stood at the far end of the room, looking out the window. He wore a gorgeous gray suit. Mira didn't know a whole lot about men's clothing, but it looked expensive. His shoulders were broad, powerful, and his long, silky black hair was tied at his nape.

The man turned and walked toward them. This was Thomas Monahan? She'd been expecting someone much older . . . and much less attractive. Mira stared because, damn, he was worth staring at.

He was built like Jack—powerful—and he and Jack were both good-looking enough to make Mira's tongue tie itself into a knot, but that was where the similarities ended.

Jack was the type to work independently, someone who didn't play well with others, but Thomas moved with the presence of a man who knew how to lead. Or that's the impression Mira had, anyway, while watching him walk toward them. He seemed to exude the perfect qualities—strength and charisma—to govern people.

"Welcome back," Thomas said to Jack as he approached.

"Glad to be here." They shook hands and Monahan pulled him into one of those manly back-clapping embraces that always made Mira snicker.

Monahan turned to her. "Mira, it's so nice to finally meet you. My name is Thomas Monahan."

She took his hand and shook it. "Nice to meet you, too." She paused. "Thank you for all you've done for me."

"I think Jack has done far more. He's the one who's risked his life."

"Yes, I—you're right." Perhaps for the first time Mira truly realized that. She turned to him. "Thank you, Jack," she said with sincerity in her voice. Even though it seemed so paltry to just say *thanks*.

A muscle in Jack's jaw locked. He didn't look at her. "Don't give me your gratitude. Please."

Mira winced at the cold tone of Jack's voice and the way he rebuffed her. She couldn't quite mask her expression. Too much had happened that day, and she had no energy left for dissembling. She wasn't very good at it anyway.

"In any case, you saved my ass this morning. Not the other way around," Jack ground out without looking at her.

Yes, but were it not for Jack, her ass would have been grass on the night the Duskoff broke her door in. Why couldn't he take a simple thank you from her? She couldn't keep the hurt and confusion from her face.

Thomas looked from Jack to Mira, his mouth tightening into a displeased line. "Jack, you look like you might need a few stitches. I know Doctor Oliver is in the house. Why don't you go find her? I need to talk with Mira alone anyway."

Jack nodded, glanced at Mira, and left the room, closing the large wooden doors on his way out. Mira shivered, feeling a tingle of dread at his absence. He was well and truly *gone* now. She felt that. Mira drew her arms over her chest, swallowing a sudden lump in her throat.

"Are you hungry, Mira? Thirsty?"

"I'm fine. Just a little tired."

"I'm sure you are." He motioned for her to sit down in a nearby chair. He lowered himself into the opposite one. "Ingrid called and filled me in on what happened this morning. There have been lots of changes for you lately."

That was an understatement. "Considering I didn't believe in magick a week and a half ago, I'd say so."

His full mouth twisted into a smile. "You seem to have come to it very well. You just need some instruction so you can harness it and use it effectively, responsibly. Annie was loyal to your parents, and it's not for us to say whether they were right or wrong in their decision to keep you from us."

"You mean to keep my magick from me." She couldn't help the note of bitterness in her voice.

He shrugged. "If she hadn't been so loyal, you would have been trained from childhood. You have much catching up to do, but from what I've heard so far you're a fast learner."

"I'm worried about Annie, Thomas. Jack said you were taking care of her?"

"I asked her to come to live at the Coven for awhile as our guest, but she refused. She told me she won't let those 'barbarian warlocks' make her change her life and that she has a store to run."

Mira smiled. That sounded like Annie. "That craft store is her world."

"Because she refused our protection here at the Coven, we sent a couple of witches to guard her for awhile, and we sent some excellent wardweavers to bind her home and business against the Duskoff."

Mira nodded, feeling somewhat better. She would give Annie a call later.

He regarded her with eyes that seemed as black as his hair. They were beautiful in a wicked, obsidian kind of way. The man truly did look like a witch. Mira wondered if there was any hint of color in those dark orbs anywhere. Jack had said he was an earth witch, but she wasn't quite sure what the magick of earth entailed.

"I have one more change for you, Mira," he went on.

She tipped her head to the side, letting her gaze travel over the handsome, yet rough-hewn lines of his face. Aside from his carriage, which was the most arresting thing about him, Thomas possessed a unique masculine beauty with his dusky skin, long black hair, and dark eyes. She loved his wide cheekbones and full, sensual-looking mouth. His mouth seemed at odds with the rest of the impression he made, something soft and lush on a man carved from granite.

Were all witches gorgeous? Was it some prerequisite for a male to have magick that he also be sexual-fantasy inducing? She wasn't as attracted to Thomas as she'd been to Jack—that had been knee-meltingly strong, and yet . . .

"I'm your first cousin."

FOURTEEN

➤

EVERY THOUGHT MIRA HAD CRASHED TO THE floor like a stack of china plates. She blinked. "Uh, excuse me?"

Thomas leaned forward, threading his fingers together in front of him. "Your mother, Eva Monahan, was my father's sister. That makes us first cousins."

Suddenly, she felt light-headed. It was almost noon, and she'd had nothing to eat. That meant on an empty stomach she'd nearly killed six men while misusing her magick and then found out she had a long-lost cousin. No wonder she felt a little woozy. She glanced at the bar. "I think I might have that drink now."

He laughed and stood. "What would you like?"

"An orange juice, if you have it"—*with half a bottle of vodka in it*—"That would be great."

Thomas came back with her orange juice and she took a sip, letting it steady her and calm her nerves. After a moment of digesting both liquid and new information, she spoke. "I noted right away that Monahan was also my mother's maiden name, but I just thought it was coincidence. I, uh, didn't even know my mother or father had any siblings."

Her chest and stomach were heavy with sadness. Annie had kept all her parent's secrets from her, everything. Even though Mira knew she'd done it to honor their wishes, it stung. Hadn't she understood how alone Mira had felt in the world? She felt betrayed.

And weary of secrets.

"I imagine they didn't want you to track down your family and discover you were a witch, Mira. They were trying to protect you because they loved you." He paused and studied the look on her face. "What do you want to know?"

Mira sighed. "Everything."

"We'll have time to catch you up. I'm sure you'll meet some of the rest of the family while you're here too."

"Rest of the family?"

"The Monahan family is directly involved with the Coven. My father, Richard, led it before control was handed to me by the council. You have a bunch of cousins who hang around here pretty often. In fact, my sister Serena should be here later today. I'm going to see if she wants to take your training over. She's an earth witch, like me."

She blinked. "Not that I'm objecting, but why Serena?"

"I only want people around you that I trust implicitly."

"Jack's been doing my training so far. You don't trust him?"

Thomas took a moment to answer. "I wouldn't have allowed Jack to be your personal bodyguard if I didn't trust him, and I still think he's the best man for that particular job, but let's try someone new for your training."

His tone seemed to prohibit any disagreement. Mira suspected not many people tried to argue with Thomas. In any case, she wanted to get to know Serena.

"All right," she said with an easy shrug. "I'm looking forward to meeting your sister . . . my cousin." She rolled the word *cousin* around in her mouth, trying to get used to the feeling of it.

"Your mom had two brothers," Thomas said, "my dad and Uncle Andrew. They both married and had kids. You have four other cousins, all around our age. There's Serena, Kathryn, Phillip, and Micah. I know you have cousins on the Hoskins side, too."

Mira couldn't even answer. She set her glass of orange juice on the table beside her.

"I'll let you rest. I can tell you're exhausted and overwhelmed. Just let me know if you need anything. You're family, Mira, and I'm happy you've found your way back to us."

Family. Wow.

Feeling a little shell-shocked, Mira watched Thomas take a photo album from one of the bookshelves. He walked over and handed it to her. "I'll take you up to your room," he continued. "You can settle in, get something to eat, maybe take a nap. That's an album filled with family pictures. They're all labeled so you'll know who is who."

She ran her finger over the leather-bound cover and smiled. "Thank you."

He led her through the huge house, past corridors tastefully decorated in neutral shades. Hardwood floors with long burgundy and gold rugs abounded. Small tables filled with vases of fresh flowers stood in corners and against walls. Beautiful artwork hung everywhere. They passed sitting areas scattered here and there, all sporting comfortable-looking furniture that invited people to relax.

As Thomas gave her the tour, he explained that the house had two large kitchens with cook staffs, a conservatory, a ballroom, a gym, and an indoor/outdoor pool.

"Who owns all this?" she asked him as they turned down a corridor on the third floor. She was well and truly lost by that point.

"The Coven is supported by donations from the wealthiest magickal families and is run through a system a little like a board of directors. The Hoskins and Monahan families both have seats on the Coven council. The council employs financial advisors who make investments that yield nice returns. We also get income from the people who keep quarters here and don't work directly for the Coven. Lastly, the Coven owns a few profitable businesses."

"So the council is the governing body, then?"

"In as much as we have one, yes. The council decides who runs the Coven and makes major decisions that affect witches in a general way."

"Sounds complicated."

He gave her a rueful smile. "It's a big job, but I love it." Thomas took a keychain from his pocket and unlocked one of the doors. "Here's your room."

The door opened into a sitting room decorated in shades of creams and gold. There was a TV, a desk with a computer, a couch and chair, and a small refrigerator. French doors led into a large, well-appointed bedroom with a king-size bed. The bathroom was enormous, with a spa tub that she couldn't wait to try out. Someone had placed her bags on the bed already.

"It's far more than I need, Thomas," she said, returning from her walk-through. "I think I could fit my apartment in here about three times."

"These are your rooms here at the Coven. Forever."

"No, Thomas—"

He held up a hand to cease her protest. "The Hoskins and Monahan families contribute a lot of money to the Coven, and you are both. Don't say another word. These are your rooms whether you decide to stay here or not. Forever." Again with the tone that said *don't argue*.

Mira opened and closed her mouth, but didn't know what to say in response to any of this.

He turned and walked to the door, but paused before he

left. "If you need anything else, let me know. You're family, Mira, and we'll do anything for you."

She flopped down on the bed the moment Thomas was gone and opened the photo album. Within were page after page of glossy photographs of people she didn't know. Strangers who didn't have to be strangers but for the overprotectiveness of her parents. They'd traded her life away in an effort to shield her, yet the danger had still found her. Indeed, the danger was double as a result of her parents' attempt to keep her safe.

Wouldn't it have been better for her to grow up knowing what she was and becoming stronger in her abilities, so strong that Crane and the Duskoff never would've even thought about coming after her?

She shook her head. She didn't know what her parents' reasoning had been because she'd never known her parents.

Mira flipped through the pages, once in awhile coming across a woman who looked a lot like her—a cousin? Sometimes she'd find a picture of a younger Thomas.

Then she turned a page and found photos of her parents. The entire back half of the album was filled with them— when they were young and laughing and surrounded by people who loved them.

Tears plopped on the plastic-protected pages before Mira even realized she was crying.

THOMAS WAS AT HIS MOST DANGEROUS WHEN HE was calm. He always went quiet and subdued when exceptionally pissed off.

Two years Jack's senior, Thomas had always been like a big brother to him, and, like a younger brother, Jack danced on the edge of his temper often.

Wincing at the soreness of his face, Jack rubbed his cleanly shaven jawline and watched Thomas pace in front of a bank of windows in his office.

Thomas never seemed to wear anything but hand-tailored suits and Italian shoes and never seemed to let his guard down. The man was wound too tight, had far too many barriers erected. He needed to lighten up a little, maybe even get laid once in a while.

The doctor had seen to Jack's injuries, stitched up the cut near his hairline, and salved the rest. He'd given himself what healing he could, which would mean his wounds would mend faster.

He'd relinquished his hold on Mira with far more pain than what he'd endured physically that morning. Letting her go had kicked his ass worse than anything he could remember.

Mira had been ensconced in her quarters, handpicked by her cousin Thomas, and was resting there now. Jack hadn't seen her all day. He missed her already, and that meant he needed to get the hell out of the Coven, needed to get far away from Mira so he couldn't hurt her anymore than he already had.

"Got any jobs for me, Monahan?" Jack prompted, since Thomas wasn't talking and he didn't want to stand there all day. "I can fly back to Minneapolis, help Ingrid bring the Duskoff hostages back down." *Just give me something to do.*

Thomas rounded on him. "You slept with her, didn't you?"

Oh, hell.

Jack didn't answer, but his silence told Thomas everything.

Thomas swore under his breath. "I could see it almost the moment you stepped into the library, the way you stood and the way you two looked at each other." Thomas swore again and showed Jack his back. He shook his head. "You thought to hide it from me, maybe, Jack, but it was all there in your body language."

Earth magick made Thomas tuned into everyone and

everything around him, every little nuance. Thomas was present and grounded in a way that made him seem psychic. Jack really wasn't surprised Thomas had picked up on it.

"Mira is your cousin," Jack replied, "but she's also a grown woman, capable of making her own decisions."

"Don't give me that bullshit, Jack." He turned to face him. "You see a beautiful woman and you seduce her, that's your way. That's why I didn't want you on this job to begin with. But I trusted that you wouldn't mess with her head because of your past, and you went ahead and did exactly that."

"I never meant for it to happen. Damn it, Thomas. I tried to stop it once we felt the strength of the magickal affinity between fire and air and the sexual attraction that came with it. But I can't say, *won't* say that I'm sorry it happened."

"The attractions are strong at first, but then you should have found a balance and they should've faded."

Jack gritted his teeth for a moment and stared past Thomas, narrowing his eyes. "The magickical affinity did find a balance, but the sexual attraction didn't fade. Not for either of us. If anything, it was stronger by then."

Thomas's face grew stormier. "Let's lay all the cards on the table. You never told her who you are, did you? You never told her the truth."

Sickening dread and guilt rose up from the depths of him. Jack hesitated before answering. "No."

"Then you should be sorry," Thomas answered in a low, dangerous voice.

"I thought you wanted me to keep that a secret," Jack growled, trying very hard not to completely lose his temper. "You told me you didn't want me to tell her anything about that until she was out of danger."

"I did . . . I *do* want you to keep that from her for now. You're the best we have to protect her, and I don't want her hating her bodyguard." Thomas cursed and turned away from him. "I just never thought you'd sleep with her. I never thought we'd have this problem."

Hating her bodyguard. The words rang through his head. "I am aware of the complication." He paused. "I'm aware of what I did. Hurting Mira is last thing I want—"

Thomas whirled to face him. "I thought I could trust you with her because of your past and the way it ties into Mira's future. I thought by having you take this job it would provide you some measure of healing. Instead you just used her."

Sudden anger stiffened his body. He felt his magick flare hot and fast in the center of his chest in response. He flexed his hands against the tickle of fire in his fingers. "I didn't use her," he snarled.

Thomas gave a short, sharp laugh of derision. "I'm counting all your women in my head right now, Jack, all your affairs."

Jack wanted to bellow at him, tell him that it was different with Mira, that he cared about her and wanted more than he'd ever be able to have from her. He wanted to yell out his frustration at the situation at the top of his lungs, but that wouldn't make anything better.

The raw truth was that he could never have Mira. She'd find out soon enough who he was, and then she'd hate him. Thomas was right. That would be the end.

"I know I have to let her go," Jack replied.

"Yeah, you gotta let her go. You shouldn't have touched her in the first place. What were you thinking?" Thomas laughed. "Oh, that's right, you weren't."

"Thomas, have you ever been with a woman you simply couldn't resist? Have you ever met a woman that, no matter how hard you tried, you simply couldn't stop yourself from touching?"

Thomas sobered, the cold smile dying on his lips. A muscle in his jaw tightened. He didn't answer.

"I'll take that response as a no." His eyes narrowed. "I hope you meet a woman like that one day. Then you'll understand how it was between Mira and me." Jack turned on his heel and walked out of the room.

"Jack," Thomas called after him. "Damn it, don't walk away from me."

But Jack just kept going.

FIFTEEN

CRANE LISTENED TO THE NEWS OF THEIR DEFEAT with rage building inside him. His fire answered the call of his emotion, flaring inside his chest until the need to set it free nearly overwhelmed him. Sparks moved from finger to finger on his right hand. Flame tickled his palm. He could spark it into a killing blast of fire with a mere thought. He could kill the messenger standing in front of him, burn him to ash in his calfskin loafers.

He slammed his fist down on the table in front of him instead, sending tiny lightning bolts of power in all directions. A deep ache shot through his arm at his movement. Everyone in the room took a step back.

Crane gritted his teeth, closed his eyes, and drew a careful breath. He hadn't come this far in life by losing control. Killing out of passion or for unnecessary reasons was a waste and a pain in the ass to clean up. No matter how much it might satisfy him to hear someone screaming in agony right now, smell the gratifying crisp of burning flesh, he needed to keep his anger in check.

He removed his hand from the desktop and opened and closed it, feeling the ever-present soreness in his body flare brilliantly to pain for a moment.

This damn cancer. He hated feeling so vulnerable, hated feeling like his body was some foreign thing that had turned on him.

He'd healed himself as much as he could, enough that he could still function, but he was nearly at the limits of his ability. In time, he'd be forced to turn himself over to weasely non-magickal doctors to poke and prod him until he took his final gasp of air, just like any ordinary human bag of bones.

More than anything, that rankled him the most.

He stared at the fine grain of the table. "Must I do everything myself?" he asked the room in a deceptively quiet voice. Fear filled the air, cloyingly sweet and luscious. He raised his gaze and everyone looked away from him. "Well?"

David cleared his throat. "We don't know what happened. All we know is that six of our men went in ready to fight and came back out on stretchers. We suspect the woman, since we sent in two highly skilled water witches to neutralize Jack. Perhaps she's even more powerful than we'd imagined."

Crane stared at him. "Powerful or no," he ground out, "she hasn't had time to learn to control her abilities."

David shrugged. "Beginner's luck?"

Crane's anger flared again, and he closed his hands, fighting to contain it. His body ached from the effort, making him shudder.

From the end of the table, Stefan spoke. "Time grows short. I suggest we substitute Marcus and hope he has enough power in him to open the portal." He shrugged an elegant shoulder. "If we cannot open the portal with Marcus, we are simply out four witches. Three we can find easily again, no? The fourth has always been a problem anyway, and good riddance. We will find a replacement."

Stefan still retained a heavy French accent, and his appearance was gentile and sophisticated. It masked the inherent dark viciousness that Crane so respected. Stefan was his son more than Jack had ever been. Still, Crane had to be careful with Stefan. He'd raised him too well and knew how much he coveted his father's position as head of the Duskoff . . . and the money and power that came with the leadership.

He considered Stefan for a moment, wondering if he was being manipulated. Yet he couldn't find a flaw in the plan. Indeed, it seemed his only option at this point.

He made his decision. "Then Marcus must be secured." Crane stood, feeling agony—real or imagined, he wasn't sure—lance through every fiber of his body. He hesitated, wincing, then moved quickly through his mansion to the room where he kept Marcus.

Their footfalls echoed down the corridor of the basement. The warlock guarding the door discarded his magazine and bolted to his feet when he glimpsed Crane, Stefan, and David turn the corner and come toward him.

"Open," commanded Crane in a curt voice.

The guard extracted his key and unlocked the door. It swung inward, and Crane fought the cry of rage and frustration that rose in his throat. All he could do was make a strangled sound at the sight before him.

Marcus hung in the center of the room with a sheet around his neck. Crane stopped in the doorway and watched the heavy witch swing gently back and forth.

Stefan came to stop behind him and clucked his tongue. "What a shame."

Crane's fingers gripped the doorknob so tightly they turned white. He fought the intense desire to raise fire and char Marcus's body where it hung. Better, he could burn the ineffective guard who currently shook in fear to his left.

He turned and fixed his gaze on the guard, his palm heating. It would make a mess, sure, but he could have someone else clean it up. The guard backed up a few paces, fell over the chair, and sprawled on his ass.

Stefan put a hand on Crane's shoulder. "*Ne t'inquietes pas*. No worries, father. I have another plan. It will even be fun." His voice carried the viciously playful tone that Crane had come to know well—and to be wary of—over the years.

Fine. It was time to take off the gloves.

MIRA REACHED AGAIN FOR HER MAGICK AND missed the edge of it. Frustrated, she blew a strand of hair away from her face. "Sorry, Serena," she apologized for the hundredth time. "I know I have it in here somewhere."

Serena put a hand on her shoulder. "Don't force it. I know you probably feel like you're playing beat the clock, but stressing yourself will just make it worse."

Mira closed her eyes for a moment and drew a deep breath. Serena, her cousin and an earth witch, had been tasked with training Mira to her magick. The problem was that her magick seemed to have all but disappeared in the last week and a half, pretty much as soon as she'd arrived at the Coven.

Thomas had given them blocks of time in the conservatory to train. The space was breathtaking, completely encased in glass and filled with nearly every plant, flower, and herb known to man. A koi-filled stream burbled through the place, with small wooden bridges to connect the cobblestone pathways constructed here and there. It was an excellent place for Mira to experiment with her magick.

Outside it was full-on winter, though winter here in Chicago was a little milder compared to winter in Minneapolis. Inside it was warm and restful, filled with soulsoothing amounts of earth, water, and air.

No fire, however.

Jack had disappeared about the same time as her magick.

She hadn't seen him anywhere in the house. The one time she'd asked Thomas about him, all she'd received in response was stony silence and a change of subject.

Mira missed Jack. She wished she didn't, but she couldn't help herself. She missed his banter, his slow sinful smile, missed the scent of him, missed his touch.

She was pathetic.

Mira focused on Serena's blue eyes. She was an attractive woman in her early thirties. Thick medium blonde hair fell to her waist, and she had an easy smile. She'd befriended Mira right away, and Mira appreciated the steadiness that Serena's earth magick seemed to lend her personality.

"I'm half inclined to get a fire witch in here and see if the affinity can raise your magick again," said Serena, frowning.

"You mean like Jack, maybe?"

Serena shook her head. "You and Jack should have found a balance by now. You need a different fire witch to trigger it, one you haven't spent any time with."

"What do you mean? Are you saying that after awhile an air and a fire witch will lose the stimulation of their magicks?"

"Exactly."

"And what about the, uh, sexual part of it? The attraction?"

Serena grinned. "That fades, too. Eventually, they find a level, a balance of magicks, and the juiced-up physical attraction eases up right along with the intensification of power."

So that meant by the time her magick had stopped reacting to Jack's . . . Realization hit her. That meant what she'd felt for Jack at the end had had nothing to do with their magickal affinity. That's why she'd sensed their magicks brush and then recede the night they'd spent in bed. The magicks had balanced, but the intense attraction had remained.

When they'd made love, that had been all them, not the magick.

Pure Jack. Pure Mira.

"Want to try again, or do you need a break?" Serena asked. "You seem kind of distracted. Thinking about a man?"

Wow, was she that transparent? "Why would you say that?"

Her cousin laughed. "Well, you did just ask about sexual attraction, Mira."

"Well, yeah." She smiled. "I guess I did."

Serena looked like her brother only in the respect that they were both attractive. Thomas's sister was light where he was dark, though they shared some of the same facial features, like the high cheekbones and the full, sensual mouth. Her eyes were a pretty shade of blue, rather than her brother's disconcerting near black.

They both had inherited earth elemental abilities, which encompassed many things, including an ability to use herbal concoctions better than any pharmacist could mix a drug. They magickally "tweaked" the potency and abilities of the potion to suit their need.

Earth magick, Mira was coming to discover, was the stereotypical sort of magick. Earth witches dealt with potions and spell casting based on plants. They were what the non-magickal population had come to view as true witches over the years.

When Mira had her period the week before, it had come with bad cramps that had kept her away from training. Mira brewed her favorite lemon balm tea to ease the pain, but not even that had taken care of it all. So Serena had offered her a store of stronger herbals to use for the cramps and told her they also acted as effective birth control without any side effects. Mira had accepted them thankfully, though she didn't know if she had need of the birth control since Jack seemed to be avoiding her quite well.

And why *was* Jack avoiding her anyway?

"Mira?"

She jerked back from wherever she'd drifted in the big sea of Jack and found Serena frowning at her. "Sorry. I guess your big brother will be upset that I can't access my magick."

"He's your cousin," she corrected gently, "not only my big brother." Mira still couldn't get used to the idea. "He just wants you to be able to defend yourself if it comes down to that. And anyway, he's more bark than he is bite. Well . . . most of the time."

"Gee, thanks. That's reassuring, Serena. What's his story anyway? Why did he take over the Coven instead of you?"

"The position isn't usually hereditary. The council chose him as the best replacement for our father based on the strength of his magick and his character. Anyway, I've wanted to be a veterinarian since I was five and that's what I became. I'm happy as a vet, and he's happy running the Coven . . . I think." She frowned. "It's kind of hard to tell with Thomas."

"There seems to be a lot of tension between him and Jack."

"You tend to get tension when two dominant witches are together. Trust me, it's even worse when they're both fire witches. Jack and Thomas are like brothers and they fight like brothers sometimes." She shrugged again. "Thomas thinks Jack is too uncontrolled, and Jack thinks Thomas needs to loosen up." She smiled. "They're both right."

"That's the nature of Jack's element. Fire can be unpredictable and uncontrolled," answered Mira right away. Funny how she felt the desire to defend him.

She nodded. "And earth is steady and solid."

"Unless there's an earthquake."

Serena grinned. "True. Thomas acts like he's got it all together, but I know that's partially a veneer meant to reassure all us underling witches. I don't really even know Thomas all that well, and I'm his sister."

"Then there's Jack. That's a man with a few secrets."

Serena pursed her lips and didn't say anything for a few moments. "Jack has tragedy in his past, and it affects his present," she answered simply. "He's a good guy and all the women love him." She paused. "Be careful with that one, Mira."

"Or I might get burned?"

"He has a tendency to do that, yes."

"You sound like you speak from experience."

Serena laughed. "Oh, no. I've never been involved with Jack. I've had a few fantasies, maybe, but . . . no. He's too volatile for my tastes."

Mira liked volatile, apparently.

"So, want to try again?" asked Serena. "Or are you ready for a break?"

"I'd like to take a break for a moment. Let me be alone with my magick for a little while?"

Serena smiled. "Of course. Just come find me when you want to practice again."

Mira watched Serena exit the conservatory, letting the wide glass doors separating the space from the main part of the house close behind her.

She found a quiet spot at the base of a tree and sat down. The sweatpants and loose white sweater she'd put on that morning were perfect for a little meditation session. A hummingbird buzzed near her, taking nectar from a trumpet-throated flower. Songbirds twittered gently from tree branches around her. They were part of the conservatory's carefully managed ecosystem. The peace of the environment washed over and through her and Mira gave herself into it. She found a comfortable position and closed her eyes.

Her magick sat in the center of her chest, just as it had since the first time Jack had triggered it with his kiss. It felt warm and comforting, a tiny ball of light residing in the heart of her.

It was there, so why couldn't she access it?

She reached into herself, parsing out a thread of it—just a thread—to pull out and form . . . and it slipped right through her mental fingers.

She tried again and again. Every time something dark and indefinable made her balk at the last moment and cause the tendril to slip from her grasp.

Mira sensed a presence nearby at the same time her magick flared a little stronger in the center of her chest. Maybe this time she could take it. Again she tried to pull a thread, again she failed. The flutter of stronger magick within her receded.

"Damn," she muttered, opening her eyes.

Jack stood near her, foliage brushing the leg of his black trousers. He wore a gray cable-knit sweater that complimented his ice blue eyes. Her heart skipped a beat.

"Hey, Mira," he said in his low, whiskey-rasp of a voice. It sent a shiver through her.

"Hi, Jack. I haven't seen you around here in a while." She hoped she sounded unaffected by his presence. Cool. Uninvolved. In reality she had her hands fisted so tight inside her too-long sleeves her nails practically drew blood from her palms.

He glanced away, into the tree towering above her. "Had to go away for a little while, but I'm back now. Are you doing well?"

He sounded so detached. It was like they'd never spent a twenty-four-hour period making love to each other over and over again, like he'd never covered her body with his, murmured sweet-dirty things in her ear, made her nearly scream as he brought her to climax.

She tried to smile, but didn't quite manage it. "I'm better than I've been in a long time." In some ways that was true, but not so much in others. Mira was happy to have found this lost component of herself, yet she missed Jack. Damn him, anyway. He'd gone and caused her to break the promise she'd made to herself, had gone and made her care for him. "Except my magick's broken."

"I doubt that."

She shrugged and forced herself to relax her hands. She really was going to draw blood soon, and Jack was doing that well enough merely by his presence and flippancy. "I can feel it there in my chest, but I can't seem to access it. I can pull the thread, like you taught me, but I can't hold it. Serena thinks maybe it's burnout or stress causing the block. I don't know."

"It could be that, but I have a suspicion I know what's causing it." Jack glanced around at the conservatory. "Have you tried to pull magick anywhere but here?"

"No. Thomas suggested we use this space and cleared out blocks of time so we could do it undisturbed."

"Well, there's your problem. You're in the wrong place to be practicing."

"What?" She laughed. "This is the best place in the Coven for this."

Jack licked his lips and smiled. He glanced around the conservatory, inhaling the flower-rich, fragrant air and closing his eyes for a moment. Mira's breath caught in her throat watching him. "Why do you like this place?"

She glanced around at the yellow and red orchids on her left and enjoyed the sound of the nearby stream. "It's beautiful, tranquil. This is an absolutely exquisite area where all the elements work in unity."

"I agree, and I understand how much you enjoy stability, tranquility, and order. But what happened last time you pulled magick?"

She shuddered and knotted her hands in her lap. "Chaos. Destruction."

"Bingo."

"You're saying that on some level I'm afraid to cause that here?"

He nodded. "Your subconscious is blocking your attempts

to take the magick because of the respect you have for your surroundings."

She glanced around, realizing he was right. She was afraid of destroying this beautiful place. Right now she was a little afraid of her magick, period, despite the rational pep talks she'd given herself.

Jack took a step toward her and held out his hand. "Come on, beautiful, let's blow this place for a little while."

She put her hand in his, and he yanked her up so fast he pulled her right into his arms. Once she had her balance, she stepped away from him and pretended to smooth the hem of her sweater and adjust her too-long sleeves. She turned a fake-bright smile on him. "Let's go."

Jack led her to a large, empty storage area in the basement. The room showed the age of the house and smelled damp. She wrinkled her nose as she stood in the center of the room, surveying the concrete floor and walls.

"It's not pretty, but you don't have to be afraid you'll damage anything in here. Try it."

She closed her eyes and reached for her magick. Carefully, she pulled a thread and managed to grab the edge of it, but it slipped through her fingers.

Mira opened her eyes. "I almost had it, but I still couldn't catch hold."

"You're afraid of it," said Jack. "Don't be. It's your magick. You control it, remember? It does what you command it to do. You need to make it yours."

He was right. It was only the fear that stopped her. She knew she could get over it, if only . . . "Will you spot me?" The question stuck in her throat from a combination of desire and apprehension, but she knew that if Jack was ready to help her control her magick, she might be able to maintain a hold on it and get over her mental block.

Jack just stood there looking stunned. Mira regretted her question in that moment a million times over. Obviously, he hadn't intended to get that close to her.

She felt her cheeks flush. "I mean—never mind—"

"No, I'd be happy to spot you," said Jack, interrupting her.

This was awkward. "No, really. I'll be fine—"

He walked to her. "Mira, shhh. Turn around."

She turned, and he moved in close to her back. His warm masculinity enveloped her and the faint scent of his cologne teased her nostrils. He brushed her hair away from her shoulder, making her feel warm, making her long for more of his touch. She had to focus, she reminded herself. He touched her because he wanted to help her access her magick, not because he wanted her.

Mira let her eyes drift closed and sighed when his arms came around her, his fingertips finding the seat of her magick nestled between her breasts.

"All right?" he murmured. Jack's warm breath disturbed the hair that fell over her shoulder. Despite the uncomfortable moment they'd just shared, Mira relaxed instantly in his arms. With Jack so near her she felt safe, protected, secure enough to draw her magick and use it.

"Uh, huh," she answered absently.

"Go ahead," Jack said softly near her ear. "I'll help you control it if you draw too much."

Mira found a thread, grasped, and pulled it without even a flicker of hesitation. She brought it up and shaped it with her mind into a nice breeze. It blew through the room, hitting both of them and making Mira shiver in Jack's arms.

"Again," Jack whispered.

Mira did it again. Then again. Then again. Sometimes she would make the breeze blow harder, or softer. Sometimes she made it go from the left to the right, or the right to the left. Once she created a gentle downdraft. She lost herself to the creation and release, tweaking here and there, learning the subtleties of her power. Mira found herself immersed in it, endlessly fascinated by the ways she could shape it to perform the task she set for it.

She didn't know how long she spent standing there in her concrete sanctuary, but when she finally opened her eyes and came back to the world around her . . . Jack was gone.

SIXTEEN

JACK CAME BACK TO HIS ROOM AT THE COVEN IN the middle of the night to find his door ajar. He stood in the corridor, his duffle bag hanging loosely in his hand, and contemplated it. He'd just returned from a trip to Minneapolis to handle the final cleanup of the destruction in his apartment and had taken a late flight back to the Coven. He was pretty sure he'd turned off all the lights before he'd left, and he was certain he'd closed and locked the door.

He pushed the door open and walked in, considering the glow of light coming from his bedroom. For a moment he imagined Mira in there, warm light spilling over her bare skin as she lay across his bed waiting for him. It made him take a step forward and then rooted him in place. If it was Mira in there, he wasn't sure he'd be able to walk away.

Who was he kidding? There'd be no way he'd deny her.

A mixture of desire and trepidation kept him standing in the living room. It seemed Mira had put a spell on him from day one. Fully immersed in it, he was doomed.

"Jack?" queried a husky feminine voice from the bedroom.

Disappointment and relief flared within him at the same time. *Ingrid. Not Mira.*

He dropped his bag on the floor near the couch and walked down the short hallway to the bedroom.

He and Ingrid had an on-again, off-again affair. They were both in it for the sex. No strings. No commitments. As two fire witches, the sex was great, but their magick made them a bad match in most other ways. They ended up at each other's throats anywhere besides the bedroom. Fire witches, as a general rule, didn't work or play well with other fire witches unless it was between the sheets.

She lay on the bed with her long, silky blonde hair spread out against the black comforter and a sultry expression on her face. Ingrid looked like a pinned-up librarian a lot of the time, but once she took her hair down and relaxed, she was a knockout. Now she wore only a pink lace demi bra and matching silk panties. Candles on the small round table in the corner of the room, his dresser, and the night table beside the bed cast a golden glow through the room. Soft music played on his stereo system.

He leaned against the doorway and took in the pretty sight of her laying there in just her silk bra and panties. She'd already secured the long pieces of hemp rope to the eyebolts in the wall over his mattress. Ingrid knew how he liked to fuck her best, and she liked to be fucked that way.

Before he'd met Mira he would've had those little pieces of silk nothing ripped off Ingrid in an instant. Now, his lust and emotion centered in another direction, she was just an obstacle between himself a good night's sleep. Still, he had to do this right. Ingrid didn't deserve to have her ego crushed.

"Ingrid, you're a nice sight for a man to come home to," he greeted her truthfully, "but, honey, I've been up since 4 A.M."

She rolled off the bed and sauntered toward him. "I'll

give you sweet dreams, Jack," she purred in a low contralto as she came to a stop in front of him.

"I'm sure you would."

Ingrid smiled and reached out to touch his cheek. He caught her hand gently and kissed her fingers.

"But really, I'm tired," he finished.

Anger flashed through her eyes, and his fire responded with a little involuntary pulse in his chest. "I bet you wouldn't be too tired for that air witch you brought to the Coven. Mira? That's her name, right?"

Jack sensed no jealousy in her, only displeasure that her plans to get laid tonight were being thwarted. Ingrid had no romantic feelings for him, as far as he knew.

"Why would you say that, Ingrid?" Was he that easily read?

She walked to the chair, where she'd discarded her clothes, and pulled her cashmere sweater and linen pants on. "I saw the way you looked at her in the limo on the way to the airport in Minneapolis, while she was injured and you were worried about her." She grabbed her glasses from his night table, shoved her feet into her shoes, and then paused to stare at him. "I've never seen you look at a woman that way before, Jack, and I've known you many years."

Damn. He was that easily read.

Ingrid walked past him, but he grabbed her hand before she could leave the room. "Ingrid?" He just wanted to make sure she was okay. He'd basically just kicked her out of his bed.

She stopped and looked up at him with a smile and a soft expression on her face. "It's okay. I was glad to see it. Made me think you might not be a lost cause, after all, Jack."

MIRA AWOKE WITH A JOLT AND SAT STRAIGHT UP in bed breathing hard. Panting, she focused on her surroundings. She was at the Coven, alone in her room. *Safe.*

Still, she reached over and flipped on the bedside lamp.

She couldn't remember the nightmare she'd had, but it clung to her like a cobweb she'd walked through. There had been whispering, whispering about plans to kidnap her, drain her of her power and her life.

Mira shuddered and hugged herself. It was possible she'd heard Crane and his minions via her still uncontrolled air magick. Once she was able to control her ability, Serena said she'd be able to tune into conversations and noises from a great distance. It had happened spontaneously as she'd been growing up, though she'd always explained it away as a dream. These days it was happening more and more frequently.

Crane probably hadn't given up on her.

She glanced out the window, where the clear sky showed a scattering of bright stars. In Minnesota a night like this in winter, without any clouds to insulate the earth, meant it was frigid outside.

It was nights like this she missed Jack's apartment and Jack's presence even more. Mira missed the scent of his skin and the feel of his arms around her. She missed the sound of his voice and heated look in his eyes. It hurt that he seemed to have no interest in her now, though she appreciated his help with her magick. Apparently, there was still some part of him that cared whether she lived or died.

It had been over a week since she'd seen him last. He'd pulled another disappearing act after the basement incident. When she'd asked Thomas where he'd gone, Thomas had said he'd given Jack another job that required travel but hadn't revealed anything more specific than that. Thomas didn't seem to want to talk about Jack much.

Mira sighed, feeling disgusted with herself. *One year*. Was one year really such a long time? Here she'd gone and fallen for someone within the first six months. Plus, her feelings were unrequited. That made the whole thing extra stupid.

She brushed her fingertips over her nipple and it tightened immediately under her touch as she remembered his hands on her . . . his mouth.

Hell, she'd take what she could get from Jack. If it was just sex, that was fine. She'd pick up the broken pieces of her heart afterward. It wouldn't be the first time she'd nursed an emotional wound.

Mira reached out and took the empty water bottle on her nightstand. She'd go down to the kitchen and get a fresh bottle. Maybe when she returned she'd be able to fall asleep again. Perhaps, miraculously, Jack McAllister would somehow be wiped from her brain.

Yeah, right.

She pushed the blankets away and found the silky black bathrobe to wear over her matching nightgown—another gift from Serena. After she closed her door behind her, she headed toward the kitchen through the darkened hallways of the Coven.

It amazed her how safe she felt here. Ostensibly, perhaps she should've felt a little more on guard. After all, the house was filled with lots of people she didn't know and therefore couldn't trust. However, Thomas had explained the system of warding and spells in place around the building and property, assuring her of her safety. She believed him. In fact, the very energy of the building felt comforting and secure.

As she passed through one of the many sitting areas throughout the Coven, she glimpsed a man in a chair. He leaned over with his elbows on his knees and cradled his head in his hands, looking deep in thought or troubled, perhaps. There was something about the shape of his body and the way he held himself . . . She stopped near him.

"Jack?" she queried in a soft voice.

The man moved his hands and looked up. "Mira?"

"Why are you sitting out here all alone in the middle of the night?"

He pushed a hand through his hair. "I just got in and felt

restless, thought I'd get a little change of scenery before I went to bed."

"I couldn't sleep either." She motioned toward the kitchen. "I was going for a fresh bottle of water. Can I get you something?"

"No, thanks."

Uncomfortable silence.

Mira shifted from one foot to another. "Well, I'll see you—"

"How's your training going?" he asked, interrupting her. "Thomas told me you're making progress."

"You solved the problem for me. Thank you. My training has been going wonderfully since then. I'm gaining a lot of control."

"That's great."

"Yeah." She smiled and nodded her head, feeling stupid. "Yeah, it is."

God. Small talk. She was reduced to making small talk with this man who'd made her yell his name fifty times in one night. This was just wrong.

Mira hesitated a moment and then sat down in the seat beside him. He eased back away from her. She masked the pang of hurt she felt by leaning down to set the empty water bottle on the floor. "It's actually pretty fortunate that I ran into you. I've been wanting to talk."

"Okay," he said. "About what?"

The dark velvety interior of the sitting area seemed so intimate. Moonlight streamed in through the windows above where they sat and shadows slanted across Jack's face, making it impossible for her to read his expression.

It was better just to come to the point, she supposed.

"Can we just quit all this bullshit? I hate feeling uncomfortable around you." She drew a breath before plunging into the speech she'd been preparing in her head for days. "I said a couple of stupid things before, and I think I gave you the wrong impression. So we had sex. So what? It's not like I want to have your babies or anything—"

"Oh, now I'm offended," came his low rumble from the opposite chair.

"Jack." She sighed. "I'm just saying there's no reason we can't be friends. We had sex, er, a few times, and it was great. But things got weird afterward, and I feel like you think I'm on the verge of pulling an emotional psycho-stalker thing on you and, frankly, while I do think you're beyond hot and great in bed, I don't think you're *that* hot or great in bed. Not enough to make me stalk you. Anyway, I'm really not an emotional psycho-stalker type because, you know, coming off a bad marriage over here, remember?" She gave a forced little laugh. Wow, her "prepared" speech had turned into a kamikaze mission. "I'm not making any sense, but you know what I mean—"

"Mira, stop babbling." He leaned across the two-foot space between them, eased his hand to the nape of her neck, pulled her to him, and kissed her. She gasped against his mouth and stiffened in surprise.

Jack threaded his fingers through her hair and slanted his mouth across hers with a sexy-sounding groan that made her quiver. She relaxed against him when his tongue glided into her mouth to lazily swipe against hers.

Her body reacted immediately to the press of his body on hers. She'd missed the feel of his hard chest against her, and the flex and bulge of his biceps under her hands where she held on to him.

He pulled her lower lip through his teeth, and Mira shivered in his arms. "If you think I don't want you anymore, you're wrong," he murmured. "Hell, I can't get enough of you. That's the problem."

"But . . . I'm confused. What about that day in the basement? You just left me there without a word."

"Because I wanted you to see that you didn't need me to

spot you in order to use your magick. That's why I left." He paused. "I also left because I knew I couldn't trust myself alone with you."

She bit her bottom lip for a moment. "But why do you feel a need to resist me, Jack?" she whispered.

He took a moment to answer. His warm breath stirred the fine hairs around her face. "I don't want to hurt you."

She narrowed her eyes, feeling a flash of annoyance. "Do you think I'm made of porcelain or something? I'm not that fragile. I don't expect marriage or anything. I meant what I said in the airport. I'm through with serious stuff for a long time. I'm a big girl and can make my own decisions." She paused. "So why have you been avoiding me?"

Jack groaned and tightened his arms around her. "Because I want you," his voice shook almost imperceptibly. "I want you so much, and the only way to resist you is to not be near you."

It left her speechless. Speechless with shock and the sudden press of questions in her mind.

He fell silent, and when he spoke next his voice was lower, a touch more feral sounding. "Then you show up in the middle of the night outside my room. Just steps away from my bed. How am I supposed to deal with that?"

Her breath came shallower and faster at his words. "I don't understand the problem. You want me. I definitely want you. I don't expect a commitment or anything, Jack. I don't *want* a commitment. If it's just about sex, that's—"

"Damn it, Mira." He slanted his mouth over hers and dragged her onto his lap. His hand found the opening of her robe and closed over her breast, making her gasp against his lips.

Her nipple hardened against his palm and he stroked it through the material of her nightgown, and then gently rolled it between his fingertips as his mouth worked on hers. She felt a little gush of moisture between her thighs.

Suddenly, she forgot what they'd been talking about.

Hunger like she'd never felt before swept through her body. Nothing would keep her from Jack's bed tonight. Consequences be damned.

She needed to feel his skin against hers like she needed to breathe.

"Jack, I want you," she gasped.

He half lifted her and she half stood, still both wrapped in each other's arms. "Here is not the place for this," he murmured against her lips.

There were places better than this? The couch near them seemed fine to her. The floor seemed great. Just about anywhere seemed just dandy. She forced herself to think through the haze that had settled over her mind and remembered they were in the public area of the house. She nodded.

He took her hand and led her down the hall and through a doorway. The interior of the room was dimly lit by a small lamp in the sitting area. These were his rooms here in the Coven. She couldn't see much of them—didn't care, really. All her attention was focused on Jack.

Jack closed and locked the door, and they sealed their bodies together, kissing each other and trying to take articles of clothing off at the same time. Somehow they made their way into Jack's bedroom and were both naked once they got there. Peripherally, she noticed that candles provided the only light.

Mira sighed at the feel of Jack's skin sliding against hers as he pressed her down onto his bed. "I missed you, Jack."

Jack covered her body with his, kissing her shoulder, her neck, and the sensitive place just under her ear. "I missed you, too. You feel like heaven to me."

He smoothed his hands over her breasts, teasing her nipples, then eased down her stomach and delved between her thighs. With his skillful fingers, he stroked her clit until it grew swollen and aroused and she moved restlessly on the mattress beneath him.

A little moan worked its way from her throat as she felt

that familiar sexual haze settle over her mind. Jack pushed her straight into a place where she could barely think just by the brush of his fingertips across her skin.

"Condom," he breathed against her lips.

He started to move away from her, and she tightened her arms around him. "Serena gave me herbs. It's okay."

"You sure?"

Mira nodded.

She found his cock and let her fingers play along his shaft until he groaned. He moved her to the center of the bed and took her wrists, drawing her hands up over her head. Languidly, she allowed him to do it.

All the while he stroked his tongue into her mouth over and over until Mira's mind stuttered through the cloud of sexual need she'd stumbled into.

Jack spread her legs with his knee, rubbing her aching sex along his thigh. Above her head, she heard the snick of a lock, then another. She tried to lower her arms and found she couldn't. "Jack?" she asked softly.

"I want you at my mercy, but if you don't like it, you tell me. I'll let you go."

She never wanted him to let her go.

Mira tested her movement, discovering the cuffs were lined with something soft and allowed her a significant amount of mobility, though she could not lower her arms or pull her hands apart. Her wrists were linked together above her head.

Jack slipped a hand under her back and drew it down her spine. She arched back into the pillows at his touch, and he kissed and gently bit his way down her throat, raising gooseflesh all over her body and making her nipples feel like diamond-points on her breasts.

"Do you trust me, Mira?"

"I do."

"Let me have you until morning. If you tell me to stop, I will. Otherwise, surrender yourself to me."

SEVENTEEN

"I'M YOURS."

He stared at her a moment, his ice blue eyes holding that at-odds warmth. Then he lowered his head and laved a nipple with the flat of his tongue. Mira watched with interest as his sensual lips worked the peak. At the same time, he stroked her between her thighs, teasing her clit until she whimpered on the edge of a climax, then easing her back and building it up all over again.

She almost swallowed her tongue when he slipped a finger inside her, then added another, and slowly—very slowly—began to thrust them in and out of her.

Death by foreplay. That had to be his plan.

"Jack," she breathed.

"Your body is mine tonight. I do what I want unless you tell me to stop. I like the way you feel, and I want to make your pleasure last." He stroked his fingers over that sweet spot deep inside her. "Do you want me to stop?"

"N-no," she answered.

He only gave her a wicked grin in response and went

back to teasing her nipple, while letting his fingers glide in and out of her.

Jack brought her to the edge of climax over and over until nothing else in the world existed but Jack, his hands, and what they did to her. She tossed her head back and forth against the pillows and moved her hips restlessly, wanting him to slide his cock into her, to allow her a release. He kept her teetering there on the edge of ecstasy, ensuring that when she finally went it would be spectacular.

Mira trusted Jack enough to surrender herself to him— her body to his touch, her will to his will for this piece of time. She trusted him enough to allow him to bind her body and know he would never do anything to hurt her, never do anything she didn't want him to do. The deep truth of that realization brought tears to her eyes.

Whatever might lie between them in the morning, in this one moment she felt comfortable giving herself over to Jack's capable hands.

He kissed his way down her body, slid his hands under her bottom, lifted her to his mouth . . . and slid his tongue deep inside her.

She gasped and grabbed the rope connecting the cuffs to the wall and held on as Jack thrust his tongue in and out of her. She watched his dark head between her thighs and the way the muscles of his shoulders and arms worked as he pleasured her. He laved over her clit and massaged it between his lips.

Her climax hit her fast and hard.

Mira arched her back and bucked beneath him. He held her by her waist, pressing her down onto the mattress as it washed over her. She cried out under the racking waves of pleasure made more intense because Jack had withheld it, built up the energy of it. Her body trembled with an ecstasy that wiped all the thought from her brain.

Jack came down over her body and let his tongue swipe

against hers, letting her taste the very faint flavor of herself in his mouth.

"That was beautiful," he murmured. "I love it when you come against my tongue. I love the feel of you and the taste of you."

Mira could barely form thoughts, let alone words. His hands explored her body, starting a fire between her thighs again. Would she ever get enough of this man?

He retrieved two lengths of rope from the drawer in the table beside his bed. She almost pulled away when he looped the rope around her knees, but instead she let herself surrender to him, like he'd asked.

Jack tied skillful knots around both her knees, not too tight, not too loose. Then he tied the opposite ends to the eyebolts.

The result had Mira's breath coming fast and heavy. She was completely opened to him, unable to close her thighs or lower her arms. "Jack," she said in a quavering, uncertain voice.

"Scary, isn't it? It's frightening to give up complete control." He paused. "But it's exciting you, too. I can see it in your eyes. I can hear it in the cadence of your breath." He reached out and stroked her exposed sex. "I can feel it."

It was scary, and yet that trust of him filled her. It made her relax and give in to the experience of it. It made her want more.

He covered her body with his, delving his tongue deep into her mouth. The ropes binding her frustrated and excited her at the same time. She liked being at Jack's mercy. It aroused her. Yet she wanted . . . *needed* to touch him.

And then he touched her.

He slid the head of his cock into her, making her gasp against his mouth. Jack gripped her hips and kissed her deeply as he entered her inch by inch until she felt completely filled by him.

Jack rested his forehead against hers for a moment and

breathed heavily. "I missed the feel of you, Mira," he whispered in an emotion-filled voice.

She couldn't respond. He held her gaze as he withdrew his cock and pushed back in slowly, letting her feel every glorious inch, every ridge, of his shaft. She watched his pupils darken and heard his breath catch when she purposefully squeezed the muscles of her sex around him, trying to hold him within her on the outward stroke.

Again and again, he thrust into her slowly until she panted and moaned, until she tossed her head and broken words spilled from her lips. Her clit had become so swollen and sensitive. She teetered on the edge of another powerful climax. He held her there, tormenting her until her whole world was only about him and only about pleasure.

She thought about how they must look, her tied to the bed and Jack ever so slowly thrusting between her spread, bound thighs. The thought alone was enough to nearly make her come and undo all of Jack's sexual torture.

He rose up a little, so he could gaze down on her, and began increasing the power and speed of his thrusts. She arched her back and spread her thighs as far as the ropes would allow, welcoming it.

Jack slid one hand to her waist and gripped the headboard with the other, steadying them both as he took her in long, driving strokes. Their pelvises met with every inward thrust and the sound of skin slapping against skin filled the air. Jack had taken complete control of her body, done exactly what he'd wanted, how he'd wanted. In the process he'd given her more pleasure than she ever could've imagined.

"Jack," she gasped as her climax blossomed through her body. He came down over her, covering her mouth with his and swallowing her cries and moans as her orgasm—teased to the point of having incredible power for the second time—overwhelmed her body.

He thrust deep within her and his cock jumped as he also came. As her body tensed and shuddered, he kissed her deeply, his tongue stroking in and possessing her mouth the way he'd possessed her body.

After a moment, he set his forehead against hers, and they both rested there, breathing deeply. "Stay with me tonight," he rasped. "I want to wake up next to you."

Mira nodded and smiled.

He undid the knots on the ropes and gathered her against him. Mira wrapped her arms around him, and Jack pulled her beneath him, kissing her. Their bodies slid together like silk. Contentment settled over her limbs like a warm blanket. She couldn't think of anywhere else in the world she wanted to be.

The candles guttered in their containers, nearly spent, and cast wavering shadows over the walls. Who had lit them? Had Jack been waiting for another woman who hadn't shown up and then settled for her when she'd arrived? Oh, that was an unpleasant thought. Or did Jack just like candles? He was a fire witch after all.

She opened her mouth to ask, but Jack answered her before she could speak. "A woman was waiting for me when I got in from my trip tonight. She wanted sex, but I didn't want her."

Unwelcome jealousy of another woman being in Jack's bedroom rose up. She pulled a bit of magick and blew all the offending candles out in one tiny burst of power, plunging the room into darkness. "How did you know I was going to ask that?"

"The question was all over your face."

"A woman tried to seduce you, and you turned her down? Jack, I'm not sure I believe you."

He traced patterns over her skin in the dark, making her sigh. "Believe it."

They lay tangled together on the mattress with the sheets and blankets pushed to the end of the bed. It was a little chilly in the room, but Mira wasn't feeling it, not with Jack's hands moving so restlessly over her body.

He stroked her nipples until they were hard little points and her breath came fast again. Then he delved between her thighs and petted her clit. It responded readily every time he touched her, making her cream for him.

They didn't talk, they only touched and kissed along each other's skin. In the darkness, Mira used her hands to see, exploring his hard chest, shoulders, buttocks, and his stiffening cock. She couldn't seem to get enough of him. She could probably give up food and water and simply get all her sustenance from touching Jack.

Relaxed, sated, and feeling safer than she had in a long time, Mira eventually let her exhaustion pull her under in the wee morning hours.

She awoke to morning sunlight and an aroused body. Mira had turned onto her stomach in her sleep and Jack hovered above her, kissing her shoulders and down her spine. He delved his fingers between the cheeks of her ass and dragged his fingers over her sex.

"Jack?"

He said nothing. She tried to turn over, but he held her in place with a strong hand to the small of her back. Damn, he was dominant in bed. He spread her thighs and pumped his fingers into her. Her breath came out in a whoosh and ended in a moan. He used her juices as a lubricant over her clit, teasing it with the tip of his finger. It felt huge and swollen. Mira shivered and shook with need. "Jack?" she asked again.

He still didn't answer her.

When she could barely stand it anymore, without a single word, he lifted her to her knees and entered her from behind. She gasped and fisted the blankets on either side of her at the feeling of his thick cock sliding into her.

She tried to rise up, on all fours, but he pressed his big body to her back and anchored her wrists to the bed.

"Mmmmm, don't move," he purred. "I have you right where I want you."

He rolled his hips back and forth, riding her slow and sure, soft and steady. Every inward stroke brushed the head of his cock over her G-spot. She lifted her hips, meeting his strokes.

Mira curled her fingers into the bedcovers, her cheek pressed to the mattress, as Jack took control of her body just as surely as when he'd tied her to the bed.

He rose up, held her hips as he shafted her harder and faster, with long brutal thrusts that sent pleasure crashing through her body. He reached his hand around and stroked her clit, regulating her orgasm until it rushed through her. Her climax triggered his.

They collapsed in a tangle on the bed and stayed there. Still, Jack couldn't seem to keep his hands off her and stroked down her spine and buttocks over and over until Mira felt so relaxed she teetered on the edge of sleep once more.

He leaned over and kissed the small of her back. "This is my favorite place on a woman's body," he murmured. He moved to the back of her knees and laid another kiss. "Here, too."

Mira turned over, scooted near him, and buried her head in the place where his throat met his shoulder, inhaling the faint lingering scent of his cologne. "My favorite place on you is all over," she sighed.

"I said those were my favorite places *on a woman*." His deep voice rumbled through his chest and into her when he spoke. He tipped her face to his. "My favorite part of *your* body are your eyes."

She laughed. "Oh, what kind of line is that? Do you say that to all the girls?"

His slight smile faded. "No, I don't."

Their gazes held for a heartbeat and Mira's smile faded too. He actually sounded . . . serious. Could it be his feelings for her went as deep as hers for him?

Oh, those were dangerous thoughts.

He eased his hand from her hip to her waist and leaned

in to kiss her. Mira's breath caught in her throat when his lips touched hers. He'd kissed her many times before, but this one seemed somehow different, more meaningful. Her arms went around him as his mouth worked on hers.

Jack broke the kiss and traveled down to her breasts, licking each of her nipples in turn. "Of course, I like these too," he said with a mischievous smile.

In Jack's eyes, with his hands on her, she felt desired. She felt luscious and sexy. This whole situation, spending the night with Jack and making love over and over, felt decadent and beautiful.

He pulled the blankets from them both, exposing her to the morning air. "Mira, you're magnificent in every way," he said, his gaze skating over her body.

Speechless at the quavering emotion she heard in his voice, she cupped his cheek and kissed his lips.

"Touch yourself for me," he murmured against her mouth.

She raised an eyebrow.

"Make yourself come for me," he growled before kissing her roughly. His pupils dilated. Darkness swallowed his eyes. "I want to see your hands on your body, between your thighs."

Mira felt heavy arousal fill her at his command. Her breath caught in her throat.

He eased back, looking at her meaningfully with heavy-lidded eyes. "Show me how you make yourself come when you're all alone."

A moment of shyness made her hesitate. Then, holding his gaze, she reached up and cupped her breast. He watched avidly as she teased her own nipple erect. She brushed the pads of her fingers over it again and again. It sent little ripples of pleasure through her body and made her cream between her thighs. Mira moved her hips restlessly, imagining Jack's cock buried deep inside her, remembering the commanding way he'd made love to her the night before.

Having her body completely bound for his every wish,

every touch, had been a serious turn-on. The memory was still a turn-on. She sank her teeth into her bottom lip, closed her eyes, and groaned. Against her leg, she felt his cock grow hard.

"That's it, baby," he whispered.

Mira eased her other hand down over her abdomen, threading through the hair covering her mons, then arched her back and spread her thighs. Her sex was swollen with arousal and well-loved by Jack. She stroked her clit until it bloomed beneath her touch, becoming sensitive and needful of a climax, then eased her middle finger deep into her heat.

Her muscles felt silken and hot. She squeezed them a little so she could feel what Jack felt around his cock. Adding a second finger, she eased them in and out of her sex, imagining it was Jack who fucked her.

Jack's eyes were dark and trained on her. It obviously really excited him to watch her touch herself. Mira closed her eyes and gave herself over to it. Biting her lower lip and closing her eyes, she worked her sex and brought herself closer and closer to climax.

He knelt at her side and leaned over her, cupped her nape and kissed her roughly, while massaging her breast and gently pinching her nipple with his free hand.

Mira moaned, feeling the first serious ripples of an impending climax. She dug her heels into the mattress and rocked her hips back and forth. She looked wanton with her thighs spread and her own hand between them. That fact only excited her more.

"You're so pretty, Mira. So sexy," he murmured as he stroked his hand down her abdomen. "Are you going to come?"

She nodded, her eyes fluttering open to see him staring down at her. He covered her hand between her thighs with his own, pressing down a little so that the motion of her rocking hips rubbed her clit against her palm.

Mira cried out as her climax exploded through her body.

The muscles of her sex pulsed around her penetrating fingers as pleasure racked her body.

"There you go, baby," he murmured. "That's it."

Mira panted as the last of her climax faded away. She opened her eyes to find a very aroused Jack staring down at her. "Up, on your knees," he said roughly. "Hold onto the headboard. Face the wall."

His terse commands, issued in that raspy voice, made her sex feel achy with desire once more. All she wanted was his cock there. She got up, feeling how wet she was between her thighs, and knelt on the mattress, facing the wall.

He put her wrists back into the cuffs and her fingers found purchase around the rope attached to the eyebolt.

Jack tossed the pillows to the floor and let his hands roam her body. He cupped her breasts, rolling her nipples between his fingers until Mira gasped. He braced his chest to her back and kissed her shoulders, easing a hand between her thighs to massage her sensitive clit. She whimpered.

"Does that feel good?" he purred into her ear.

"Yes."

"Part your thighs and I'll make it feel even better."

She parted them, and, groaning, he slid his cock up into her sex from behind. She gasped at the sudden, overwhelming sensation of having all that width and length stretching her muscles.

Mira turned her head to glimpse his body against hers and caught their reflection to her right. A full-length mirror stood in the corner of the room. She hadn't noticed it the night before, maybe because it had been dark. Now it was morning and the angle showed them perfectly—Jack's big, muscular body cupping hers, the consumed, aroused look on his face as his hands explored her body.

Her own expression was slack, her eyes wide and dark, her hair mussed, her body bound to Jack's bed. For a moment, she could hardly recognize that sexual creature as herself.

He moved her hair to one side, gripped the headboard, and braced his other arm around her abdomen.

Then he began to thrust.

The reflection showed the leverage he used to push up into her body. The muscles of his thighs and buttocks rippled with every upward stroke into her body. Pleasure coursed through her at the friction of his cock tunneling in and out of her sex, stretching her and filling her to the limit.

Jack nipped at her neck and let the hand on her abdomen dip to rub her clit. "You feel good, Mira," he murmured. "So hot, so sticky sweet."

She watched his hand move between her thighs in the mirror's reflection as he stroked the pad of his finger over her clit. He increased the tempo of his thrusts—faster, harder. Sensation flowed through her, overwhelmed her.

"Jack!" she cried as her body found itself caught in another amazing release. She held onto the rope with everything she had.

Jack growled something low, still pounding up inside her even as her climax drove all thought from her mind. It stripped her, laid her bare, then filled her with only Jack and what he did to her.

He came as well, thrusting deep into her and groaning.

Both panting, both sweating, he released her wrists and they collapsed onto the mattress.

"Oh, Jack," Mira gasped. She was sticky wet between her thighs and she ached everywhere. Still, she'd never felt better or more satisfied in her life. Her body still tingled with the memory of his hands on her and his cock inside her.

Jack pulled her to him and covered her body with his, kissing her eyelids, her cheeks, and her throat.

They stayed that way, collapsed in an exhausted heap and tangled together for a while. Jack finally pulled the blankets over them and they cuddled beneath them, drowsing in and out of sleep.

"Mmm, this was a nice morning," Mira murmured against the curve of his throat.

His arms tightened around her. "More than nice." His voice rumbled through his chest, making her feel safe and comfortable.

"I suppose we should think about leaving the room at some point."

He took a long moment to answer. "Yeah, sure. I'll take that under advisement in an hour or two."

Mira laughed softly, but someone pounding on the door cut her off. "Who's that?"

Jack glanced at the clock on his night table. Mira followed his gaze. It was almost 10 A.M.

He slid off the bed and pulled on a pair of sweatpants from one of his drawers. "Stay there. I'll be back," he said as he walked out the door, pushing a hand through his sleep-mussed hair to tame it.

JACK OPENED THE DOOR TO FIND THOMAS ON THE other side.

"Went by her room this morning," Thomas greeted him in a clipped tone. They both knew who he meant. "She's here, isn't she?"

Jack just nodded.

Last night had been another nail in his coffin. Jack had tried to stay away from her, but he simply couldn't say no. The scent of her had intoxicated him, and the spill of moonlight over her skin had tempted him and that had been it. He had zero self-control when it came to her.

He wanted Mira so much it made him ache. Wanted her not only in the carnal sense, but the long-term one. What was it people said about human nature? People always wanted what they couldn't have. Except Jack wanted Mira because he loved her, not because he couldn't have her. He knew that now.

He loved her intelligence, her insecurities and her strength, her compassion and desire not to hurt others even when they meant her harm. He loved the sound of her laughter and the look she got in her eyes and on her face when she was aroused.

Jack loved Mira, every aspect of her.

Thomas took a moment to answer. "You know I have no problem with you, Jack," he spoke softly so Mira couldn't hear them in the other room. "If it wasn't for your history and how it intersects with hers, I'd be happy you were together. I'm just trying to protect her."

"I know that, Thomas. I care about her, too. I wish I could make you see that."

"Perhaps it's time to tell her who you are."

"I thought you wanted me to wait until this was over."

"I do. I still think you're the best man to be protecting her from Crane, and telling her who you are interferes with that." He paused and then growled, "I just wish you'd stop sleeping with her. Is that so hard?"

It was that hard. What Jack couldn't say was that it wasn't just about sleeping with Mira. It wasn't just about sex. It was about connecting with her in the one way he could, the one way he knew how. It was about joining with her, becoming a part of her, even if it was only for a short time.

Jack remembered the night before, how he'd glimpsed the faint red marks on her wrists and legs made by the rope and cuffs before the candles had gone out. He'd felt a flash of pure satisfaction in that one moment of having marked Mira. Every primal male cell in his body had rejoiced in that one split second of knowing that Mira was his and his alone. His to love. His to cherish, protect, and adore.

No, it was hardly just about the sex.

But Jack couldn't voice any of those thoughts to Thomas. Instead they stared at each other for a long moment in silent challenge.

It was Thomas who finally glanced away. "Get dressed.

Get Mira dressed. Both of you come to my office," he bit off in a voice made of steel. "I have news." He turned on his heel and strode away.

Jack closed the door and made his way back into the bedroom. Mira lay tangled in the sheets, her long hair spread over his pillows and one slim calf and foot peeking from under the blankets. She had her eyes closed. No wonder. They'd really made a night—and morning—of it.

He wanted to walk over and kiss her awake. Wanted to crawl back into bed, pull her into his arms and hold her. He wanted to spend the whole day in bed with her, order something up from the kitchen when they were hungry, but otherwise spend all their time immersed in each other.

Cold reality slapped him in the face. *Fuck.* He kept making this situation worse.

Thomas wanted him to wait until all this was over before he revealed that he was actually Crane's son. Jack wanted to never tell her. He never wanted to see that inevitable look of hatred in her eyes when she learned of his parentage and discovered that he watched her mother die right in front of him . . . and had let it happen.

"Mira," he said gruffly.

Her eyes drifted open.

"That was Thomas. We're supposed to meet him in his office. He's got something to tell us."

She pushed the blankets away and stood, cloaked in nothing more than morning sunlight. She raked a hand through her long, loose hair. Tight little pink nipples peeked from where the dark skeins lay tumbled over her shoulders. The curve of her waist and hip begged for his lips and tongue.

His cock started to rise. *Down boy.* He turned away and busied himself with finding clothing.

"I need to go back to my room. All I have here is my nightgown and bathrobe," she said.

He turned toward her, a pair of jeans in his hands. "That's probably for the best. If you stay here any longer, I'm going to push you back down onto the bed and keep you there all day."

"Would that be such a bad thing?"

"Considering Thomas's mood? *Yes*."

She laughed and slipped her nightgown over her head. "I've noticed he can be a bit prickly sometimes. *Moody* is perhaps a better word to use." She grabbed her bathrobe and breezed past him. "I'll meet you down there."

He grabbed her around the waist and dragged her against his chest for a final kiss, wanting the taste of her in his mouth awhile longer.

They broke the kiss, and she stayed there for a moment with her lips parted and her eyes half closed. "Mmmm," she sighed and bit her lower lip. "Do we really care if Thomas is a little upset?"

"Go." He slapped her ass playfully.

She went, throwing one last glowing smile over her shoulder at him.

Hell, he loved her.

And he was going to lose her soon. He felt it.

MIRA HURRIED BACK TO HER ROOM, NODDING AND smiling at people as she passed them in the hallway like it wasn't at all odd that she should be walking around the corridors in her nightgown and bathrobe this late in the morning.

She ached in intimate places, places that hadn't received much attention since she'd left Jack's Minneapolis apartment. Jack had loved her well. It made her shiver just to remember it. Made her want more.

She reached her room, took a shower, and dressed in a green sweater, a black skirt with a hem that hit her about midcalf, and a pair of cute black wedge heels that Serena had been kind enough to give her after her cousin had gone on a shopping expedition. Mira was pretty much stuck at the Coven, unable to leave the tightly warded property.

Serena had stepped in and decided to be her fairy god-cousin, bringing all kinds of goodies from the outside. Mira didn't put on any hosiery. She was lucky to have skin dusky enough that she didn't need them, not even in the dead of winter.

Before leaving to go to Thomas's office, she quickly curled her hair and put on a bit of mascara, blush, and lipstick. Okay, so maybe she did care a little more about her appearance these days. Was that so wrong? She felt beautiful in Jack's eyes.

And, staring at her reflection in the mirror, she realized she was once again starting to feel beautiful in her own eyes, too.

After the divorce, she'd lost that. Her self-esteem had hit rock-bottom. Finding her magick and learning how to control her latent power had a lot to do with the fact that she was finally recovering a positive sense of self.

In fact, finding her magick seemed to be reflected in all she was, even her appearance. Her hair seemed glossier and thicker. Her eyes seemed brighter, her lips fuller. Even her skin seemed creamier. Perhaps it was a side effect of recovering that missing part of herself and integrating it into her whole.

Mira stared at her reflection in the mirror and tipped her head to the side, letting her heavy hair slide over her shoulder. Or perhaps she was just seeing herself through different eyes.

She left her room, locked the door, and headed down to Thomas's office, where she found both men waiting. As soon as she entered she felt the tension in the room, thick like honey being smeared across her skin. Since she'd begun training her magic, she'd noticed her ability to sense emotions—something she'd always had to some degree—was growing stronger.

"Mira," Thomas greeted her.

"Thomas," she answered cautiously. She wanted to ask

what the tension was from, but thought better of it. The edge of a storm shone in Thomas's black eyes.

"Have a seat." Thomas motioned to the chair opposite Jack.

She sat, crossed her legs, and tried to get comfortable in the leather chair. It should have been easy to do, but the testosterone in the room had reached near unbearable levels. Obviously, there was something going on between Thomas and Jack that she was not privy to and, whatever it was, it was serious.

Thomas leaned against his desk, framed by the wide window behind him and the snow falling outside. He pressed his lips together. "We have new information about Crane. I didn't want to tell you until it was verified." He glanced at Jack. "Crane has cancer. Bone cancer. That's why he needs the demon circle. His prognosis is grim. If he can't call a demon for healing purposes, he's going to die."

The room went silent.

"So, I guess he's pretty motivated then," Mira said finally. It was a fairly unnecessary comment and fell into the quiet air like a rock.

Crane wanted to sacrifice four lives to save his own. More than that, maybe, depending on what the demon asked for in return for the healing.

"He's rejected traditional medical treatment, out of hubris, most likely, and doesn't have much time before he'll lose his mobility," answered Thomas. "There's only so much self-healing a fire witch can do, even one as powerful as William Crane. He's going to move fast, maybe even a little desperately. That's going to make him both sloppy and dangerous. We've alerted all witches in the Coven to be on guard, especially the air witches."

"But that means he won't waste his time coming after Mira, or trying to kidnap one of the powerful air witches." Jack rubbed his hand over his jaw. "He'll put Marcus in the circle."

"Marcus is dead," Thomas answered.

"What?" answered Mira and Jack at the same time.

"Marcus contacted an air witch in our employ right before he killed himself. Hung himself with a sheet. That's how we know about the cancer. After you foiled the Duskoff warlock's attempt to take you from Jack's apartment, Marcus assumed he'd be put in the circle and committed suicide to prevent it."

"Oh," said Mira. "Poor Marcus."

"He may not have been very powerful, but he had admirable courage at the end," answered Thomas sadly. "And he gave us a valuable heads-up on the situation. Seems they never truly broke him."

"I assumed the Duskoff hostages gave you information," said Jack.

Thomas shook his head. "They've been very tight-lipped."

"So without Marcus to use, he'll come after Mira for sure, since she's the most powerful air witch around with the least ability to use her magick," said Jack thoughtfully. "He'll be pulling out all the stops."

"That's why as much as I want you gone from the Coven, you need to stay here." There was a brutal quality to Thomas's voice, something oddly aggressive, that Mira wondered at. "And stay near Mira."

"I will," answered Jack without hesitation.

Thomas seemed to grind his teeth for a moment. "I know."

They glared at each other in challenge.

"Okay." Mira popped out of her chair. "Can someone please tell me what's going on? *Please?*" Both men went silent as she looked from one to the other.

EIGHTEEN

❦

THOMAS CROSSED HIS ARMS OVER HIS BROAD chest. "Nothing's wrong."

"Everything's fine," Jack said at the same time.

"Bullshit." She put a hand on her hip. "Don't make me pull my new super-duper witch powers on you and read your minds."

"Telepathy doesn't lie in the realm of air, Mira," answered Jack.

She raised her hand. "No speaking unless it's to tell me what's going on between the two of you, because it seems to have something to do with me. That means I have a right to know."

Jack sighed. "Your cousin is being overprotective of you, and rightly so."

"Overprotective?" Her gaze swung to Thomas. "What does he mean?"

He shifted uncomfortably. "I've known Jack longer than you have. That's all. You're a nice woman and he's a nice guy. Jack is the best of men. I respect and trust him.

But Jack is also . . ." He faltered and started again. "Jack is . . ."

"Not good enough for your cousin?" she ventured with raised eyebrows.

Jack just kept staring straight ahead as though he couldn't hear their conversation, like he wasn't even in the room. His face had gone blank, unreadable.

"No, it's not that at all. I'd be proud . . ." Thomas trailed off again. She'd never seen him at a loss for words before. "It's just that Jack is . . ."

"A man who likes to play the field?"

Thomas glanced at Jack, who didn't react. He just kept staring stoically out the window at the falling snow. "That's not an untrue statement about him. Nice way to put it, actually. I might call it something different," Thomas finished wryly.

"I appreciate your concern, Thomas. Really." She sighed. "But I wish everyone would stop trying to be so careful with me. I'm a grown woman. I can take care of myself. Make my own decisions. Set myself up for heartache if I choose to." She shrugged. "Anyway, sorry to disappoint you both, but I'm just using Jack for hot sex."

Jack jerked his gaze from the window to Mira's face and blinked. Finally, a reaction, even if his expression remained indecipherable.

She tilted her head to the side and grinned. "Sorry, Jack."

She only wished it was true. Mira had a feeling Jack was bound to break her heart, so she preferred not to wear it on her sleeve. She'd take what she could from him, dealing with him with her eyes open, then she'd nurse the wounds he dealt her after it was over.

Someone knocked on the door and Thomas called for them to enter. Serena stuck her head in. "Is Mira going to be able to practice at all with me today?"

Jack cleared his throat. "I'll do it today. It's good for her to switch instructors once in a while. Anyway, I've got orders to stay close to her." He paused. "Right, Thomas?"

Thomas hesitated before answering. "Jack will take over for today, Serena, if Mira is okay with that."

A whole afternoon with Jack to herself? She tried not to slobber when she answered, "Of course."

"Okay, then. See you later, cousin." Serena winked at Mira and shut the door.

"Just stay inside Coven walls, Mira," said Thomas unnecessarily. "Stay near Jack. Concentrate on learning to control your magick because the more powerful you become, the less of a target you are. We'll do the rest."

"If I can help with anything other than protecting Mira, let me know," Jack said.

"You have all the responsibility I plan to give you."

Jack glanced at Mira. His blue eyes seemed strangely hot. "It's a job I take very seriously."

"I know," answered Thomas.

"About Annie," said Mira.

Thomas held up his hand to stop her flow of words. "I called her this morning, tried to reason with her again. She will not agree to come into the Coven. I'm sorry."

That sounded like her stubborn godmother. She swallowed the lump in her throat.

"Annie is working now, but you can call her this evening and try to talk some sense into her, if you like. Now go concentrate on learning how to better control your magick. It's important."

Yes, now more than ever.

She and Jack finished up with Thomas and left to find a place to train.

"Hot sex, hmmm?" Jack asked as they walked down the corridor leading away from Thomas's office. He gave that familiar lazy grin that had the capacity to stop her heart. "I'm flattered."

After stopping at the conservatory to pocket a feather and rock—he wouldn't tell her why—Jack led her into the basement again.

"Uh, Jack?" she said once they reached the bottom of the stairs. "I'm okay with the conservatory now. You helped me get over my block."

"I'm not taking you to the storage room. I'm taking you to the ballroom."

"The ballroom? Why?"

He led her across the basement, up another flight of stairs, and down a wing of the Coven she hadn't even known existed. Her shoes sank into the plush red carpeting of the richly decorated corridor. He didn't answer her until he opened a set of double doors. "Because there's a mirror."

The room was enormous and completely empty. More plush red carpeting covered the floor, though the center of the room had an area covered in hardwood, probably for dancing. A chandelier hung from the ceiling and a mirror lined one wall, giving the illusion the room was twice as big.

She stepped within, and Jack closed the doors behind her. "And why do we need a mirror?" she asked with a raised brow and a leer on her face. Her voice echoed in the large space.

Jack laughed at the insinuation. "I know you can levitate objects, but I want you to try and do it when you're disoriented. The mirror is there to mix you up."

He led her to sit cross-legged on the carpet, facing the mirror, and set the feather and rock a distance behind her on her right. She could see them, but it was a reflection and therefore disorienting. She'd relied a lot on her sight to accomplish these tasks in the past. Obviously, Jack knew that and wanted to break her reliance.

"Levitate them both at the same time," he said, leaning back against a wall. "Do it so that they're held at equal levels in the air."

She blew a strand of hair away from her face, her

expression grim. This was going to be tough. Not only had she never levitated objects of such varying mass at once before, she'd never done it using a reflection.

He read her expression. "It's important that you gain full control of your abilities. Hopefully, you'll never need to use them to defend yourself, but if you do, you need to be ready. You're a strong witch. You don't want to end up like Marcus, your fate in the hands of more powerful warlocks."

Mira thought of Marcus for a moment. She'd never even met him, but she felt a kinship with him because they were both air witches. He'd ended up dangling from the end of a makeshift rope, alone and used up. "No, I don't want that."

He nodded at the stone and feather. "Then levitate."

Mira drew a thread and manipulated it under the two objects. Creating air movement was fairly easy, but fine work like using wind to levitate objects was much trickier. Several times she blew the feather too far away and had to carefully draw it back using little puffs of air. She regulated the air currents to what she needed for each object— much, much stronger and tightly contained under the rock and hardly a breath for the feather.

It took all her concentration and several false starts, but she finally got the right recipe and very slowly lifted both the rock and the feather at the same time, then set them back down. Perspiration sheened her forehead by the time she'd finished the task. She had no idea how long it had taken her. Time had slipped from her as she'd worked.

"Good job," said Jack. "I'm impressed. You've taken to your magick well."

She had. To go back to who she'd been before her power had nestled, purring, in the center of her chest would be like tearing off an arm or leg.

"Now do it again," said Jack.

She glared at him.

"Go ahead," he prompted.

She raised the rock and feather five more times. Each time it became easier and faster. Mira looked at Jack with triumph on her face when he told her to stop.

"Okay, now do it with your eyes closed."

"Jack!"

"Mira, do it."

She sighed and settled in for a long afternoon, but she finally managed to master the task. When Jack told her to stop, she felt exhausted from having her concentration so centered on her lesson.

"Have you done anything to tap into your ability of hearing conversations from far away?" he asked.

"My super-duper eavesdropping ability? It's been happening spontaneously." She drew a breath and told him about the whispering she'd heard early that morning. "That's why I'd been going to the kitchen when I saw you. I couldn't fall back to sleep after that. I wanted to think it was just a nightmare." She shuddered. "But I know it wasn't."

"It was a nightmare, all right, but one of the waking variety."

Mira dropped her gaze, feeling a mixture of dread and panic wash over her. She didn't like being a target, a potential victim. It made her all the more motivated to gain control of her power. She raised her gaze and met her own eyes in the mirror. "Okay, give me another lesson, teach."

"Find me a conversation somewhere in the building." He hesitated, thinking. "No, find me either Thomas, Ingrid, or Serena and tell me if they're having a conversation. If so, eavesdrop on it. You know them, so it should be a little easier to locate them in the Coven. Plus, we can verify it afterward."

"Uh, aren't they going to mind if I drop in on their private discussions?"

"They know there's an air witch in the building who's training. That's warning enough."

"If you say so, Jack." She closed her eyes and let her consciousness drift into deeper places. Mira had been meditating every day, training to let her awareness steal a bit of magick and go exploring.

Soon she lost most of her physical connection with the room and unfurled the thread of power she'd taken along for the ride. It reached into the house, sorting through the vocal vibrations it found disturbing the air currents. Mira discarded the ones that didn't seem familiar and stopped to investigate ones that did.

Finally, she found a pattern that seemed very familiar and honed in on it. Using her magick, she adjusted the frequency so that it became less a humming buzz and more and more like a conversation. It was Ingrid.

Mira heard only her half of the discussion. Either Ingrid was talking on the phone, or Mira didn't have a good grasp on the person Ingrid was speaking with. Reaching out a tendril of magick, she sought the answer and discovered the second person. Again "tuning the frequency," she forced the other person's voice to come in clearly.

She'd half been wishing for some juicy gossip, but instead got a discussion about garbage pickup. *How scintillating.*

Carefully, she unhooked the tendrils of her magick and withdrew. Their voices faded as Mira gradually came back into her body. She let her eyes slowly open and found Jack sitting on the floor, his legs and arms around her. She'd been so involved with her project, so out of her body, she hadn't even noticed him settle in behind her.

Mira snuggled back against his warm chest. Now this was what she'd been wanting all day long. "Well, that was boring."

"Good. What did you hear?" He slid his hand under her sweater and rubbed his thumb back and forth over her lower stomach. It made it hard to think.

"I overheard Ingrid and an unknown person discussing

the entertaining topic of arranging new garbage pickup for the Coven."

"Fascinating. If you can remember specific details, we'll verify them later."

"I can."

"Good." He held his free hand in front of her, palm up. "One more task for the day," he said, his deep voice rumbling through her back. A spark ignited in the palm of his hand. "Make it brighter. Make it flare."

Her magick responded to his instantly, growing warmer and tingling in the center of her, wanting to be free, wanting to play with his magick. She pulled a thread, molded it into the shape she wanted and let it slide sinuously around the flame, like a cat rubbing up against a person's leg, silky and soft.

Behind her, Jack shivered, and she wondered if he could somehow feel what she did. Obviously, he couldn't see the tiny air current. She teased the flame over and over, making it flare in the center of his hand.

Finally, she fed her magick into his fully, causing the fire to grow bigger and brighter until she was able to pull it completely from his hand and allow it to hang before them. Their combined magick danced, suspended in the air, in shimmering colors of red, orange, yellow, and blue. It looked like a fiery version of the northern lights.

Jack pushed his hands under the hem of her sweater, and Mira faltered in her control of the magick. "Don't lose it," he breathed into her ear. "Don't let me break your concentration." He nipped at her ear gently, making gooseflesh erupt over her body.

"You're evil," she murmured, trying to maintain her grip on the light show in front of them. "But I don't really mind this particular lesson."

"Mmm," he purred as he dragged his hands up her abdomen. "Who said training couldn't be fun?" Her fronthooking bra came undone.

Jack cupped her breasts in his hands and rubbed his thumbs over her nipples. She moaned deep in her throat, keeping her gaze on the fire in front of them. The heat she felt from the flames was nothing like what came from Jack.

"You have gorgeous breasts, so sensitive and responsive. I love to touch them." As he spoke, he traced every ridge and valley of each of her nipples, making Mira feel the effects of his touch much further south. "Sometimes you become so aroused when I play with them, I think you might come by that alone."

"Uh." Her voice came out breathy from her arousal. "You may be right about that."

"Really? Let's see how excited you are." He eased a hand down her stomach.

The magick slipped, and she nearly lost it all together.

"Let it go, Mira," he murmured into her ear. "Training's over. Time to play."

NINETEEN

SHE LET THE MAGICK COLLAPSE, EXTINGUISHING the fire and revealing their reflection in the mirror they faced. He had one hand up her sweater, stroking her nipple. The other lay on her thigh, his fingers playing idly with the hem of her skirt.

He lifted a brow, catching her gaze in the mirror's reflection. "Hmmm. This has possibilities," he whispered in her ear.

"I knew the mirror played some part in your nefarious plans," she answered breathlessly. In the mirror's reflection, Mira could see how her pupils were dilated in arousal, making her eyes look dark. Her jaw was a little slack and her expression relaxed. She had the look of a woman already under the influence of Jack's powerful, sensual touch. Mira recognized this woman as the same one she'd seen that morning in Jack's corner mirror. It was an aspect of her personality only Jack had been able to coax forth.

"You caught me." He looked like a predator, like he

knew exactly what he was doing . . . and what he meant to do was make her climax right here on the ballroom floor.

She had no real objections to that.

Jack held her gaze in the mirror as he pushed his hand past the hem of her skirt and dragged his fingertips upward over her skin. He stopped where her inner thigh met her sex and brushed back and forth over that sensitive place until her breath caught. Then he moved to the damp panel of material covering her sex and caressed her clit through it, stroking over the aroused bundle of nerves.

Pleasure warmed her between her thighs and spread out. She made a small noise in the back of her throat as she felt herself find that now familiar place on the edge of an orgasm.

"Let's take your panties off," he murmured into her ear. He grasped the edge of the small lacy undergarment and pulled. Silk tore.

Mira gasped in surprise. "Those were a perfectly fine pair of—"

"I'll buy you new ones." He held up the small blue bikini briefs. "Those were pretty insubstantial anyway."

"If you want me to wear granny panties, I'm sure I can find some."

He tossed her panties to the side and gripped the hem of her skirt, pulling it upward until she could see her mons. "Mira, less talking," he purred into her ear, "more moaning." He covered her sex with his hand. "Now where were we? Oh, yes, you were going to watch while I make you come."

Mira's mouth went dry.

Jack caressed her clit with one hand and eased his other hand up to cup her breast. Mira moved restlessly against him, feeling drugged and needy. He eased a finger up into her heat and it drew a moan from her. He added another, stretching her deliciously.

"You like to watch, don't you?" he murmured in her ear.

She found his gaze in the mirror's reflection and nodded.

He gave her a slow smile. "I noticed that this morning. Drop your gaze now, Mira. Watch what I'm doing to you."

She did as he asked and watched his big hand working between her thighs, the muscles of his forearm flexing as he pushed her straight to a place where Mira's whole world was focused only on pleasure.

She wanted him badly. Wanted to feel him inside her, but Jack wasn't teasing her today, he clearly meant her to climax against his hand . . . and she was going to do just that.

She dug her heels into the carpet and arched her back. Jack worked his thick fingers in and out of her as he rolled her nipple back and forth with his other hand.

"Jack, I'm coming," she whispered. She closed her eyes, feeling the beginnings of it skitter through her body.

"Eyes open," he ordered gently. "Watch yourself."

She opened her eyes and took in the whole decadent, exciting picture. Her gaze caught his and held steady. His eyes were dark, his expression serious.

"Hell. You're gorgeous, baby," he murmured.

Mira came hard against his pistoning fingers. Her muscles clamped down and pulsed around them as pleasure slammed into her body. She held his gaze as long as she could, then she threw her head back and shuddered and moaned her way to heaven and back.

When the final ripples faded, she let herself sag in his arms. He smoothed her skirt down and kissed her tenderly on her temple. "I wanted you to see how beautiful you are when you come."

Mira forced herself to form a response. She raised an eyebrow. "Well, at least I'm obtaining what I set out to get from you."

A low chuckle rumbled through him. "I'll give you all the hot sex you want, woman."

She turned over and pushed him back onto the carpet. "That's good, because there's something I've wanted to do for a while now, and you keep stopping me."

"What's that?"

She only gave him a mischievous smile and kissed him, first on his lips, then down his chest, pushing up his beige sweater to put her lips on his flesh. When she reached his jeans, she ran her tongue over the top of the waistband and looked up at him with a sultry expression on her face.

He dropped his head back and groaned.

Then came the soft noise of a button being undone, the sound of a zipper coming down . . . and his gorgeous cock came free and stood at attention. She ran her fingers down it, smoothing the glistening pre-come over the crown.

Jack shivered, and Mira smiled.

"I want you at the mercy of my lips," she murmured, "and my mouth. I want to feel your body totally vulnerable to the mere lick of my tongue . . . until you give me everything you have to give."

"You're going to drive me insane."

"I don't want to drive you insane. I just want to make you come."

She caressed him a little while longer with her fingers, feeling every groan, every shudder, every tightening muscle as if through her own body. Mira licked the smooth head, let the tip of her tongue dance around the sides of his shaft, and lowered her lips around his cock.

His fingers twined through her hair as she worked him in and out of her mouth. Once in a while, he gently thrust so the head of his cock touched her tonsils.

When he finally came he pushed deep into her mouth and groaned. He tasted warm and musky against her tongue, down her throat. Mira closed her eyes, enjoying the knowledge that she'd made this man, who loved to be in control, completely lose it to the caress of her lips.

Jack lay for a moment, breathing hard, and then pulled her up his body, sinking his fingers into the hair at her nape. "Damn," he groaned before he rolled her beneath him and kissed her deeply.

She'd never known how good sex could be—this sweet give-and-take of breath, emotion, and body. No shame. No shyness. Just pleasure. No matter what happened between her and Jack in the end, he'd given her that.

They spent the rest of the day together, and that night she went to his room instead of her own.

In the evening she called Annie and tried to cajole her godmother into coming to the Coven. Annie flatly refused, saying she had a store to run and a life to lead. After she hung up, Mira stared at the phone in the living room, a ball of roiling emotion in her stomach.

Jack walked into the room and held his hand out to her. She let him pull her from a sitting position into his arms. He tipped her chin up and kissed her softly, not needing words to comfort her.

She followed him into the bedroom where they undressed each other and curled up naked under the covers, taking pleasure in the feel of their skin touching and their mingling body heat.

Jack guided her face to his and, without a word, kissed her. His lips slipped over hers, soft and slow, as though he savored the taste of her. She made a little noise in the back of her throat and kissed him in return. His tongue feathered against her mouth and she opened to him.

When he dropped his kisses to encompass her throat and her breasts, she let him. When he planed her inner thigh with his broad hand, she spread her legs for him. Patiently, with his skillful touch, he readied her.

When she was slick and swollen, he slid inside her. He rode her slow, then even slower. He held her gaze steadily with his own, breaking it only once in a while to kiss her or murmur into her ear. It was intimate and arousing and made emotions swell within her and tears sheen her eyes.

He made her feel protected and even, almost, loved and cherished.

She climaxed with her legs twined around his hips and

his cock thrust way up inside her. Her orgasm triggered his, and they stifled each other's cries with their mouths and tongues.

When they slept, it was in a perspiration-drenched, satisfied tangle of intertwined bodies.

Mira couldn't remember the last time she'd slept so deeply.

ANNIE BUSTLED INTO HER KITCHEN AND SET HER bag of groceries down on the kitchen counter. This early in the morning it was colder than a witch's tit outside. She'd always loved that expression.

She shrugged out of her winter coat and busied herself unpacking the bags. Today was an eventful day at the store because of a couple of craft classes she was hosting, so she'd done her shopping early. Thank heavens for grocery stores that were open twenty-four hours.

After everything was put away, she poured herself a cup of coffee and sat down at her small kitchen table. Early morning light filtered in through the window above the sink. From her seat, she gazed past the light green curtains, trying to think of everything she had to do that day, but ending up only thinking about Mira's phone call the night before.

Her goddaughter had sounded so worried about her. Annie felt guilty for not rushing to the Coven for shelter just for Mira's sake, but she felt a need to stand her ground. The Duskoff always sent everyone running for the hills, and she was sick of it. If the bastards wanted her, they could damn well try to take her. She wasn't unfamiliar with how to use magick in a fight.

Annie's gaze shifted. On the shelf over the sink, next to a small pot of miniature roses she'd managed to keep alive indoors all winter, was a high school graduation picture of Mira.

Her goddaughter had always been beautiful and talented in so many ways. She was very empathic, a side effect of being a witch, and would've made a great psychologist if she'd finished school. Annie had been against her marriage to Ben from the start. She'd sensed he was no good for Mira. Annie had let her concerns be known, but she hadn't pushed Mira too hard on the subject. It was Mira's life. Mira's choice.

But even Annie hadn't suspected Ben would turn out to be the schmuck he was. He'd betrayed Mira badly, just as her own godmother had.

Annie closed her eyes, feeling the bitter taste of remorse well up. She keenly regretted deciding to honor Mira's parents' wishes. If she'd told the Coven about her, Mira would've grown up with the training she needed, and she never would've found herself hunted the way she was now.

Her parents had simply wanted her to have a normal life as a non-magickal person. They'd known the dangers facing a powerful air witch, as Mira had been fated to become from conception. They'd meant well and so had Annie, but that saying about good intentions paving the way to hell was true.

She wondered how Mira fared at the Coven now. They hadn't talked for long on the phone the night before. Annie trusted Jack McAllister to keep Mira safe from physical harm, but how was she doing mentally, emotionally? Besides the night before, she'd only talked to Mira once since she'd reached the Coven, and Mira had seemed distant on the phone, confused and overwhelmed by the fact that she had family she'd never known about.

Family that Annie had kept secret from her.

Did Mira hate her now? She had a right to, Annie supposed. She hoped Mira knew she loved her like a daughter. A tear slid down her cheek and she wiped it away.

Outside on the street were the two bodyguards the Coven had sent to watch over her. She was forever bringing the men hot meals and tea, but they always declined her offers to come into her home or the store. Thomas Monahan had also sent top-rated wardweavers to create powerful wards around her home and business. They worried about her because of her connection to Mira.

But Annie only worried about Mira.

One day, when this was all over, she'd try to make amends for keeping things from her. She only hoped that Mira would forgive her.

Her heart heavy, as it had been for weeks now, Annie got up, put her coffee cup in the sink, grabbed her purse and coat, and headed out her back door to begin her day.

Her heels did not slip on the perfectly clear walkway she managed with her magick. Tall hedges grew on either side of her yard, concealing what she did from non-magickal eyes. Snow removal was easy for her, being comprised of water. She heated it up until it melted, or simply moved it to either side of the walkway.

She reached the alley and her car. The green sedan with the two witches was parked a little further down. She waved at them as usual, but they didn't wave back. Annie frowned, lowering her hand and sensing something amiss. She narrowed her eyes—she had a bit of astigmatism—to get a better view.

The witches were slumped over in their seats. They looked incapacitated at the least, dead at worst.

That couldn't bode well.

Footsteps sounded on the cleared walkway behind her. *Two men.*

Adrenaline surging through her, Annie pulled a strand of magick as she turned to confront the two Duskoff warlocks behind her. One was earth, the other fire.

She gave them no time to react. She drenched them in water and cooled it so fast neither of them could retaliate. They both froze in place.

Then she whirled around, expecting more to be behind

her. It was a common tactic. The first were just cannon fodder. When the Duskoff wanted to take a powerful witch, they overwhelmed her, confused her.

Two more came from around the corner of the garage, a water witch and an earth witch, both pulling magick so fast she feared she couldn't stop them. With honed reflexes, she pulled strands and dowsed them, freezing them solid.

Breathing hard, she turned a circle, waiting for the rest. No more warlocks met her view . . . but no way had she finished this battle.

A man in a long black trench coat stepped from the alley.

Like some gunfighter on the streets of Deadwood, Annie pulled her magick and directed it at the man, but he moved his hand, and her water flared in a sudden flash of fire and evaporated. She tried again and again as the man neared her.

He was a master of his element. She'd never felt a more powerful fire witch in her life. Annie cast about in her mind for alternatives, ways to defeat this one. Some water witches could manipulate the water in a person's very body, but she didn't possess that ability. Out of options, Annie backed away from him, into one of the men she'd frozen.

As he grew near, she could see his face more clearly. He was ruggedly handsome, with thick, curly blond hair and gray eyes. *Stefan.* The whole witch community knew who he was. Stefan was almost as well-known as his bastard father.

He threw his arms wide as if greeting an old friend and smiled. "Annie, so good to meet you." Flames sparked in both palms.

He embraced her.

Annie screamed.

TWENTY

JACK AWOKE TO FIND HIS BED EMPTY. SENSING
Mira still in the room, he turned over, glancing around for
her. She stood in her nightgown at the window looking out
at the morning-draped front lawn.

"Mira? What are you doing? Come back to bed."

She turned. The look on her face chilled him. She'd
gone pale and her expression seemed perfectly stark. Her
eyes seemed to hold nothing.

He got out of bed and went to her. Her arms were cold
to his touch. "Baby, what's wrong?"

She stared for a long moment before finally blinking.
"Nightmare."

Jack pulled her against him, but she felt like a board. He
rubbed her arms, trying to get her warmed up. "Must have
been a bad one," he murmured with his cheek pressed
against her hair. "It's still early. Come back to bed." He
wanted to hold her, chase that haunted look out of her eyes.

She pulled away from him, blinking twice rapidly. A

smile flickered over her mouth. "Sorry. It really freaked me out."

His heart started beating again. "Sometimes training magick can produce nightmares. It's not uncommon."

"Really?"

"When the magick is first disturbed, the mind can sometimes be disturbed too. Nightmares are a problem for adolescent witches because of that. Since you're only now being trained, seems likely you'd have them."

She shuddered. "It was very vivid, like I was there in reality."

"Witches dream vividly. They're prone to spontaneous lucid dreams too. I don't think I have to tell you how much being lucid in a nightmare can suck."

"I think I just found out."

"Come on." He led her back to bed. Once they were both under the heavy blankets, he pulled her against him and spooned her, nestling his hand between her breasts to cover the seat of her magick. "You can tell me about it, if you think it would help."

"No," she answered quickly. "I just want to forget it." She pulled his hand to her mouth and gave the back of it a kiss. "But thanks."

"Okay." He glanced at the clock. Tucked against his body, she was finally starting to warm up. It was 8 A.M. They had another half hour before they had to get up and begin training for the day.

They'd spend it just like this.

MIRA HELD OUT HER HAND AND HELPED JACK TO his feet. Grimacing, Jack stood and stretched his back and neck. She was kicking his ass today, and she felt guilty about it.

He'd taken her training over from Serena, figuring it was time to start concentrating more on defensive magick, which was his specialty. They'd gone back to the storage room, where he'd instructed mats be placed on the floor. She was making progress, although it was hard for her to concentrate with the remnants of the dream clinging to her. Still, she managed to best Jack every time he came at her.

Jack had told her it was just a nightmare, and she desperately wanted to believe him. The alternative was too gruesome to consider.

"I'm going to add in my fire now." Jack had been serious all day about her training, driving her to try new things, tweak her magick this way and that way. He was intent that she learn new defensive techniques. She was grateful for his focus because she shared it. Something was building. She could feel it. And it was something bad.

"How does air have any defense against fire, Jack? Air only makes a fire burn hotter and brighter."

"Think for a moment. What it is that fire needs to burn in the first place?"

It hit her instantly. "Oh."

Jack nodded. "Defensive magick is a lot like a game of paper-rock-scissors, although that's a deceptively simple description. A lot of it depends on an individual witch's abilities, how creative and quick they are, and their level of power."

He extended his hand and a fireball formed. It grew larger rapidly, forcing Mira to draw a strand of magick and use it to encase it in a bubble and draw all the air out. It took a lot of concentration, but she finally got the fireball to extinguish.

"Good. Very good, Mira."

She smiled, proud of herself.

"Now let's try it when I'm not standing still and waiting for you."

Her smile faded.

Again and again they practiced. Jack made the fire bigger, smaller, threw it across the room, and tossed it directly at her. Finally, Mira could sense and extinguish fire with her eyes closed. By the time she'd mastered the ability she felt exhausted and had a splitting headache, but the hard magickal workout had blessedly wiped away the last vestiges of the nightmare from her mind.

Jack watched her across the room with unmistakable heat in his eyes as she leaned over and braced her hands on her knees, breathing heavy from chasing fire around the room. He stalked toward her and bustled her back against the wall behind her. Jack pinned her there with his hands on either side of her head and stared intently at her.

She blinked. "Er. Is there something you want to say to me, Jack?"

"Just that I think you're incredible, beautiful, smart, and sexy."

She felt herself flush under the praise. "Got anymore adjectives you want to throw in there?"

"I've watched you meet every challenge that's been thrown at you over these past few weeks. You've never once whimpered, never once whined. In that time period you've gathered as much magickal knowledge as it takes some witches years to learn."

"Um, thank you." She never knew what to do with praise. "I'm kind of motivated, you know?"

His voice lowered seductively. "Did I mention the sexy part? The beautiful part?" He leaned toward her and gently brushed his lips across hers. The slight touch made her body hum with awareness of him. He rested his forehead against hers. "Damn, Mira. I think I—" He bit off the end of his sentence. "I care about you a lot. And there's no way I'm letting you use any of this defensive magick you've learned. Crane and his minions will get near you over my dead body."

She smiled at the vehement protectiveness in his voice. "Well, that's the last thing I want, Jack, because I care about you, too."

Something dark moved in his eyes. "Last task for the day. Throw me back. I'm the enemy. Repel me."

She shook her head. "No, I'm finished for the day. You probably already have ten bruises—"

"Do it."

"No."

"Do it."

"No!"

His eyes turned a terrible shade of red and flame seemed to flicker in their depths. "*Do it, Mira,*" he growled low.

She did it.

Jack went careening backward and landed on his ass about ten feet away. He didn't move.

Stupid man! Mira ran to him and knelt by his side. His eyes were closed. "Jack? Are you all right?"

He opened his eyes and had her beneath him so fast she couldn't even yelp in surprise. "Great . . . now," he murmured right before his mouth came down on hers.

His lips worked over hers, and his knee insinuated itself between her thighs. Mira's aches and pains from the day, her headache, all faded under his touch. She let her hands play over his broad shoulders, let her fingers tangle in the silky hair at his nape as he kissed her.

She loved him.

Mira could never tell him that, but she did. There was nothing she could do about it. The feelings had hit her like a Mack truck.

Jack slid his hand under her shirt and rubbed his thumb back and forth against her waist, making her shiver. She pushed up, forcing him over onto his back so she could straddle him. Her mouth worked over his as she yanked the hem of his shirt up, wanting to kiss over his chest.

He cupped her face in his hands before she could lower her mouth to him. "Mira . . ."

Just then someone opened the door. Thomas stuck his

head in. He surveyed the scene for a moment before speaking. "Glad to see the training is going well."

Mira stood and dusted herself off while Jack got to his feet.

"Mira, I need to talk to you," said Thomas. He gave a pointed look at Jack. "Alone."

"Okay." She glanced at Jack before heading out the door with Thomas.

They walked to his office, not saying a word. He wore a grim expression that made all the dread Mira had felt from her nightmare come rushing back to hit her right in the solar plexus. "Thomas, I—"

"Not until we get to my office."

Finally, they reached their destination, and he closed the door behind them. She sank into one of the leather chairs. He sat on the edge of his desk and pinched the bridge of his nose between his thumb and forefinger.

Mira braced herself. She focused her gaze on one of the legs of the desk. "I had a nightmare last night. I dreamt that a powerful warlock had Annie." She paused, drew a steadying breath and raised her gaze to Thomas's face. "Just tell me, Thomas."

Thomas only looked up. Everything was on his face.

A cold blast of air rushed through the room, a result of Mira's sudden uncontrolled burst of emotion. The despair faded until Mira felt made of wood. "Tell me more."

"We received a messenger about fifteen minutes ago sent by Stefan, William Crane's adopted son. Do you know who Stefan is?"

She nodded.

"He is a very powerful fire witch. Apparently, he killed the two guards we sent and took Annie from her home this morning while she was on her way to work."

Mira drew a shuddering breath. She should have a million questions, but her mind had gone perfectly blank.

"Annie is bait." He paused. "For you."

She forced herself to think through the numb haze she'd stumbled into. "You said the Duskoff contacted you?"

"They sent photos."

Mira swallowed hard, feeling nauseous. Photos had to be bad.

Thomas continued in a matter-of-fact tone, but Mira could hear the tremble of emotion beneath it. "She's been burned by Stefan. She needs medical treatment. Plus, they say they'll kill her if you don't hand yourself over to them within twenty-four hours."

Mira let all that information sink in. Her life for her godmother's life.

"You will not do this," he commanded.

Her numbness melted into searing rage. She stood, and another blast of air rushed through the room, scattering the papers on Thomas's desk. His long black hair blew around his head, but his grim expression didn't change.

"Like hell you'll tell me what to do, Thomas. Annie is the only mother I've ever known. I will *not* leave her to die in Crane's clutches in order to save myself. I will not allow Crane to take any more of my parents away."

"You need to calm down. I have no intention of letting either you or Annie die. Please, sit."

She remained standing, crossing her arms over her chest.

"I know you're spoiling for a fight, and you're going to get what you want after a fashion, but we're going to be smart about this. We've got the resources to meet this challenge if we adequately anticipate their moves."

Thomas could obviously think much clearer about this than she could. All she wanted was to go, and go now. Do anything in order to get Annie back safely.

"You're not ready to fight warlocks, Mira, I'm sorry."

"I *am* ready, Thomas. I fought six of them in Jack's apartment."

"And nearly killed yourself."

"I've been training. I've come a long way since then. I have more control now."

"You're not ready. Trust me."

She stood fuming for a long moment before yelling, "I *will* be a part of anything the Coven does, Thomas!"

He didn't say anything.

A breeze born from her impatience and anger buffeted their hair. "Thomas, I mean it. You treat me like I'm made of glass. Just like Jack. I'm stronger than you both think I am, and there's no way I won't make Crane pay for everything he's done to me. I want your word now that I will be a part of anything the Coven organizes. It's my choice. It's my life. Annie is my godmother."

Thomas stared at her for a long moment. "You are definitely a child of both Hoskins and Monahan houses. You have my promise."

"And I don't want Jack to know anything about this," she added. "Not a word."

Shock and anger spilled across Thomas's face for a moment, but he managed it quickly, letting that familiar blank mask settle over his features. "Why? He can help."

"He's so damned protective. He'll stop me, or he'll get in my way. It's just easier if he doesn't know it's happening."

"It's a mistake."

She shook her head. "Promise me as my cousin, Thomas. As family. You said you'd do anything for me. *Swear it.*"

Thomas closed his eyes and sighed in defeat. "I paired him with you for a reason. He's the best man to guard you, Mira. He'd give his life to keep you safe."

"Yeah, I know. That's the problem."

TWENTY-ONE

❦

THE DAY DAWNED COLD AND GRAY. SHE STEPPED
out of the limo on some swanky street in New York City.
Mira had never visited this place, knew nothing about it,
and she was hardly paying close attention to their surroundings at the moment. The best she could do was note
the winter-barren expanse of Central Park that lay across
the street. At least, she suspected it was Central Park. It
was a really big park at any rate. They were at Thomas's
apartment, not very far from Duskoff International.

Mira glanced at the lightening sky, her breath showing
white against the cold air. She'd slipped from Jack's bed
during the night. He'd be waking up soon to find her gone,
but she wasn't going to think about that.

Thomas placed a proprietary hand to her lower back
and steered her into the building, past the doormen, the
front desk person, and to the elevator. Several witches
trailed them. More would follow.

Thomas's New York digs were all Mira had come to

expect—hardwood floors, expensive furnishings, huge floor-to-ceiling windows with a view of the park. It was beautiful, but Mira noticed little beyond the obvious. All her thoughts were centered on Annie.

She pulled her coat off, and one of the accompanying witches took it for her, shuffled it away somewhere. She sank down onto Thomas's couch and stared out the window. Behind her the phone rang. Thomas picked it up and spoke in muted tones to the person on the other end.

Thomas approached her after hanging up the phone. She didn't bother to look at him. "They know we're here. They say 4 P.M., at Duskoff International. The pretense is that you've agreed to exchange your life for Annie's, but we all know that's not the way this is going to happen. We're here to fight. They know that well enough. They'll do all they can to take you from us. We need to be ready."

Mira only nodded and kept staring out the window. A curious sense of power had stolen over her, a feeling of confidence. All her fear was locked somewhere deep inside her. She couldn't afford fear right now, not while Annie was with Crane and needed medical attention. There was no time to waste on feelings that did no good, did nothing to get Annie back. Everything seemed so crystal clear to her.

"Where is Duskoff International in relation to your apartment?" she asked Thomas mildly.

"Five blocks north of this building."

"Thank you." She stood and walked down the hallway, seeking a quiet place.

"Mira? Where are you going?"

She turned. "I'm a witch. It's time I started to act like one."

"Do I need to worry about you? You seem too calm."

"You don't need to worry, Thomas." Mira turned back around and continued down the hallway, finding one of the bedrooms at the back of the apartment. She sat cross-legged in the center of the bed, closed her eyes, and let her consciousness drift deeper, drift until she couldn't sense her physical body anymore.

She heard a little *pop* as her consciousness freed itself, and she directed it out of the room and into the main part of the apartment.

Her awareness was the air itself, and she could point her attention anywhere she chose. Regulating the sounds of the witches in Thomas's apartment so they faded to nothingness and managing the loud clamor of the street beyond, Mira turned northward and sought the Duskoff Building and Annie.

The gunmetal gray building stood on the corner of a large intersection. A tall, wide, carved granite sign in the common area in front marked it as the building she sought. Despite it being Saturday, many people walked the street outside the frosted double glass doors. Mira tried to send her consciousness into the building but couldn't get past a heavy barrier that ran around it.

Warding.

She'd forgotten that the Duskoff Building would probably have some serious protective wards around it. She remembered what Jack had told her once. The barriers were meant to allow non-magickals through, but not just any old witch. No magick other than what the wardweaver had decided was safe could pass.

That meant she was definitely locked out. She was not safe to them.

Mira slid along the barrier, finding what felt like a seam in the magick. She followed. Maybe she could find an imperfection of some kind, a mistake or a back door. That's what the wardbreakers had found at Jack's apartment, according to Thomas. Completely perfect wardings were a fluke. Some wardings were better than others, but no witch could get a barrier up that was completely solid.

This warding seemed perfect.

She explored for what felt like hours and found nothing. Mira searched until she felt despair rise up from the center of her. There seemed to be no imperfections anywhere in the sleek magickal barricade or along its perfect seam.

Just as she was about to admit defeat, she found a tiny crack at the base of the southern wall. She went right over it at first because it was so small. Mira came back to it and worried at it with her own magick, trying to make it rip, but it held fast. She was incorporeal after all; she couldn't hope to have that much effect.

Taking a different tact, she pushed and squeezed until she forced her awareness through the miniscule tear and into the building. She felt her consciousness ooze through like a viscous liquid.

Now to find her godmother.

The moment she put her focus on Annie, Mira experienced a *zoom stop* straight to her, as though merely thinking of her had some kind of magnetic attraction. Her godmother was being kept in a storage room somewhere in Duskoff International.

Annie lay on her stomach on a cot. Black and red, blistering burns marked her back where her very clothing had ignited and burned away. Shivers wracked her body, either from the cold or from her injuries.

The amount of damage that had been done to Annie stunned Mira into nonreaction . . . a moment before perfect rage filled her. Mira could feel her physical body shaking from it back in Thomas's bedroom.

Mira attempted something she'd never tried before. She pulled a thread of magick and created a warm breeze in this remote location. It caressed Annie until she no longer shivered.

Annie pushed up, wincing at the pain the movement caused her. "Mira?" she whispered.

Mira could feel tears running down her physical cheeks, but she had no way to answer her. Instead she created another steady breeze in the room, warming the air for her. It was all she could do.

She let herself drift out of the room, examining the building and the location where Annie was being held. She could tell by the views out of the windows that it was somewhere high. By finding the lobby and elevator, she discovered which floor it was for certain.

Eventually, she came to a large boardroom. Two men stood near the long table in the center. The older man had his back to Mira. The younger, handsome man she recognized right away as Stefan. As the two men spoke in low voices, she noticed that Stefan's visage had a brutal set that he didn't allow the world to see.

This was the man who'd taken Annie and who had burned her.

Mira's anger flared, and Stefan jerked his head up. He put his hand on the older man's shoulder, helped him into a chair, and then circled the room, looking up at the ceiling. He knew they weren't alone.

Had she inadvertently caused a disturbance in the air, or was Stefan simply sensitive to other magicks?

She had no time to wonder further. Stefan flicked his wrist, and all Mira saw, tasted, and felt was fire. Her consciousness slammed back into her body, making her gasp. The coppery scent of burnt blood filled her nostrils and the persistent sense that she'd been seared lingered along her skin. She touched her face and chest, making sure she hadn't truly been burned, but it had been an illusion.

She collapsed to her side and closed her eyes, her heart thumping wildly. Her legs had fallen asleep, and she suffered through the pins and needles. When her heartbeat had slowed to an acceptable level and the pain in her legs had receded, Mira opened her eyes. She knew where Annie was being held within the building, and she knew what they had to do. They wouldn't wait until it was time to meet and battle it out.

They would take them by surprise before then.

She slid off the bed, stalked into the other room, and told Thomas as much.

"You're forgetting about the warding, love," said Thomas. "They'll drop the warding before 4 P.M. so we can get in. We can't break through before that time, not even with our top wardbreakers working nonstop between now and then. They need more time."

"But I know where there's a chink in the warding, Thomas. It's how I got in. It's a hairline crack at the base of the southernmost wall, but maybe it can be exploited with the right magick. I know exactly where it is."

"Whoa, calm down." He took her by the upper arms and guided her to sit on the couch. "What are you talking about?"

"In the bedroom I just . . . I don't know . . . traveled to Duskoff International. I wanted to see if I could locate Annie. I ran into the warding, but after spending some time exploring the seams, I found a little chink and worked my disembodied awareness through it."

Thomas shared a look with a male witch standing behind the couch. The guy was about six three, blond, and built like a tank. Mira thought his name was Brandon or Brian or something.

"She's powerful," said Brandon or Brian.

"First, it's incredible that you managed to do that." Thomas shook his head in disbelief, sending his loose hair sliding over his shoulders. "But it's because you have the magick of air. It needs only the tiniest of cracks to squeeze through. Getting in physically is something altogether different."

Mira closed her eyes for a moment in frustration. "Stop telling me what *can't* be done, Thomas. If I can give the wardbreakers the exact location of the imperfection, can't they worry away at it until it rips?"

Thomas pushed a hand through his hair. "Andrea?"

A sleek redhead who was leaning against the foyer wall with her arms crossed spoke up. "Maybe."

"Mira, this is Andrea, our best wardweaver and breaker."

The redhead smiled. Mira let a ghost of a smile pass over her lips in return. She didn't have time to make new friends at the moment.

"Try it," said Thomas.

JACK STRODE DOWN THE CORRIDOR TOWARD THE office of the one person who would know where both Mira and Thomas had gone. He'd woken to a cold, empty bed and the knowledge that Thomas, Mira, and the top fifteen most powerful witches—except him—in the Coven were gone.

Anger made his magick restless, made sparks jump from finger to finger when he wasn't actively suppressing them.

Last night, Mira had kissed him, curled up against him to fall asleep . . . and then left him sometime this morning to put herself in Crane's way. He was sure of it.

He'd believed her yesterday when she'd told him that her meeting in Thomas's office had been of a personal nature. She'd told him that it had been about her family. She'd seemed depressed and subdued all evening, but he'd equated it to her nightmare. Now Jack suspected that for unknown reasons, Thomas had whisked Mira away from him.

Fear flicked through him. Was Thomas in league with Crane? *No.* He gave his head a sharp shake to rid himself of the notion. *Impossible.* But what other reason would cause Thomas to take Mira and leave him behind when he'd been the one tasked with keeping Mira safe?

He reached Ingrid's office and stood in the doorway, watching her shuffle papers on her desk.

She looked up, caught sight of him, and sighed.

"Tell me."

She shook her head. "I can't. I'm sorry."

He stalked to her. "Tell me."

"I can't tell you anything. You're wasting your time."

"Ingrid, I love her."

She looked away. "I'm under orders, Jack."

Jack took her by the shoulders and made her look up at him. "I love her, Ingrid," he repeated. "Don't do this to me, please."

Ingrid sighed, swore, and softened. "Stefan kidnapped the godmother to draw Mira out. They're holding her at Duskoff International. Mira went with the others to try and get her back." She paused. "What are you going to do?"

"I'm going to make sure she's safe. I'm killing anyone who gets in my way."

She nodded slowly. "That's a good plan. Simple. Brutal. Effective. Easy to remember."

"I think so."

"They didn't tell you because—Jack? Jack?"

He was already on his way to New York.

MIRA GOT A FASCINATING CRASH COURSE IN wardweaving and wardbreaking with Andrea, an earth witch. Apparently, only earth witches could construct or deconstruct a warding because it was all done with plants and potions and things that remained elusive mysteries to Mira.

She and Andrea set up operations in Thomas's kitchen, using a dozen small vials and beakers of various liquids and powders. It looked more complex than chemistry class.

They brought in a sample copy of the warding where Mira had found the rip from around the Duskoff Building, sort of like a metaphysical carbon copy, and set about trying different combinations of potions to tear it down. Mira helped by describing the texture of the fissure. She was the only one with that knowledge since she'd squeezed through it. Andrea and another earth witch named Devon worked to exploit it.

Finally, at 2 P.M. something in the kitchen went boom. Not a big boom, just a little one. Enough to make Mira's ears pop.

"Bingo," declared Andrea.

Thomas walked into the kitchen. "Damn, you're good, Andrea."

"Yes, I am. I deserve a raise," she answered, beaming. "I must say that Mira made it happen, though. Without the knowledge of the inconsistency and location of that tear, I couldn't have broken it."

"So, we're going then?" asked Mira impatiently.

"We're going in five minutes," said Thomas loudly as he pulled Mira to the side. Everyone jumped to get ready to leave. "Listen, about Jack. I think you should know before we go in that—"

She held up her hand to stop him. "I can't think about him right now. I feel bad about leaving him behind, and it's important I channel all my concentration on getting Annie out."

He pursed his lips together. "Okay. I just want you to know that you always have a place at the Coven. You always have a job with us. When this is over—"

"You mean if we don't get killed," she added.

He inclined his head a degree. "If we don't get killed, you have a home and a career waiting for you in Chicago."

She gave his shoulder a warm squeeze. "Thank you, Thomas. If we make it through today, I'll consider your offer."

"We could use someone like you. You've grown incredibly powerful over these last few weeks, so I'm not asking you just because you're family. I'm asking because soon you're going to be kicking some serious magickal ass, and I want you at my side."

Mira smiled and hugged him. "I'm glad you're my cousin, Thomas."

"*Now* I'm speaking as a cousin. I know I'd have to tie you up and lock you in the bathroom to keep you from coming with us and not even that would work because of your magick. So, I'm putting you with Brian," he pointed at the blond witch who was built like a tank. "And Craig, and Alex," he pointed at two more witches built like tanks.

"Thomas . . ."

"And James," he pointed to a good-looking witch with curly short-cropped red gold hair, glasses, and power that fairly radiated from him. James was an earth witch, she could feel it. A strong one.

She started to protest, but he put his finger to her lips. "No. Not a word. You left Jack behind. That means I get to say who you go in with. You don't leave their side. Do you understand?"

She nodded.

Thomas sighed. "I wish Jack was here."

Mira did, too, but she didn't say it.

THEY HAD THE ELEMENT OF SURPRISE UNTIL THEY were actually in the building. When the warding broke, all the witches in the Duskoff Building knew it.

Mira clapped her hands over her ears when Thomas and Andrea used the potion to dissolve the warding. It twanged like a heavy cable on a bridge snapping when it went.

Thomas had taken fifteen of the best and brightest from the Coven, but more witches had joined them in New York. They all had converged at Thomas's apartment during the day, trickling in by twos and threes. He'd broken them into groups and given them instructions before they'd left to break the warding. While they were busy breaching the Duskoff's defenses, the witches left his apartment piecemeal so they wouldn't attract attention.

Even though their cover was blown, Thomas sent in witches with the specific task of taking down the building's surveillance, so that Crane and his minions wouldn't know exactly where in the building any of them were located.

The group that went in right after that group had orders to engage the warlocks who would rush forward to defend their building. Those witches were their first line of defense . . . well, *offense* in this case. The Duskoff were on the defensive now.

Mira liked that a lot.

The rest of the Coven witches entered from several different points on the ground floor after Thomas had confirmation the security cameras were down.

Mira and her men entered from a side door that led into a long corridor with many doors leading off on either side into offices and meeting rooms. Their shoes were silent on the tan marble floor, though Mira was sure everyone could probably hear how loud her heart was beating as they progressed.

The good thing was that the Duskoff had driven their only air witch to suicide, so at least they couldn't tell where Mira and her guards were remotely. The bad thing was that Mira wasn't experienced enough yet her in her abilities to send her consciousness out while she was nervous and distracted and therefore could not tell where *they* were remotely.

Another good thing was that this battle would take place within the walls of the Duskoff Building, well away from the awareness of any non-magickals.

They progressed down the corridor as quietly as they could. Their goal was to make it to the fortieth floor. That's where Annie was located.

Noise came from further down the corridor. Mira and her guards all ducked into empty rooms, but no one came down the hallway. Mira cautiously peered past the doorframe. The sounds seemed to be coming from the main lobby at the end of the corridor.

Well, hell. They had to go through there to get to the main stairwell or the elevator.

The witch beside her, James, crept out of the room and inched down the hallway. He waved them out behind him when he deemed it safe. Together they made it to the end of the corridor. From the lobby came loud voices, yells, and the sound of a fight already underway.

Mira crouched down and peered around the corner of the hallway where it opened into the lobby. Coven witches had engaged the warlocks, but were getting their metaphysical asses kicked. They needed help. Plus . . .

"We have to get through them to get to Annie," Mira whispered to James. Was there an edge of panic in her voice? *Shit.*

"Then let's go," answered James eagerly. His magick seemed to pour off him in waves of steady, crushing power. Mira could tell he was chomping at the bit to let all that luscious, rich magick off its leash.

Mira drew a steadying breath. They could do this. *She* could do this. For Annie's sake, and her own, she had to.

She wouldn't go in cowering, afraid. She'd go in there like the powerful witch she'd become and put the fear of the Goddess in them.

It was time to make an entrance.

"Okay. Everyone ready?" she whispered to the men beside her.

Brian and James nodded. She couldn't see the others, but no one objected.

Her stomach swarmed with nervous butterflies, but underneath that lay Mira's absolute resolve to get Annie out of there alive.

Mira closed her eyes and pulled a thread of her magick, a sizable one, and readied it. Around her she heard and felt the men get their magick ready too.

She rose from her crouching position and stepped around the corner, raising a tempest along with her. Wind rose gently but became stronger fast. It ripped her long black coat and blew her hair around her head until she probably looked like Medusa. Adrenaline surged through her body, but she put everything she had into maintaining an aura of dangerous confidence. She even swaggered a little.

There were about thirteen warlocks in the lobby and only a couple of Coven witches left standing.

Once the wind kicked up, all eyes turned to them. She couldn't do the tornado trick like she'd done in Jack's apartment because the effort might leave her unconscious, and also because she couldn't be sure she wouldn't hurt any of their own people.

The warlocks advanced on them. Her guards engaged, and fighting began around her, but she never faltered in her forward march. Walking toward them, she lifted her hand and tossed a warlock backward to hit a wall when she felt him raise a strand of power. Another tried to throw fire at her, but she sucked the air out of it like Jack had taught her. One of the warlocks doused her in water. She felt it grow colder and colder, but she raised a warming wind around her, drying her skin, hair, and clothes before the warlock could freeze her.

Mira kept advancing on them, but now they were retreating. One by one, feeling her power rising within her, she tossed the warlocks backward to get them out of their way.

She almost felt giddy. Now she understood the power of air. No one could defeat air. It was too vast, too supple, and easily managed by the witch who wielded it.

Who could stand against her?

No one, that's who.

New power skittered over her skin—dark and strong. Earth magick. A spell woven from the magick of the earth herself. A strand released itself from a curvy, diminutive blonde warlock to her right. Mira turned just in time to block her blast of energy with a wall of air, dissipating the spell before it reached her.

"Come on, guys," she shouted, elated. "Is that all you've got? I could do this all day!"

Something hit her throat. She gagged and reached up to feel a pointy object sticking out of her neck.

TWENTY-TWO

OH, THAT WAS NEVER A GOOD THING.

Sharp pain washed through her veins, bleeding quickly into a hazy, numbed nothingness. Suddenly, she felt wrapped in cotton, her mind, her body . . . everything. The wind in the room ceased, and she heard people cheering and clapping as if from a distance.

Mira collapsed to her knees, trying to pull another thread. Her mind felt fuzzy. Thinking was like trying to pick up a grain of sand with swollen fingers.

Without her air magick to shield them, the Coven witches she'd come in with were unprotected. There was a strained moment of silence after the applause before chaos let loose around her.

A man walked toward her. The cacophony surrounding her faded until she could hear only his leather shoes on the polished floor. They seemed to echo in her mind. He stopped in front of her, and she glanced up with effort.

Stefan.

He walked around her once more, humming the song "Behind Blue Eyes," and obviously enjoying her helplessness.

Oh, please.

Rage bubbled up within her, but it was impotent. She couldn't reach her magick. He'd drugged her with something that made it impossible for her to access her seat. She felt numb, slow. She couldn't move her limbs. Even now her ability to move her head was fading. Mira tried to speak, and only an incomprehensible gurgle came from her throat.

Stefan laughed low. It was a beautiful laugh, like rich velvet whispering over her skin. "Did you think that air magick was invincible, *ma jolie sorcière?*" He clucked his tongue. "A witch is only as good as her ability to wield her power. That means even a witch such as you can be defeated. You gave us a nice surprise today, however. I will give you kudos for that."

He resumed his humming, allowing her to witness what was happening in the lobby. Around her the Coven witches fell to the Duskoff one by one. Craig went down. Then Brian. Then James.

Rock. Paper. Scissors.

Stefan forced her to watch it all to the irritating sound of his circling footsteps and his little song.

Her thought process seemed sluggish and confused, though her mind seemed to be growing a little clearer with every passing moment. Even though she wanted to, she couldn't fight when Stefan pulled her to her feet and picked her up, cradling her in his arms like a lover. Her skin tried to get up and walk away without her at the intimate touch of him against her body.

"I do not like it when people try to hurt William Crane, Mira," Stefan whispered as he bore her through the lobby toward the elevator. "He is the only father I know. Therefore, I understand your desperation to help your godmother. I do not fault you for it."

Well, that was a load off her mind.

They traveled up to the fortieth floor, and he carried her down the empty corridors of Duskoff International, past the gleaming silver and gold of the offices and receptionist areas, and into a long boardroom. A wet bar and mirror lined one side and a long table with swivel chairs dominated the center. The windows looked out on the New York City skyline.

A man sat in a chair on the far end of the table. The older gentleman turned as Stefan entered the room. Mira caught a glimpse of his face before Stefan laid her on top of the table.

Crane.

"What's all the fuss about?" demanded Crane.

"Thomas and his witches surprised us. They managed to break the warding and enter the building ahead of our scheduled meeting. Our people still fight them, but it matters no longer. I have brought you the witch you covet, Father."

William Crane struggled to rise and make his way around the long table to look down at her. His eyes were blue in his craggy, ashen face. They were like Jack's, that distinctive pale hue you didn't see just anywhere.

He wrinkled his nose. "Pretty, but she stinks of my son. His magick is all over her."

Her mind fumbled for a moment. *His son?* Did he mean Stefan? But Stefan was standing right beside him. Why talk about him as though he wasn't in the room?

Crane leaned toward her. His breath smelled of sickness. "You've been in Jack's bed, haven't you? Your skin has rubbed against his numerous times. I can tell." He touched his nose. "One of my special abilities, see, girl? I can scent out magick like a bloodhound."

Realization slammed into her. She felt like she'd just been thrown through a plate glass window. Shards of brutal truth glittered around her, ran her through and made her bleed.

Jack was Crane's estranged son. Lord and Lady.

Things made more sense now. The ring she'd found in his apartment bearing the initial *C*, the way he'd never looked her in the eye when he spoke of his family, and why he always appeared uncomfortable when discussing Crane and Stefan.

Apparently, she wasn't very good at masking her expression because Crane laughed. "He didn't tell you I'm his father, did he? Jack has always been a little ashamed of his family."

Stefan's cell phone rang and he stepped away to answer it, leaving Crane peering down at her. "Don't take it too hard, dear. Jack sleeps with all the pretty ones, I hear. Never gets close enough to any of them to tell them all his secrets. He was there, you know, the day your mother died."

Dread settled in the pit of her stomach.

Crane nodded. "I remember that day well, because it's the last time I was able to call a demon." He frowned. "I don't even remember why we had to raise it." He scratched his head, thinking, and then waved his hand in dismissal.

Stefan snapped his cell phone closed and tucked it back into his inside suit jacket pocket. "Thomas and his witches are still in the building, but David is bringing the others here so we can complete the ritual. There is no sense in wasting our time."

"Fine. We'll have the demon for a while. It can take care of Thomas and his witches. We'll tell it it's a perk." He gave a harsh laugh and wavered on his feet.

Stefan put a hand to Crane's elbow to steady him. "After it takes care of you, Father."

Yuck. Stefan really did care about this monster. Monsters fathering monsters.

Did that make Jack a monster?

No. Of course not.

Still, why hadn't Jack seen fit to tell her this bit of monumental news? He'd lied to her, concealed his true self from her, and betrayed her trust . . . just as Ben had done.

Tears trickled from the corner of her eyes, but she lacked the ability to wipe them away. She was done with men for the rest of her life. It would be an easy oath to keep, since it looked like her life would be over in about fifteen minutes.

"Where was I?" continued Crane. He wandered over to pour himself a drink at the bar. Crane and Stefan both seemed totally unconcerned that the Coven had infiltrated their building. "Oh, yes. Jack watched your mother die. Hmmm, yes. She lost the will to live after your father went the day before her." Crane shook his head. "It was very sad, truth be told. I felt badly for her."

"Tell her about taking them, Father. I love that story," said Stefan from his place beside her. He reached out and caught one of her teardrops from the edge of her eye and let it dangle on his fingertip for a moment before it fell.

Mira felt like she was in some horror story, paralyzed and alive while everyone around her thought her dead. And they were just about to slip her into a coffin and bury her that way.

"They were hard to kidnap," Crane said after he'd taken a sip of his cocktail. "You can be proud of them on that score. You have to be very committed to go after an air witch of any talent, and we went after two at the same time. It was one of the Duskoff's finest hours." His voice held a great amount of pride.

"Your parents killed ten of my best witches before we finally got them into custody. Your father almost died during the kidnapping. He was burned very badly while we tried to subdue him and your mother. In the end we could barely keep your father alive until the ritual. He was a powerful witch. Enough power in that one to open three portals." He tipped the glass toward her before draining it. "Your mother too."

"I've sensed the power in this one," added Stefan, smoothing his fingers through her hair. "She has inherited their ability, though she lacks their control."

"How long do those drugs last?" Crane asked, eyeing her with a little trepidation.

"Long enough for us to perform the ritual, Father, *ne t'inquietes pas*."

Mira felt nauseous. She wasn't sure if it was from having to listen to Crane talk about the murder of her parents like a fond memory, or if it was because the drugs in her system were wearing off. Unobtrusively, she wiggled a toe in her shoe.

The drugs *were* wearing off. Mira felt a moment of triumph. Maybe Stefan had mistaken the dosage, or the drugs reacted slightly differently in her system.

"Jack watched the whole of the ritual that killed your mother, but he ran before the demon was birthed." Crane grimaced. "I thought it was a sign of weakness, but it turns out the boy wasn't weak at all. His failings were my own. If I'd raised him differently, he would've turned out fine."

The door opened, and several warlocks entered with three gagged and bound witches in tow. Last to come through the door was Annie.

Mira was able to move a little more now, a fact she would closely guard. Incrementally, so no one would notice, she moved her head to watch Annie's captor lead her through the room.

Annie's salt-and-pepper hair had none of its normal luster, and her face appeared pinched with pain. Her gaze brushed Mira's before the warlock leading her plopped her into a chair on the other side of the room, making her grimace in pain and her face go white. The burns along her upper arms and the exposed skin of her back looked angry, irritated, undoubtedly infected. Her godmother's gaze locked with hers across the room and didn't budge.

A moment later another group of warlocks came in. "Sir, the Coven witches are all over the building," said a small, greasy looking man with a bad toupee. He sounded worried.

"Yes, let's not waste any more time," answered Crane. "Stefan."

Stefan scooped her up into his arms while the other warlocks positioned the three bound and gagged witches in the empty area at the end of the room near the bar. The witches all struggled against their captors and were wrestled into submission and forced to kneel. They went submissive, their faces slack. Had they been drugged too? Mira wasn't sure.

No visible circle marked the floor, but Mira sensed a metaphysical one. Earth magick signaled north, south, east, and west.

Stefan began to ease her down to lie on her side in the position of north.

Knowing she had only this small window of opportunity, she pulled her ace. When he'd laid her down, she shot to her knees and bolted forward into Stefan's waist. Her muscles felt like rubber, and she had less ability to move than she'd supposed. All the same, she knocked the French bastard back a few steps before falling forward onto her face.

The ace hadn't really been much of an ace.

The warlocks in the room snickered.

"Shut up," Stefan snarled at them. "She has spirit and a will to live. Give her the respect she deserves. *Merde*."

Stefan braced her shoulders, and she tried to fight him as he pulled her upward. Her muscles just wouldn't cooperate. Another few minutes and the stupid drug would wear off, but she sensed she didn't have that kind of time.

No more minutes for her.

"The tranquilizer did not work very well on you, did it, *ma chéri*?" he murmured into her ear. "I was not sure how much to use on a witch like you. *Bon*, no matter."

He plopped her back down in position, and she panted from the exertion of trying to fight her body's paralysis. She looked at the other three witches in the circle as Stefan backed away. There were two women and one man. The man was perhaps in his early forties. His hair was clipped so close to his head she couldn't tell if it was gray or blond.

The two women were both brunette and appeared similar in face and body, sisters perhaps. The Duskoff sure did like to take families. Maybe they'd been a two-for special.

Crane began snapping orders at everyone to get into position. "Hurry up," he groused. "Once we get the spell started, we'll be safe. No Coven witch will be able to penetrate the barrier of the magick."

Oh, shit. There went their last chance at rescue.

The two women fought their bonds, their wide eyes glancing around the room, still hoping, perhaps, for a last-minute reprieve. It wouldn't come. The man had gone incredibly still and knelt with his eyes downcast, resigned to his fate.

Near them, the warlocks organized into a separate circle to their left and the chanting began. It was a foreign language, nothing that Mira could place. It sounded and felt old, powerful, and very, very dangerous.

At first their voices were separate, like a badly timed chorus. Little by little, they merged and became one single voice.

The magick rose in the air and soothed her. It felt soft against her skin, smelled like rich vanilla or sugar cookies baking. It was nice, nothing to be feared. Mira relaxed into it, suspecting it was an illusion to make her passive, to allow the warlocks to rape her, but, strangely, she didn't mind.

Then the magick changed, became aggressive.

The power shifted, prickling over her skin. The chanting became louder. The comforting, pacifying magick had been a lure for this more powerful trap, and now all the witches were locked inside it.

Mira grimaced. This is what her mother had felt, what her father had endured. This was the power that had killed them.

The magick pulled her to her knees like a puppet, and the texture of the power changed further. Now it tasted like a fine wine on her tongue, filled her nostrils with an old, faintly musty smell. The flavor of the magick held the nutty hint of earth infused with a clear, light note of water, shot through with threads of spicy fire.

The magick was mostly of earth and felt like bottomless earthen fissures and high mountain peaks. It felt rich and fathomless and so, so powerful.

The sound of the chanting grew louder and became one long drone in her mind, each word no longer separate. The prickling discomfort became actual pain. All of the witches in the circle gasped. Mira's spine arched and her head snapped back as she tried to endure the sensation in her near paralysis.

The magick caught her, caught all of them and held them in thrall. The expressions of everyone in the room appeared rapturous as the chanting intensified. It grew louder, fading into one long hum of power.

Vibration filled her body, gentle at first and then stronger and stronger until she *hurt*. It wasn't any ordinary kind of hurt, it was hurt with a capital *H*. It infiltrated every pore of her body and her mind with an intensity that made her wish to pass out, but apparently she would not be allowed that luxury.

It was the feeling of her magick being extracted from her.

She was dying.

Images of her life flashed before her eyes, just like they always said happened at the moment a person died. They flickered through her mind so fast she could only focus on a few of them.

She saw Annie smiling at her as she picked out library books when she'd been a child. The small burst of rain in Annie's backyard. She saw images from high school, prom night, and graduation. She saw Ben, their wedding, the day their divorce was final.

Then flashes of Jack. Jack smiling at her. Jack leaning in to kiss her. Waking up in the morning and turning over to find Jack tangled half naked in the sheets beside her.

The *hurt* flared brilliantly through her body, and all the images disappeared.

Everything disappeared.

TWENTY-THREE

❧

JACK TRIED TO OPEN THE FROSTED DOUBLE GLASS doors of Duskoff International and found them locked. The warding was broken, so he knew Mira and Thomas were inside and the alarm system was likely off thanks to the Coven, not that he cared if it wasn't. He waited until no one was near him on the street and used his magick to melt the outside of the door where the lock and bolt were located, and cautiously stepped inside.

Bodies lay strewn on the marble floor of the lobby, the grisly result of a magickal fight. The windows fronting the building were also frosted, shielding the interior from normal eyes, but it wouldn't be a good thing for a non-magickal to wander in through the doors from the street, so Jack welded the lock shut from the inside.

He made his way through the lobby, searching for Thomas, Mira, or a conscious Coven witch, but aside from already fallen bodies, he could find no sign of anyone. Clearly, he was late to the party.

"Damn you, Thomas," Jack muttered. He flipped open his cell phone and tried to call him, but no one answered.

Knowing it was his only shot in a building this huge, he went to the elevators. He leaned against the wall across from the bank of doors and watched, anxiety for Mira and anger gnawing a hole in his stomach.

Nothing.

Then finally the display showed movement for two of the elevators. One went to the twenty-second floor, the other to the thirty-eighth. It was a toss-up. Impatiently, he pressed the Down button to call a car and hit the twenty-second floor.

The muzak in the elevator was an orchestral version of the song "Witchy Woman." Right now having to listen to piped-in music, especially some warlock's idea of a cutsie inside joke, made Jack want to hit something. Jack planned to do just that.

Finally, the doors opened on the twenty-second floor, revealing Thomas and a handful of Coven witches. The unconscious bodies of several warlocks lay collapsed on the floor at their feet. The Coven witches had obviously taken a beating in the lobby. Jack was encouraged to see the Coven had won this little skirmish, at least.

That knowledge did little to ease his temper.

Thomas turned to see him standing just outside the elevator. "Jack," he said in surprise.

Jack rushed him, grabbing him by his shirt front and slamming him back against the receptionist's desk. "Where is Mira?" he snarled into his face.

Several Coven witches grabbed Jack and pulled him off Thomas. He fought them, but they held him fast by his upper arms, allowing their boss to straighten. "There are a number of Coven witches in the building now. She's with our strongest."

"Have you seen the carnage in the lobby, Monahan?" He yelled it.

"We're all on the same side here, Jack. Calm down."

His gut said Mira was in danger. "Crane has her."

"How do you know that?"

"I can *feel* it," he growled. He wanted to punch Thomas bloody for leaving him behind. Jack shrugged off the men holding him. "Bang-up job you've done here, Thomas," he muttered and sought one of the still barely conscious warlocks sprawled on the floor.

No time to waste on small talk, he showed the earth warlock a ball of very hot fire. The man's groggy eyes widened. "Where would they do the ritual?"

The warlock said nothing. His lips moved mutely. The man was obviously too drained to call any power in his own defense. All the better.

Jack raised his eyebrows. "Don't think I won't burn you."

Something in Jack's expression made the warlock stammer out, "F-fortieth floor. Conference floor."

Jack let the man slump back to the floor, extinguished the fire, and turned back to the elevator. Thomas and the other Coven witches followed him.

As soon as the doors opened on the fortieth floor, cloying power rushed in to fill the elevator. It smoothed along their skin like black silk, seductive and dangerously lulling. All the men in the elevator groaned under the crushing weight of it.

It was familiar to Jack.

The sound of the chanting filled his ears. He remembered that sound and the feel of the magick tickling through his mind and over his body. It dropped the Coven witches to the floor of the elevator, but Thomas and Jack struggled out before the door could shut on them again.

He glanced back at the closed elevator car. *Great.* Apparently, they were going to have to take on a whole room full of power-rich warlocks on their own.

Jack blinked and pushed through the nauseatingly strong power. He made his way through the lobby and down a polished corridor on the heels of the sound. Jack staggered and lurched his way to the room where they had Mira under the weight of it. Thomas followed him, stumbling and tripping.

He lunged into the room through a sheer force of will and caught himself on the back of a chair before he collapsed, but no one even noticed him. Thomas wobbled in after him and fell to his knees. The Duskoff had counted on the magick being their watchdog. They hadn't assumed any witch would be able to travel through it, but he and Thomas had the strength because of their deep love for Mira.

Mira.

She knelt in a circle with three other witches, all of them hanging suspended on their knees in the magick of the circle. Her expression was blank, her eyes closed. Her face appeared sheet-white, her lips and eyelids purplish. The sight of her like that made adrenaline surge through him and denial scream through his mind.

No, she couldn't already be dead. Gods, no. It simply wasn't possible.

"Help her," sobbed a woman tied to a nearby chair.

Annie? He glanced at her right before a surge in the magick nearly brought him to his knees.

Like velvet, the power rubbed along his bare skin. Within the magick he could pick out a strand of Mira, that distinctive scent of fresh linen and lemon filling his senses.

In that moment, Jack understood what he hadn't as a child. The power filling the room was the raped magick of the witches in the circle—the more powerful the witches in the circle, the more potent the "recipe" of the magick.

This mix was pretty damn heady.

Jack helped Thomas to his feet, and together they made their way to the end of the room where William Crane and the highest of the Duskoff stood chanting. The men and women in the circle had looks of beatific joy on their faces. They had no idea anyone else was even in the room.

Jack shoved Crane hard, breaking the warlock's circle, but the chanting didn't stop. Crane stumbled and fell to the floor, taken by surprise. He flipped over and looked up at Jack with disbelief on his face.

Thomas yanked warlocks from the circle and either threw them across the room, or punched them. The chanting stammered to a halt, the powerful magicks eased, and the more comforting sounds of a fight filled the room.

Of course, he and Thomas were outnumbered thirteen to two.

The witches in the circle all slumped to the side with their eyes closed, let down like puppets on strings as the heavy magick dissipated. All of them appeared unconscious.

That was the best-case scenario.

"Jack?" breathed Crane, coming out of his stupor.

"Long time no see, Dad," he snarled before he grasped him by his lapels and pulled him up from the floor.

Someone grabbed his shoulder and spun him around, making him lose his hold on Crane. He had half a second for Stefan's face to register before a fist connected solidly with his cheek. A crack of pain echoed through Jack's head, making him stagger back.

Jack held on to the edge of the boardroom table, his head ringing. Stefan had a good punch on him. The warm glow of fire magick rose right before Stefan launched a ball of it at him. Jack lunged out of the way. It hit the leg of the table, setting it ablaze.

Coven witches swarmed into the room and magick flared hot against his skin as they began to wield it against the still recovering warlocks. One of them doused the table with water, making it sizzle and steam. It was no one's interests to burn the building down right now.

Unwilling to use his fire magick in such close quarters and with the witches in the circle unconscious and vulnerable, Jack launched himself at Stefan.

They rolled on the floor, punching each other. Jack got a

few satisfying hits in, and took a couple as well, before a new power began to swirl around him. It whispered over his skin at first, growing in intensity.

He and Stefan stopped trying to take each other's faces off. Everything in the room halted under that eerie fluctuation of the magick in the room. A breeze tickled his face, and he sensed Mira's distinctive power. The scent of clean linen and lemon filled the room, much stronger than he'd ever experienced it.

The breeze became a wind. Jack struggled to separate himself from Stefan and looked up to see Mira standing in her place in the demon circle.

She stood with her head thrown back and her eyes closed. Wind buffeted her coat around her body, sent her hair flying around her head.

Jack and everyone else who wasn't already standing struggled to their feet, their eyes on the witch who radiated so much strength. Her lips peeled back from her teeth in a grimace of pain.

"Mira?" he asked tentatively, taking a step toward her.

Without looking at him, she held up a hand to stop him. He halted in his tracks.

Several things happened nearly at the same time. Fire from his left side flared magnificently. Jack turned to see Crane kindling a white-hot fire ball and throwing it straight at his face at close range. Jack threw his hands up to shield himself, knowing it was too late. Suddenly, the fire was gone.

And so was Crane.

Glass broke. A man's terrified scream filled the air, fading into the distance. At nearly the same time, the room filled with the sound of bodies hitting the surrounding walls, the room awash in flying men and women.

Silence.

Then groaning. Cursing.

Jack glanced around. Mira had thrown all the warlocks,

just the warlocks, against the walls. His gaze went to the window, understanding that Crane had been propelled through it. Shattered glass glittered on the expensive tile and cold winter air rushed in to chill the boardroom.

Mira was crumpled on the floor, but conscious. She pushed herself into a sitting position, holding her head. Her gaze locked with his.

Mira had killed William Crane.

Jack shifted his gaze and stared transfixed for a moment at the broken window. William Crane, the man he hadn't thought of as his father in a very long time, was dead.

"Where's Stefan?" Thomas's voice sounded sharp in the sudden absence of the magick.

Jack broke his fixation on the broken window and glanced around the room at the witches and the warlocks. The warlocks were peeling themselves up from the floor. No one was fighting. Everyone seemed stunned by what had happened.

Stefan was nowhere in the room.

His gaze met Mira's and held. She'd struggled to her feet and looked ready to cry.

Thomas rattled off orders to the Coven witches to go find Stefan, but Jack was done. In several wide strides, he caught Mira in his arms and held her tight, kissing every part of her body that he could find. "Are you all right?" he asked between kisses.

She nodded.

He cupped her face in his hands and kissed her lips, tasting salt from the tears running down her cheeks. She wrapped her arms around him and deepened the kiss.

He was so happy she was safe that the anger he'd felt at her leaving him behind and endangering herself disappeared. All that mattered was that she was out of harm's way.

Gods, it felt so good to have her back in his arms. He would never let her go again.

Mira broke the kiss slowly. She stayed in his arms for a

moment but would not meet his eyes. Gaze downcast, she licked her lips. "Thank you for coming, Jack," she said. Then she raised her eyes and whispered, "I know what you hid from me. I know all of it."

Shock and dread jolted through him at the resolute look in her eyes. He'd forgotten about all that in his haste to see her safe.

She took one step back from him, out of his arms. It was like a chasm opening up between them. She gave him one last lingering look and then rushed to her godmother's side.

"WE HANDLE OUR OWN INJURED," SAID THOMAS.

Mira shook her head. "No. Not my godmother. I want someone to call an ambulance for her right now. *Right now*, Thomas." She wouldn't take anything less than that for Annie.

He stared at her a moment, but she was wearing her don't-mess-with-me face. She felt a lot more comfortable wearing that one these days.

"Adam, take Ms. Weber back to my apartment. Tell the doorman to call an ambulance," Thomas said.

"Thank you."

Adam, a fire witch who had the body of a weight lifter and a nose that had been broken more than once, helped Annie to her feet with a gentleness that seemed at odds with his obvious physical strength. Annie stopped in front of her, and Mira cupped her godmother's face in her hands and kissed her cheek. "I love you, Annie."

Tears streamed down Annie's cheeks. "I love you, too, kiddo."

"Now go. I'll be right behind you."

Adam helped her out the door.

Mira could feel Jack's gaze on her back. She stared at Thomas, struggling not to turn around and go to him.

"Mira," Thomas said. "Jack is a good man. He can't help who fathered him."

She went stiff. She shifted her gaze so she looked through Thomas, instead of at him. "I don't care about that, Thomas. I don't care who his father was or that when he was a little kid he saw my mother die. But I do care that he lied to me about it," she said tonelessly. "I love him, Thomas, but he lied to me."

Thomas sighed. "It's my fault. I asked him not to tell you who he was. Thought it would interfere with the job if you knew. I never thought you two would fall in love."

"And he obeyed you blindly. I don't accept that. He should have told me." Mira pushed past her cousin without looking at Jack and left the room to follow Adam and Annie.

At Thomas's building the doorman called an ambulance. She knelt beside the couch in the lobby, where Adam had helped Annie sit down.

Annie fisted her shaking hands in her lap. "I thought maybe you hated me."

"Hate you?" She covered Annie's hands with her own. "I could never hate you, Annie. You've been a mother to me my whole life."

"But I kept things from you."

"You did what my parents asked of you. You're loyal. When everything started to go down, you did your best to protect me." She shook her head, her eyes filling with tears. "I don't hate you, Annie. I love you."

The ambulance pulled up to the curb and the paramedics rushed in, tending to Annie. Adam told them that she'd received the burns from a space heater incident gone awry. The paramedics looked askance at that, but they didn't ask questions, they just bundled Annie into the back of the ambulance.

When Mira tried to climb in the back with her, the paramedic stopped her. "You'll have to follow in a car. We're taking her to Mercy General." He slammed the door.

The ambulance drove down the street. Mira watched until it turned the corner. She felt Jack come up beside her before she glimpsed him out of the corner of her eye. They stood for a moment in silence.

Every part of her body seemed to ache from the knowledge that he'd deliberately misled her. He'd concealed and twisted the truth.

"I expected you to break my heart in the end, Jack, but I never thought it would happen this way," she whispered. She turned and walked down the street and didn't look back.

TWENTY-FOUR

❧

MIRA SLUNG PLATES OF TURKEY, GRAVY, AND mashed potatoes, the special of the day. Lunchtime at Mike's Diner was in full swing, and Mira should've hit her groove by now.

But Mira doubted she'd ever again find her groove in the diner.

That was gone, along with a wicked, gorgeous, and ultimately deceitful blue-eyed man.

Mira dropped her order off, refilled drinks, and went to clear off a table. Her body went through the motions because her mind was a million miles away.

Annie had been released from the hospital two days after she'd been admitted, and they'd flown home from New York. Mira had gone back to work at Mike's the next day, needing something to occupy her in a major way. They'd hired a part-time waitress to cover her while she'd been gone, but Mike had still given her old job back without a moment's hesitation.

Not that she was enjoying it much.

The world had changed in her eyes during the last few weeks, and she had changed with it. She no longer found the tentative satisfaction she'd once known at the diner. Not now, after she'd tapped her power and found her magick. That made everything else seem awfully pale in comparison.

Or maybe she was just depressed.

Mira picked up a tub of dirty dishes and carted it to the back. After she dropped it off for the dishwasher, she stopped to wash her hands. Plucking a clean dish towel from the cabinet near the sink, she walked out behind the counter to survey the half-full restaurant. She caught sight of the TV on the corner platform above the counter and did a double take. The afternoon news was on and the picture showed the Duskoff Building. She grabbed the remote by the coffeemaker and increased the volume.

Police are still investigating the mysterious death of billionaire W. Anderson Crane, the CEO and president of Duskoff International. Last Saturday, he fell through a window of the Duskoff Building in New York City and plummeted forty stories to his death. Police have no witnesses and no leads in the case; however, suicide is suspected. His adopted son, Stefan Faucheux, reportedly revealed that Crane suffered from advanced bone cancer. Crane was not expected to survive and had purportedly expressed suicidal intentions. . . .

She muted it and put the remote back down, shuddering with the memories of the shattering glass, the scream, and the silence. It was only now that she was beginning to deal with the fact that she'd murdered someone. Even though it had been a case of self-defense, she'd still taken a life.

Would Stefan come after her for what she'd done? She'd seen and felt how powerful he was, and Mira wasn't sure she could stand against him if he did.

The tinkle of the diner door opening caught her attention. The familiar large form of Jack McAllister filled the doorframe. He searched the diner and caught sight of her standing there in the act of drying her hands on the dish towel.

This was the last thing she needed. Sighing, she threw the towel onto the counter.

He looked magnificent, as always, though a bit worn. Stubble darkened his jawline. He wore a pair of jeans, black boots, a black sweater, and his navy peacoat.

Jack took a booth in her section as luck would have it. Or perhaps he'd been watching from his car before he came in so he'd know where to sit.

Mira took care of all her other customers before walking to Jack's booth with a pot of coffee and a cup in her hands.

She set the cup down and filled it, then tossed one packet of sugar down beside it. She didn't have to ask how he took his coffee. "What are you doing here?"

"I came to apologize."

She raised an eyebrow. "Really? You came to apologize for *lying* to me?"

"I didn't lie. I simply concealed some things."

"Yeah, that would be another way to say you *lied*, Jack," she retorted furiously.

"You're right. I lied." He rubbed his hand over his chin. "I made a mistake, and now I'm paying for it. I just wanted to come and apologize. I know you must hate me now that you know who my father was and I just wanted—"

She set the pot down on the table with a clunk, making coffee slosh back and forth. The family in the next booth over gave her a curious look.

Mira leaned in toward Jack. "I don't care who your father was! *You* were the one I fell for. Your parentage means less than nothing to me. What *does* matter is that you didn't see fit to tell me about it. You didn't trust me enough to reveal that very pertinent bit of information."

They stared at each other for a long moment.

"I care about you," she whispered, feeling her eyes well

up with tears. She blinked them back. No way was she going to let him see her cry. "But I went through this with Ben, and I can't do it again."

She picked up the coffeepot and walked away. When she turned back, Jack was gone. He'd left his coffee untouched.

SHE OPENED THE FRONT DOOR OF HER APARTMENT and tried to turn on the light in the hallway, but the switch flipped on and off, dead.

"Great," she groused, pushing her way through the door with heavy plastic grocery bags hanging from her arms and cutting off her circulation. She slammed the door closed with her foot.

Thomas had sent her a check to pay her bills and rent. She'd mailed her payments yesterday, but that hadn't stopped the electricity company from declaring her late and shutting off her power, apparently.

It was cold in the apartment, too.

"Double great," she muttered.

After tripping and knocking her knee against the kitchen chair and cursing a blue streak, she managed to deposit her bags on the counter. She fished out a few emergency candles from her junk drawer and lit one. By that guttering light, she proceeded to find and light more. Soon her apartment was light enough for her to function without bruising herself.

By candle glow, she put the groceries away. Ripping into a bag of sugar cookies, she snatched one and sank onto her kitchen chair with her coat still on. Munching the cookie, she stared at the flickering flame of the candle on her small table.

Why did he have to come and see her today? She'd been doing fine—okay, she'd been pretending like she'd been doing fine—until he showed up.

She sighed. He probably hadn't told her about being Crane's son because he was ashamed, or because he thought she'd hate him for it. Maybe she'd been too hard on him? Plus, Thomas had said he'd been under orders not to tell her.

Just like Annie had been under instructions from her parents not to tell her about her magick. She'd forgiven Annie, so why not Jack?

The gooshy, hopelessly in-love part of her wanted to use those reasons to forgive Jack for his deception . . . but she just couldn't let Jack off the hook so easily. Deliberate deceit hit her in a very tender spot. Loving him as much as she did only made it hurt that much worse.

Mira didn't care who'd fathered him. That was beside the point. If he had known her a little better, trusted her a little more, he would've, *should've*, realized that.

Her magick stirred restlessly in her center. She put her hand between her breasts. It had been a few days since she'd used any magick, and it acted like a puppy needing a walk. She pulled a thread and allowed a very soft warm breeze, not strong enough to blow out her candles, to waft through the room. She closed her eyes and enjoyed it stirring her hair.

She was not the person she'd been when she'd left this place with Jack a month ago. Now she was no longer happy to stay in this apartment, work as a waitress, and struggle through college for a job she wasn't sure she wanted.

Her magick was a part of her, and she wanted to use it every day if she could. Thomas had offered her a job at the Coven, and once she got a handle on her emotions where Jack was concerned, she would take it.

The soft, warm, barely breeze heated her apartment enough for Mira to take off her coat. She filled her sink up with water. Life went on. She had men to get over and dishes to wash.

Someone knocked on her door, making her jump. Mira

closed her eyes, sensing who had come to visit her right away.

Here she was at the start of everything again, except the man at her door this time had the capability to wound her heart instead of her body.

She fought herself a moment, her hands plunged deeply into the soapy water, and then sighed in defeat. Mira grabbed a dish towel and dried her hands on the way to the door.

"Mira," Jack said as soon as she opened the door. "I messed up."

"You can say that again." She leaned her head against the doorframe, fisting the dish towel in her hands, and gazed up at him. He looked miserable. Ben had never looked that miserable, that repentant.

And Ben had lied for far longer and about far worse things.

Had she overreacted because of her relationship with Ben? Her emotions were so jumbled, she just didn't know. She couldn't keep the emotion out of her eyes, off her face. She wasn't any good at faking that stuff, so she knew he could see her hurt and vulnerability.

"I'm so sorry. I need you. I need you like I need to breathe. I'm here to ask your forgiveness."

She hesitated a moment, then turned and strode into her apartment, leaving the door open behind her. She went to sit in her tiny living room. The door closed, and Jack's footsteps sounded in the short hallway.

He leaned against the wall separating the living room and hallway and looked miserable. "Can we start over somewhere near the beginning? Do you think you can give me another chance?"

"Jack—" She started and then stopped. Damn it, she loved him. She loved him so much it hurt to have him anywhere near her and not be able to touch him. "You hit me right where I was most defenseless. Don't you understand that? Ben lied to me over and over, kept things from me . . .

secrets." She shook her head, feeling tears prick her eyes. "I can't do that again. I can't be with a man who does that to me, Jack."

He walked over and knelt at her feet. "I know, but I am *not* that man. I screwed up by not trusting you enough to think you could handle the knowledge of who I really was, but *I am not Ben*. Please, acknowledge that."

He *was* nothing like Ben. She felt that at the core of her. Yes, he was a man who loved women, there could be no doubt about that. Yet Mira understood that Jack was not the sort of man to two-time a woman, not the type to casually discard a woman's emotions for his own selfish, sexual desires. The fact that he had come after her for forgiveness and even now knelt at her feet was proof of that. "You're not like Ben, Jack."

He shook his head. "No, I'm not. I'm not stupid enough to let a woman like you slip through my fingers without a fight." His voice trembled with emotion. "Damn it, Mira. I never expected this. I never expected to find someone like you. You just . . . crashed right into me when I least expected it."

Neither of them said anything for a long moment.

He drew a breath. "I love you, Mira."

Her breath caught in the back of her throat and a tear slid down her cheek. She hadn't been expecting to hear those words. Mira brushed the teardrop away.

"And, yes, I messed up. I messed up so badly. It's just that I was afraid you'd hate me for being who I am and for being there"—he paused and swallowed hard—"when your mother died that I hid it from you, even knowing that it would hurt you when you eventually found out."

Emotion caught in her throat, making it hard for her to speak. "Jack, I love who you are, regardless of who your father was. That day you watched my mother die, you were a *child*. Why would I blame you for standing there and letting it happen?"

He looked away from her, but she saw the breathtaking pain and guilt in his light blue eyes before he dropped his gaze.

Mira understood something in that moment. Jack had been carrying this heavy guilt and perceived responsibility in his heart since the day it had happened. That day Jack's soul had been branded with the emotional weight of her mother's death and his inability to keep it from happening. The fact that he'd been a kid was inconsequential. Logic had no place in wounding events like Jack had endured. He blamed himself for her mother's death.

Was it any wonder he'd wanted to keep it from her?

Understanding what he needed, even if Jack didn't, she took his chin and forced his gaze to hers. "I forgive you, Jack. I, as my mother's daughter, absolve you of whatever it is you think you did wrong that day."

"Mira, don't—"

"*Jack.* Did you hear what I just said?"

"Yes."

Mira didn't think he'd done anything to merit forgiveness, but, somewhere deep inside him, Jack needed to hear that he had it. "I forgive you for being there. I forgive you for observing my mother's death. I forgive you for not being old enough to do anything about it. I forgive you for being too frightened to try and stop it. I forgive you for being sired by William Crane."

He glanced at her before turning his face away. She glimpsed relief in his eyes. Maybe he wasn't yet ready to absolve himself of responsibility, but hopefully that had given him a starting place to heal.

She paused, feeling her eyes fill up with fresh tears. "And I love you back." Her voice shook. "I love you so much."

He leaned forward and took her into his arms, laying a sweet kiss to her mouth. "I'm so glad to hear those words from your lips," he murmured. "I'm so relieved."

She felt another tear roll down her cheek, and he kissed it away. Mira rolled her eyes and gave a little laugh. "Please, Jack. I've loved you ever since that day you kissed me in your kitchen and set my magick free."

"Do you think that some day you might be able to forgive me for hiding the truth from you?" He cupped her cheek in his hand. "I'd happily spend the rest of my life working for it."

"Wow." She gave a short laugh. "The rest of your life. And I thought you were just in it for the sex."

"The sex is great." He ran his thumb down her cheek. "But I love the whole package. In fact, I can't imagine living without you."

A smile flickered over her mouth. "Ditto, Jack. You made a mistake in not telling me the truth, but we make mistakes sometimes. I can forgive you."

"I wasn't kidding about taking the rest of my life to make it up to you."

Her breath hitched in her throat. That had sounded like a proposal and he was down on his knees . . . and now he was pulling a small jewelry box out of his pocket.

No! She couldn't get married again. *Never, ever.*

He cracked the box, revealing the most gorgeous diamond and sapphire ring she'd ever seen. It wasn't a traditional engagement ring, but it was close enough to make her worry.

"Jack," she said warily.

He must've seen the horrified look on her face because he chuckled. "I'm *not* asking you to marry me, Mira." He took the ring out and slipped it on her finger.

It fit perfectly. She stared at it glittering there on her hand. It looked so much better than her wedding band ever had.

He pressed his forehead to hers and cupped her cheek in his palm. "But I am asking you into my life on a permanent, forever-type basis," he murmured. "Maybe one day you'll decide that marriage to the *right* man might not be so terrifying, and this ring can become an engagement ring instead of simply a gift from someone who loves you deeply."

"Jack," she started, and then stopped, trying to find the right words. They never came. She smiled so broadly she thought her face might crack. "Okay."

He kissed her sweetly at first, then his tongue feathered across her lips, urging them to part. They did, and he slipped within her mouth to rub his tongue against hers. She heard the jewelry box drop to the floor as Jack pulled her into his arms and off the couch. He laid her on the floor beneath him, his mouth still working on hers.

The way he kissed her, the heat of his body, and his sheer masculine presence overwhelmed her and stole her breath.

She slid her hands over his shoulders, down his back, and pushed them beneath the hem of his sweater, seeking warm flesh. Her body responded so easily to his kiss. Her nipples grew hard and her sex reacted, growing warm and aroused.

"Jack," she gasped, when they broke the kiss. "I want you." Mira pulled a thread of magick, and the candles extinguished, plunging the room into darkness.

"Honey, I'm yours."

Turn the page for a preview of the next book
about the elemental witches by Anya Bast

WITCH
BLOOD

Coming soon from Berkley Sensation!

HOW TO CATCH A WARLOCK 101. ISABELLE COULD teach that class.

The pounding beat of the club music thrummed through Isabelle's body as she enjoyed a respite from what had so far been a wretched evening. The trap she'd set for the warlock had also trapped her.

Eyes closed, she stood in the center of the floor and let inner calm fill her as she swayed her hips, though she danced more to the ebb and flow of the subtle emotions around her than to the music. The sea of euphoria and lust intoxicated her. For a moment, caught in the seductive, primal weave, she could forget. Dancing had been an escape for her when she'd been a little girl. As an adult, escape came in the form of a passport and an airline ticket.

A man's hands encircled her waist. A lean, muscular body pressed against hers from behind. She knew that touch, those hands, and the scent of his expensive cologne. It was the warlock she hunted. The one who thought she was a woman just like any other. Her eyes came open, the moment of serenity vanquished by his presence.

Anyone able to see her face would've glimpsed revulsion pass over her features before her lips curved into a coy smile. She snuggled back into Stefan Faucheux's arms. He rocked her back and forth, changing the sway of her body to the beat of the music instead of the soft waves of emotion. Stefan had no empathy.

Somewhere nearby a camera flashed, then another. Paparazzi. The media fawned over Stefan, an ultrarich playboy. Any woman he dated was a source of particular interest. Isabelle had managed to stay on Stefan's arm longer than most. She was the mysterious red-haired, green-eyed woman on whom no reporter could find much information. Isabelle had paid a lot of money to ensure that was so. She'd gone to a lot of work to make certain she interested Faucheux for a while, too. A lot of planning had brought her to this night.

Of course, the photographers didn't know she was a witch and Stefan a warlock. Those were secrets best kept from the non-magickal population. That was the only thing the Coven and the warlock-controlled Duskoff Cabal could agree on. The non-magickals greatly outnumbered the magickals and, historically, showed a lot of bloodthirstiness for those perceived to be different.

Stefan moved his body with hers in a teasing semblance of sex that made her stomach roil. Soon, this would all be over. That was the only positive about having to suffer his closeness.

Isabelle pasted a smile on her lips and closed her eyes again. She thought of deep, rushing streams furrowing their way through the earth, the recesses of the ocean, where the water lay still and silent, the gentle eddies and ripples at the edge of a lake. She felt her power rise in response to the mental stimulus, just a little. It bled off a bit of her stress, blunted the sharp edge.

Stefan's arms tightened around her and he nuzzled her throat. More cameras flashed. They'd be on the front page of every tabloid in the country by tomorrow. She'd probably be touted as pregnant and making plans for a wedding. The Lady only knew what stupidity they'd come up with.

And then the *other* story would break. The darker one. The far more violent one.

Soon, she assured herself. Tonight. Because she was not a woman like any other and today was no ordinary day. It was time Stefan Faucheux paid for his sins.

Emotion welled in her throat for a moment. She'd barely had time to grieve. These days she was running on rage, sorrow, and little else.

Use it. Don't let it use you.

Immediately, the sudden swell of vulnerability faded into cold resolve. It was a lesson she'd learned long ago and learned well. She'd had lots of practice stuffing away her pain, transforming it into a far more effective force. Her emotion had become a well-honed weapon.

He leaned into her, spoke into her ear loud enough for her to hear over the pounding music. "Time to leave, *ma chéri*."

It was, indeed, time.

Anticipation coursed through her, leaving a tingle of sweetness that warmed her more surely than Stefan's skill with fire could ever do. Stefan was a fire witch, one of the more powerful she'd encountered. Though he couldn't claim the title *witch* anymore. He'd betrayed the Coven, broken the rede too many times to count. Now he was nothing more than a warlock with magick that lay in the element of fire.

Her own ability resided in the realm of water. That meant she and Stefan were direct opposites magickally. It had complicated her plans somewhat. Normally, fire and water had a natural repulsion, whereas fire and air had a built-in attraction. Isabelle had had to work double time to snare her quarry because of that, especially since she couldn't hide her abilities from a witch like Stefan. He had a nose like a bloodhound for different types of magick.

He took her hand and led her through the crowd toward the door. The photographers detached themselves from the partying throng and followed. She could see them scuttling like crabs out of the corner of her eye. Stefan's bodyguards flanked them, not allowing them to get too close, not allowing anyone to get too close. Earth charms helped. He'd had several made that worked to make people keep their distance.

They made their way out of the club and the heavy doors closed behind them, not quite blocking out the bass of the music within, seemingly making the entire club throb on its foundations. Early morning chill instantly raised goose bumps on her bare arms and legs. She took a moment to inhale the fresh, not quite clean, air of the city, ignoring the surprised whispers and gasps of those in line to enter the club.

"Come, darling," Stefan said, placing a proprietary hand at the small of her back and guiding her toward the limo.

She stopped in front of the car and whispered into Stefan's ear, "Send your bodyguards away." Isabelle dragged his earlobe between her teeth and felt him respond with a shiver. Cameras flashed in abandon.

He spoke a few words to the warlock muscle near him while the driver opened the door for her and ushered her within. Isabelle had a moment of unease at the dark closing around her like a velvet fist. Close spaces weren't her thing. Regulating her breath, as she always had to do when entering a small area, she climbed into the cool interior of the limo and sank down onto one of the leather seats. Stefan sat down next to her. As soon as the door was closed, he was on her.

Not coarsely or clumsily. That was not Stefan. He was a perfect gentleman until he decided not to be. He slid his hand to her waist, tilted her chin toward his face, and pressed his lips to hers. Suave, undemanding, seductive. His fresh breath invaded her mouth as his tongue sought entry. She suppressed a shudder and placed her hands on his broad shoulders, the fabric of his suit cool against her skin. She hesitated, unwilling to allow him a deeper kiss. Isabelle simply couldn't help it. He pressed the issue and she allowed it, using every ounce of her willpower not to push him away.

Outwardly, to the non-magickal world, Stefan was a benevolent social icon, known for his goodwill and his generosity. In reality, as head of the Duskoff Cabal, the violent little club warlocks kept, he pillaged and plundered his way through witches as though in his personal stockyard, slaughtering here and there when he felt like it. Like any sociopath worth his salt, Stefan was a charming, handsome monster. The world should thank her for what she was about to do, even though she'd had to turn warlock herself to do it.

He leaned in toward her, burying his nose in the curve of her neck and sliding a hand past the hem of her short, black Versace. "We're finally alone," he whispered, "as you requested." The car pulled forward, rocking her against his body.

She tilted his face to hers and kissed him, pressing herself into the curve of his body. She cupped his groin through his black pants and felt his hardness. "So we are."

"Then why so shy? Tonight you will not escape me, Isabelle," he breathed against her skin in his smooth French accent.

Part of her plan had been to tease him sexually. It had been a little like taunting a starving tiger with a slab of meat, but she'd been successful. It had hooked him, made him want her more, and allowed her limited intimate contact with him. Although any contact was too much.

She raised an eyebrow. "I think it's you who won't escape me, Stefan." She unbuttoned his pants. "Take them off."

He grasped the hem of her skirt. "You first," he purred.

"Nooo, you," she shot back coyly.

He shook his head. "Take off your dress for me, Isabelle." His voice held a thread of steel and his eyes had a brutally cold glint in them.

Her sly, sexy smile faltered. Damn it! This was not going the way she'd envisioned it. In her head, she'd been fully clothed when she brought him down. Having no choice unless she wanted to raise suspicion, she allowed him to draw her dress over her head, leaving her in only a lacy red bra and panty set and her shoes.

"Mmm," he murmured in appreciation right before he pressed his lips to the swell of her breast. Oh, yech. Yech, yech, yech!

She yanked him forward by the waistband of his pants and kissed him roughly, biting his lower lip hard, and making him jerk a little. "Off now," she commanded.

"I adore a woman who likes it a little rough."

Then he'd love her.

He slipped his shoes and pants off. She glanced down and lifted a brow as if in sexual speculation. He gave her a cocky smile, the smile of a man who's sure he's about to get laid. How wrong could he be? He was about to find out. She reached out and took him in her hand.

And she squeezed. Hard.

At the same time, she flooded her body with magick. It exploded from the center of her chest with a warm pulse. Power shot down her arm, centering in her fingers. They tingled and twitched as she fought to retain the heavy burst of emotion-drenched magick. The water in his groin responded instantly to her will, the molecules jumping to do her bidding. They grew cold, then even colder.

Stefan's eyes bulged out of his head and shock took his expression from arousal to terror in under a quarter of a second. A soundless scream erupted from his mouth, his lips forming a yawp of unvoiced pain.

"I thought you liked it rough, Stefan?" she asked through gritted teeth. She had him right where she wanted him. She'd known she'd had to get him by the balls . . . literally. There was no other way to trap a warlock as powerful as he. She'd needed to get close enough to get him in a susceptible position, without his hired muscle present, make him let down his guard, and then take advantage of his vulnerability.

She squeezed the soft flesh of that vulnerability in her hand a little tighter. "Awww . . . not having fun? I'm sorry." She twisted until he gasped. "Really."

Stefan made a gurgling noise somewhere in his throat.

"Does it frighten you to stare into the eyes of your own mortality, Stefan? Do you ever wonder what happens to us when we die? Do we blink out like a light, or do we live on?" She paused, tilting her head to the side. "Is death only another life? Hmm . . . What do you think?"

"I don't . . . know," he gritted out.

"I think you're about to find out."

"Who . . . are you?" His lips formed the words, but there wasn't enough breath to give them life. She eased up a little. He'd pass out otherwise and it was too soon for that.

"That is not the relevant question at this juncture. The real question is about Angela, Stefan."

Confusion clouded his eyes.

Oh, that was the *wrong* answer. Power flared down her arm, making her fingers ache. His head snapped back in pain and she forcibly eased up on him.

"Angela?" he gasped.

"Angela Novak. The last witch murdered by your demon." She clamped down harder. "You can't even remember her name?"

His lips peeled back in a grimace. "Not . . . my . . . demon."

"Well, no. Maybe not technically. Your father, William

Crane, raised the demon that killed Angela. Crane and his minions. But your father is dead and you've taken his place at the head of the Duskoff. The Duskoff is the reason the demon exists in this dimension. Therefore, the Duskoff is responsible for Angela's death and the death of Melina Andersen, the first witch it killed."

"But I wasn't with the Duskoff . . . when . . . they raised the demon."

"Oh, spare me. You've done enough horrible things to warrant this, Stefan, and don't try to tell me you wouldn't raise another demon if you could."

"No," he whispered, his head falling back from the pain.

"No? What do you mean, Stefan? Wasn't it you who were going to sacrifice those four witches last winter to raise one? If it wasn't for the Coven, you would have succeeded. That alone makes you deserving of punishment." She cocked her head to the side. "And aside from all that, what about Naomi Nelson, that earth witch you roasted when you were eighteen? What about Robin Taylor—"

He pulled his head forward and focused on her. "I can help you. Help . . . help find the demon. Right the . . . wrong."

He was making bargains now, was he? She opened her mouth to respond, but heat flared white-hot against her palm. They both cried out in pain. Isabelle snatched her scorched hand away. Damn it, she'd lost focus for a moment and he'd taken control from her.

Stefan rolled to the side, his hand between his legs, cupping his privates. Her hand hurt like she'd been holding it over a flame, but he had to be in more pain than she was. He'd burned himself in a very sensitive place in order to unseat her.

Isabelle raised power as fast as she could, despite the pain. The air crackled with power as Stefan also drew magick to defend himself. In the same moment, the entire limo lurched to the side. Isabelle slammed against the opposite seat and cried out as her back twisted. The limo came to a swerving, squealing, smoke-under-the-tires halt. She fell back to the floor of the limo, her face contorting from the pain searing down her leg and through her lower back.

She glanced up through her tangled dyed dark red hair, seeing Stefan kneeling on the floor of the vehicle in front of her, looking as though he might retch. They'd both stopped drawing power. Outside the sounds of boots pounding on pavement and shouting reached her ears.

Fighting through the pain, she raised magick and directed it at Stefan. Sensing the swift buildup within the confines of the limo, his head snapped up and he also tapped power. The air snapped with electricity with their combined efforts. It was a magickical showdown and they were both fighting through injuries.

But his were worse.

Isabelle shot her hand out in a near unconscious effort to increase her power, commanding the water in Stefan's body to do her bidding—to freeze.

The limo door opened and she felt the press of confusion, then fury from the unknown observers. The intense emotions around her settled like a bitter wine on the back of her tongue, but she focused all her attention on Stefan.

"No," came a commanding male voice. "Stop it now."

She ignored the order. Stefan's spine snapped back as she intensified the freezing process. She had him now and, dear Lady, it had to hurt. It was nothing compared to what the demon had done to Angela, though.

Isabelle had been the one to find her body. Her sister had died the one way she'd always feared, by a demon's hand. Angela had had nightmares about that since she'd been a child and one of their "uncles" had related to them how demons killed their victims. The memories of finding her sister, well, Isabelle still couldn't bring herself to visit them. Not in detail. Her mind had blocked them and she was grateful for that.

In front of her, Stefan keened.

Funny, Isabelle thought she'd feel satisfaction when this moment came, perhaps a release and a lifting of the heavy emotion that had weighed her down for so long. But she felt none of those things. She only felt sorrow.

"This is for Angela, Stefan," she said woodenly. "This is my sister saying hello from her grave."

Where was the fulfillment she thought she'd feel? Where was the righteous justification? She stared into Stefan's eyes, watching pain explode within the pupils. Her magickal grip faltered. She couldn't do this . . . *Damn it!*

From her left, a man approached her. "Isabelle," he said gently. "He's the scum of the earth, but he didn't kill your sister."

Her face contorted, her eyes filling with tears. "He did. He's the head of the Duskoff. Without the Duskoff, the demon wouldn't exist."

"I'm asking you for the last time. Stop."

This revenge, once a red-hot, pulsing, living thing in her heart and mind, now tasted bitter and cold. Still . . . Angela.

"I can't," she whispered. "I can't stop."

The man threw himself at her, breaking her hold on Stefan. Her back screamed with agony, making her cry out, but she still fought the heavy weight on top of her. He pinned her down, struggling to gain control of her limbs. Exhaustion and the pain in her back forced her to go passive. Her magick sparked and died in her chest, spent like a candle burned too long. She made a choking sound of grief.

He stared down at her, his face shadowed by a long fall of blue-black hair. Thomas Monahan, head of the Coven. The hair branded him. She didn't even need to see his face. She winced and let out a small sob. "It's because of him, because of the Duskoff, that my sister is dead."

"He won't get away with what he's done, Isabelle," came his low voice. "But his punishment can't be like this."

"How do you know my name?"

Behind them she could hear witches subduing Stefan. The limo rocked with the motion. "You said you're Angela's sister. I can only assume you mean Angela Novak, the water witch who was killed by a demon a couple of months ago. That makes you Isabelle. We're on the same side. If I let you up, will you be good?"

Her mouth snapped shut and she nodded.

He moved away from her, Monahan's face—set in handsome, brutal lines—finally coming into view. She glanced around the limo's interior, seeing Adam Tyrell and Jack McAllister, both fire witches she was well acquainted with. Both restrained the injured Stefan, who wasn't fighting anymore. He knelt with his hand between his legs, looking like the only battle he could wage was against unconsciousness.

"We are not on the same side," she growled at Thomas. "You are preventing me from—"

"Taking your revenge. I know."

"I didn't kill her sister," spat Stefan.

Thomas cast a look at Stefan that reminded Isabelle of how a cat might regard a worm, beneath his bother but something interesting to play with. "In general I'd prefer Stefan dead, but we need him."

Cradling her injured hand, Isabelle only glowered at him through her hair in response.

"Ah, Isabelle? Not that I mind the view, but . . ." Adam looked at her pointedly, helping her remember her state of undress.

She glanced down, seeing her lack of clothing. Hell. Could anything more go wrong?

Making sure Jack had a hold of Stefan, Adam tossed her dress to her, and she gingerly slid it over her head, wincing at the pain in her back.

Thomas jerked his head at Stefan. "Incapacitate him for transportation."

Jack glowered at Stefan—his expression dangerously dark. For a moment Isabelle wondered what he'd do. The warlock had tried to kill Jack's girlfriend last winter. Jack glanced pointedly at Stefan's privates. "You should see a doctor about that." Then he punched him—hard. Stefan slumped to the floor of the limo, unconscious.

"You could've just drugged him," said Thomas with a twist to his lips.

Jack glared down at Stefan. "That was one option."

"You could've just let me kill him, too," Isabelle inserted. "That would have been much less trouble for everyone. I know I would have been far happier."

Thomas turned and regarded her with eyes that seemed blacker than obsidian. They were unsettling, yet beautiful, and they matched the hair that swirled around his shoulders. The man truly did look like a witch—a very, very wicked one. "Really? That would have made you happy, Isabelle? Tell the truth."

She glanced away from him, suddenly feeling far more naked under his gaze than when she'd been undressed.

The head of the Coven was better looking in person than he was in his pictures, like some beautiful fallen angel. Although the rough-hewn lines of his face saved him from the more perfect type of male prettiness. His sensual, lush mouth seemed at odds with the rest of him, set with deep lines on either side. He had a powerfully built body, long of leg and broad of shoulder. She'd felt every inch of that massive body a moment before and it had hurt. Her back twinged with the memory, making her wince.

"How's it going, Isabelle? Long time no see," said Adam as though they'd met up by chance at Starbucks or something.

She grinned. Grinning at Adam Tyrell was something you had to do because of his charm, especially if you were female. Even under these circumstances, she couldn't help it. "Not too great, Adam."

"Get him out of here," Thomas growled at Adam. He turned to Jack. "Can you heal her back and hand?"

"Isabelle's hand and back, yes. Stefan's dick, no. My hands aren't going anywhere near that."

"We'll let Stefan heal on his own, I think. It's the least he deserves."

Adam heaved Stefan out of the limo and Thomas followed, casting one more piercing look at her over his shoulder before he went. "I want to talk to you. Don't disappear."

She grimaced at his back and narrowed her eyes. Asshole! He had no right to order her around. She'd left the Coven. Hell, what she'd just done made her a flat-out warlock. Thomas Monahan held no power over her.

"Give me your hand," said Jack.

She unlocked her jaw and raised her hand, shifting on the floor of the limo and snagging the heel of her shoe in the carpet.

He took her hand between his. Jack was a fire witch and, therefore, could heal. She'd always found it odd that the power to heal resided in such a destructive element. Her hand grew warm, tingled, and the pain receded. When he released her, the skin was pink and healing quickly. He jerked his chin at the seat. "Sit down with your back to me."

Carefully, she pushed up and slid onto the seat. Ripples of pain shot through her back and down her legs. She blew out a careful breath as nausea swamped her.

Jack sat behind her and placed his hands on her spine. His hands, completely businesslike on her back, grew warm, making her feel instantly better. "I don't remember your hair being this dark a shade of red or your eyes being green, Isabelle."

"I colored my hair and I'm wearing contacts."

"All the better to stalk your prey, hmm?"

"I guess. Stefan prefers redheads."

"Good disguise. None of us recognized you in the tabloids. We didn't know who you were, or that you were even a witch. It wasn't until tonight, when we saw you up close, that we realized your identity. All we knew was that this evening Stefan's flavor of the month had finally convinced him to shed his bodyguards for sex."

She let out a small laugh. "You guys were piggybacking my seduction as a way to take Stefan hostage?"

"Yep. We were watching, waiting for an opportunity. You gave us a surprise when we opened the limo door. Never saw that one coming." He paused. "I'm sorry about your sister. I understand why you went after Stefan."

She had a million questions, but they all caught in her throat. They were questions for the head of the Coven, anyway, not Jack McAllister, Thomas's right-hand man. "I hunted the demon for a month and couldn't find it."

"We've been hunting it, too, without any luck."

"I went after the cause for the demon's existence instead." She swallowed hard. "I just . . . needed to do something, and Stefan can't be allowed to bring any more of those creatures into our world."

Jack slid away and she turned toward him on the seat. Her back was still sore, but the worst of the pain was now gone. "I get that. Still, bad girl, Isabelle. You should have come to us instead of playing vigilante. We had always planned to take down Stefan and we're definitely going after the demon." Jack shook his head and *tch-tched*. "Bad, bad girl."

"So what's new?" she muttered in response. Angela had always been the good one. Isabella had always been the one getting into trouble.

He must've known she wasn't asking what was new with him, but he answered that way all the same. "I'm going to be a father." The words were spoken with such pride that she smiled.

She fussed with the hem of her skirt, happy to change the subject. "I heard that. Knocked up that little air witch of yours."

"Mira."

Lady, the look in his eyes when he said her name. Such love. Such devotion. A man had never looked that way while speaking her name, and Isabelle had to admit a part of her regretted that fact.

"That's right, her name is Mira," Isabelle answered. "Everyone's hoping she'll turn up with a baby air witch of her own." Of all the elemental witches, air was by far the rarest and the most powerful. "What do you think, air or fire?"

"I think she'll take after her mom and be an air witch. We're going to name her Eva, for Mira's mom, if she's a girl. David, for her dad, if it's a boy."

Eva Hoskins, maiden name Monahan. That had been the air witch who'd been sacrificed in the circle that had brought the demon into existence over twenty-five years ago. Four witches—one for each of the elements—had been killed to bring in the demon who had murdered Angela. How poetic one of their names should be spoken on this night.

She patted him on his shoulder. "Good luck to you both." She scooped up her purse from the floor of the limo and exited the vehicle.

Isabelle found herself on a darkened side street in a commercial part of town. The front of the limo had been rammed in by a Hummer. Behind the limo was another car crash, a tangle of metal where sedan had met heavy SUV. The sedan had been the vehicle carrying Stefan's muscle.

She cast a glance at Stefan, who they were lifting into the back of Thomas' car. Thomas stood nearby. He stared at her for a moment, his black-as-sin hair spread over his shoulders and his expression intent. Then he crooked a finger.

Oh, no. Hell would freeze over first.

Isabelle gave him a little wave and walked away.

"Isabelle," he called after her. "I need to talk to you."

Ignoring him, she turned a corner and pulled on her remaining magickal reserves, scraping the very bottom of her capacity. Isabelle gathered the water molecules in the air, condensing them around the dust particles and cloaking herself in the resulting thick fog. By the time she heard his footsteps behind her, she'd disappeared and had left him standing in zero visibility.

She heard him swear loudly and smiled. Isabelle needed to talk to him, but she wasn't about to do it on his terms.